Mango Thief

A Mango Bob and Walker Adventure

by

Bill Myers

www.mangobob.com

This book is a work of fiction. Names, characters, places, and incidents are either the product of the author's imagination or are used fictionally. Any resemblance to actual persons, living or dead, or to actual events or locales is entirely coincidental.

Copyright © 2023 Bill Myers. All rights reserved including the right to reproduce this book or portions thereof, in any form. No part of this text may be reproduced in any form without the express written permission of the author.

Version 2023.04.20

Chapter One

I was in my motorhome, parked in the vacant lot behind Taco Bell in Titusville, Florida. According to the web, it was one of the few places where I could park a rig as big as mine and watch a rocket lift off from Cape Kennedy just across the bay.

There were better viewing spots on the Space Coast, but none that I could get my RV into, unless I had planned ahead and reserved a site six months in advance.

I hadn't done that, so my best option was the lot behind the Bell. It had plenty of room for my motorhome and as a bonus, if I got hungry while waiting for the launch I could walk across the lot and order up fresh tacos.

I'd been parked there for three days. Two days longer than I planned. The launch had been postponed twice due to high winds, but it looked like today might be the day. Or maybe not. The winds were still blowing.

There were six other RVs in the lot, all there for the same reason. To watch the launch.

No one had parked close to me or felt the need to come over and start a conversation.

That suited me just fine.

It wasn't that I was anti-social. Just that I didn't feel like making any new friends right away. It was nice not having to listen to strangers tell me things I didn't want to hear.

Sometimes though, you don't have a choice. When you're in an RV, people sometimes come up and talk to you whether you want them to or not.

This was one of those days.

I was outside, scraping bugs off my RV's windshield when a woman walked by with her dog. She was about my age. Nice looking, but not in a beauty queen kind of way. More of a wholesome farm girl look.

The faded jeans she was wearing fit her well. The oversize gray sweatshirt hid the rest. Maybe on purpose. Or maybe just to fend off the morning chill.

The woman, busy with her phone, didn't see me. But her dog, a beagle mix, did and bolted in my direction. She had him on a leash, but didn't have a good grip on it. Still focused on her phone, the mutt got away and headed straight for me.

By the time she caught up with the dog, he was at my feet, laying on the ground, belly up, wanting a pet. He looked harmless, so I bent over and gave him a belly rub.

Putting her phone away, the woman walked over. "Sorry, about that. He got away from me. Hope he's not bothering you."

"He's not. I needed to take a break anyway. What's his name?"

"Biscuit. I'm Norah. With an 'h.'"

I couldn't think of a reason I'd need to know how to spell her name, but if it came up, I now knew to add an 'h' to the end.

"Biscuit? His name is Biscuit?"

"That's what they told me when I picked him up at the shelter. Kind of fits him, don't you think?"

Norah with an 'h', had just scored two points with me. First, she had a dog named Biscuit. And second, she'd rescued him from a shelter.

She pointed to an older motorhome parked near the back

of the lot. "We came down from Knoxville to see the launch. You here for that too?"

"Yep."

That's how I answered. Just one word. "Yep."

I could have said more. Maybe tell her about the two launches that had been delayed or the menu choices at Taco Bell.

But I didn't.

I just kept rubbing Biscuit's warm belly. He was laying there with a grin on his face while kicking one of his back legs in the air, like dogs do when you rub them in the right place. I guess I'm the same. Rub me in the right place and I'll shake a leg too.

Since my three-letter answer of 'yep' had done nothing to keep the conversation with Norah going, I figured she'd get the hint, pick up the leash, and carry on with Biscuit's morning walk.

But she didn't.

Instead, she pointed back to her RV again and said, "I think yours is the same as mine. A Winnebago Aspect, right?"

I looked over my shoulder to see where she was pointing. Near the back of the lot sat a motorhome like mine. A few years older, but the same make and model. Probably with the same floor plan.

It would have been rude not to answer her question, so I said, "Yeah, they're the same. I guess that makes us twinkies."

She frowned almost like I'd offended her. "Twinkies? What does that mean?"

"You know, Twinkies. Two of a kind. Like the cupcakes."

Still frowning, she shook her head. "Where I come from, Twinkies means something else. Not so nice."

The logical thing for me to do, was to ask where she came from. She'd brought it up, so it was reasonable to think she might want to talk about it.

But since I'd already offended her once, I decided to keep my mouth shut.

Maybe it was time for Norah (with an 'h'), to pick up Biscuit's leash and get back to her walk. I did nothing to encourage her to stay.

I figured she'd get the hint, grab the dog's leash and they'd be off.

But that's not what happened.

Norah (with an 'h') didn't pick up the leash. And Biscuit made no move to get up.

Instead, she said, "I might need your help."

Had I known then, how those five words would change my life, I would have gone back into my RV, locked the doors, and not come out until she was gone.

But I didn't.

Instead, I asked what kind of help she needed.

And boy was that a mistake.

Chapter Two

Norah (with an 'h') was standing near the front of my RV. Biscuit, her dog, was on the ground on his back, with a smile on his face. I was down on my knees, rubbing his belly.

"You're going to spoil him. You do that and he'll never leave you alone. Every time we walk by, he'll expect you to come out and give him a rub."

I shrugged. "That's fine with me. I like dogs. Sometimes more than people."

She laughed. "I kind of got that impression when you didn't bother to tell me your name after I told you mine."

"Sorry about that. I'm Walker. With a 'W'."

She smiled. "Okay, Walker, with a 'W', nice to meet you."

She pointed back to her motorhome. "I just bought it two weeks ago. Hadn't planned on getting one, but needed a place to stay in Orlando for a couple of months. Normally I rent an apartment or a suite at an extended-stay hotel. But when I called around, I couldn't find anything. Everything was full.

"I asked my booking agent to find me a place. He was the one who signed me up for the gig, so I figured it was in his best interest to find me a place to stay. His commission depended on it.

"He struck out too. Nothing available. At least not at the kind of places I usually stay. So, he started looking for alternatives. AirBnB's, that kind of thing.

"He struck out again. Everything was full. But he kept looking and found an RV park that he could get me into. It wasn't fancy and didn't have room service, but it was available.

"The only problem was, I didn't have an RV. In fact, I'd never even been in one. My agent said not to worry. Said an RV was the perfect way to travel between gigs and have a place to stay wherever I was.

"So he went ahead and booked the site and told me to start looking for an RV."

She paused to take a breath. I took the opportunity to ask a question.

"You have a booking agent? Are you famous? Should I know you?"

She smiled. "No, I'm not famous. I'm a traveling nurse. I move from job to job, usually filling in when hospitals are short-staffed or doctors need extra help.

"I just finished a gig at the cardiac center in Knoxville. I start at Orlando Regional in two weeks."

I nodded, giving her a signal to continue her story.

"So, like I said, my agent told me to get an RV. He didn't tell me what kind of RV. He just said to get one. I figured the place to start looking was at the local RV dealers around Knoxville.

"I visited the three biggest ones. I figured they'd have the best selection and I'd have no problem finding something affordable that would work.

"Boy, was I wrong. There's no such thing as an affordable RV. At least not a new one. Prices started at a hundred thousand dollars and went up quickly. The cute little van-sized one I liked the best was over two hundred thousand dollars!

"When I told the salesman there was no way I could afford it, he said not to worry. Just sign a buyer's agreement and they could get me a thirty-year loan with easy payments of almost a thousand a month.

"After hearing the same spiel at three different places, I gave up going to dealer lots and started checking Craigslist and Marketplace. But soon learned they are full of scams. People want you to pay in advance for rigs that don't even exist.

"I was telling one of the nurses at the cardiac center about my failed RV hunt, and she mentioned that one of the doctors had a motorhome for sale. She gave me his number and said to call him.

"Long story short, I made the call. He told me the RV was his father's. He'd bought it new and had kept it in tip-top shape. His parents had traveled in it all over the country and had planned to travel even more. They had just updated the brakes, tires, shocks, and everything else to make it safe for a long trip they were planning.

"But then, life got in the way. His father's eyesight was fading, and he decided it wasn't safe for him to be out on the road in a big RV.

So they decided to sell it.

"I went and looked at it, took it for a test drive, and after hearing the price, bought it on the spot.

"I don't know whether I got a good deal or not, but it doesn't matter. I wanted it and it was within my price range.

"The sellers were sad to see it go but seemed to be happy they were selling it to someone like me who would enjoy it.

"The wife mentioned that on their trips, they towed a car so that when they set up camp, they could use it to get around locally. She wondered if I'd be interested in it. It was a five-speed manual, and she didn't like driving it in the hills around Knoxville.

"My car was a Camry, with an automatic. I liked it, but it

couldn't be towed behind the RV.

"The doctor's wife said she'd be willing to trade straight across. My Camry for her tow car. The two cars were about the same age and probably worth about the same. I couldn't think of a reason not to do the trade.

"They showed me how to drive the RV, how everything worked inside, and how to hook up the tow car. They even went with me to the DMV to get the titles changed over.

"Three days later, when my gig at the cardiac center ended, I filled the big RV with gas, and me and Biscuit hit the road.

"My plan was to get to Florida, watch the rocket launch, maybe spend a few days relaxing on the beach. Then head to Orlando for work."

She paused, then said, "You probably didn't need to know all that, did you?"

I gave Biscuit one last pet, and stood, groaning as I did. At thirty-five, I shouldn't be making old man noises when I stand, but I was. Way too soon. There was no real pain involved, just the noises. Like my father before me.

Norah was waiting for me to say something. So I did.

"Let me get this straight. You've never been in an RV before. Never driven one. But you buy a used one. Jump in it with your dog, and head to Florida. Then you walk up to me, a total stranger, and start telling your life story.

"You do things like that a lot?"

Chapter Three

"No, I don't. I usually don't talk about my life. It just sort of came out. The last few months have been really stressful, what with everything that's been going on. I guess I just needed to tell someone. But probably not you."

She paused, then said, "I think it's time for me to leave."

She tapped Biscuit's leash to get his attention. Still lying on the ground, the mutt looked up and grunted. But didn't move. He stayed where he was, in no hurry to go anywhere.

I kind of felt the same way about her leaving.

Norah was turning out to be someone who I might want to spend some time with.

"Norah, no need to rush off. You mentioned you might need some help. With what?"

She hesitated, scratched her head, then said. "I don't know if I should tell you or not. It's kind of embarrassing."

I grinned. "It can't be that bad. Just tell me."

She shook her head, looked back at her RV, then back at me. After thinking about it for a few seconds, she said, "Okay, but you have to promise not to laugh."

When people tell you that, it usually means you're going to laugh, no matter what you say. I needed a good laugh, so I said, "Norah, I won't laugh, I promise."

She shook her head, then said, "It's the toilet. In the RV. I can't get it to flush. I step on the pedal but no water comes out. The pump runs, but there's no flush. Nothing goes down. It stays in the bowl.

"Same thing with the sink. I turn on the tap, the pump starts, but no water comes out.

"It was working fine when I first got it, but not now. No water means I can't use the toilet or wash my hands. At least not in the RV.

"I've been using the bathroom over at Taco Bell. I can't do that forever though. The people there are starting to wonder."

"You think I broke something? Or maybe I'm doing it wrong?"

I was doing my best not to laugh. It was hard not to, thinking about her going back and forth to Taco Bell to use the bathroom. It gave a new meaning to their catchphrase 'Make a run for the border.'

I was holding back the tears of laughter, I had to, because I didn't want to embarrass her any more than she already was. I mean having to repeatedly go into Taco Bell knowing the employees are watching you head to the bathroom, is plenty embarrassing enough.

So, instead of joking about it, I thought about her toilet problem and ways to solve it.

Having lived in a motorhome full time for almost three years, I'd dealt with lots of RV related issues, including a no-flush toilet. I knew from personal experience it wasn't fun. You either had to use a bucket or find public facilities. Neither is an optimal solution.

When the issue cropped up for me, I searched Google and found out it was a common problem for RV newbies. In most cases, an easy fix. I decided to see if it would work for her.

"Norah, you said the toilet worked when you first got the RV. But it doesn't work now, right?"

"Yeah, it worked before. But not now."

"Okay. Did you stop and fill up your fresh water tank on your way down here?"

"Yeah, in Charleston. At the KOA there. That's where I spent the night. I hooked up to campground water. Filled the tank until water ran out onto the ground. Then turned it off.

"Isn't that the way I'm suppose to do it?"

"Yeah, it is. As long as you turned the RV's water input valve back to 'city fill'. Do you remember doing that?"

She shook her head. "I don't know. All I did was hook up the water hose, move the setting to 'tank fill', and let it run until the tank was full. Then I unhooked the hose, put it away, and locked the compartment.

"Was I supposed to do something else?"

"No, you did everything right, except when you were done, you should have set the water valve back to 'City Fill'. If you left it on 'tank fill', the water pump will run, but no water will come out of your faucets.

"That's why your toilet won't flush. It's easy to fix. Just go back to your RV, open the outside utility panel, and set the water valve to 'city fill'."

She shook her head, made a pouty face, then asked, "Would you mind coming over and showing me how to do it?"

I didn't have to think about my answer. It's not every day that a woman as good-looking as Norah invites me to her place. Even though it wasn't going to be a social visit, I wasn't going to turn down her invitation.

"Yeah, I'll go over there with you. But first, I need to go inside and let Bob know I'll be gone."

She gave me a strange look. "Bob? Is he your partner? I don't want to take you away from him if you two have something planned."

13

I laughed. "Bob is not my partner. He's my cat. He lives with me in the RV. Just the two of us."

She wasn't impressed.

"A cat? You're living with a cat? So I'm guessing that means you're single? Most grown men who live alone with cats, are."

She was right.

"Yeah, I'm single. But I don't think it has anything to do with the cat. He came along later."

She nodded. "Uh, huh. I'm sure it's not the cat's fault that you're single."

Before I could come up with a spiffy reply, she had another question.

"You down here on vacation? Or did your boss let you off?"

Her question kind of bothered me. But I answered anyway.

"I don't have a boss. And I'm not on vacation. I live full-time in my RV. I pretty much spend most of my time just traveling around Florida. Trying to stay out of trouble. But it seems to follow me. Usually involving women I meet in Taco Bell parking lots.

"Like you."

She smiled. "Yeah, you've got to watch out for women like me. We're always on the prowl, looking for a man we can corral. When you get to be my age, the pickings are pretty slim. You have to take what you can get.

"But don't worry. I'll do my best to resist your charms. Can't make any promises, though. Sometimes it just happens."

She pointed to her RV. "I'll meet you down at my place after you tell Bob where you're going. Bring your driver's license with you."

She tugged Biscuit's leash. He slowly got up on his feet and they walked back toward her rig.

I should have asked why she wanted my driver's license, but didn't.

That was a mistake.

Chapter Four

Back in my RV, I washed my hands and changed out of the shirt I'd been wearing for the last two days into a clean one. It wasn't that I was trying to impress Norah. It was just it didn't feel right going over to her place wearing a sweat-stained shirt.

After changing, I checked on Bob. He was back on my bed sleeping. His head on my pillow with a paw over his eye to keep the light out. He sleeps like that a lot. I personally think it's kind of cute. And have lots of pictures to prove it.

But Bob doesn't really like me taking his picture while he's sleeping. The shutter noise bothers him. He wakes up grouchy and is no fun to be around. So even though he looked cute on the bed, I didn't pull out my camera. I just let him sleep.

I checked his food and water bowls and made sure both were at least half full. If they get lower than that, he starts to think he'll soon starve. He'll let me know with repeated howls, regardless of the time of day, and won't stop until the bowls are refilled to his satisfaction.

So I check his bowls several times a day. And always before I go out or head to bed.

He's trained me well.

It was a cool day in Florida. The RV's overhead vent fans were pulling in fresh January air off the Atlantic. They are temperature controlled and would automatically speed up, or slow down when needed. They'd keep Bob comfortable while I was gone. And add a bit of white noise to make sleeping under them easy.

With Bob's needs taken care of, I grabbed my wallet and went outside. After locking up the RV, I headed to Norah's. On the way, I remembered what she'd said about women her age looking for men to corral.

She probably meant it as a joke. But sometimes, jokes are based on truths. Then again, it was possible she was just flirting with me.

It didn't matter either way. I wasn't getting involved with another woman any time soon.

At least, that's what I thought.

Chapter Five

She was waiting for me outside her RV.

"Did you bring your license?"

"Yeah, why?"

"Because my Momma told me to never invite a man into my home unless I knew who he really was. So hand it over."

Reluctantly, I pulled out my license and handed it to her.

She laughed when she saw the photo. "Bad hair day?"

"Yeah."

She pulled her phone from her back pocket and took a photo of the license. Without waiting for me to ask why, she handed the card back and said, "Let's just see what comes up."

"What do you mean, 'what comes up?'"

She pointed at her phone. "I have this app that does deep background checks. All I have to do is scan a person's driver's license, and it'll tell me everything about them.

She smiled, waiting for me to say something.

The best I could come up with was, "Will it tell you anything about my cat?"

"No, not unless he has a criminal record."

"So, you're not kidding? You're really doing a background check on me? Why?"

She smiled. "Because so far, all I know about you, is you're an unemployed, homeless drifter, with no visible means of support, living with a cat. That's pretty much the resume of most serial killers.

"So yeah, I'm checking you out."

Her phone beeped with the results. She looked down at the screen and started nodding. "Okay, so far, it's looking pretty good. No warrants for your arrest. You're not out on parole. Not a sex offender. Not currently married. And surprisingly, a decent credit score."

She looked up and smiled. Then back at the screen. "You were in the Army. Got a few medals while you were there. Honorably discharged. Followed by a college degree in computer science. Impressive work history."

She frowned. "Then for three years, nothing. No job, no source of income. Plenty of money in the bank, though."

She looked up. "I guess you'll do. Let's go inside."

"No, let's not. Let's do you. Tell me what the app says about you."

"Really? You want to know about me? I'm flattered. But I'm afraid you'll be disappointed. There's not much to know that I haven't already told you.

"I'm a divorced traveling nurse, living with my dog in an RV – which I just bought last week. My work history will show I've had a number of jobs, most lasting ninety days or less.

"I don't have any warrants. I'm not a serial killer. And I'm not on any sex offender registry. At least that I know of. But that could change, depending on how you and I work out.

"Anything else you want to know?"

"Uh, No. That's plenty."

"Good, follow me inside."

She stepped into her motorhome. I went in after her.

Biscuit was waiting for us, just inside the door. His tail was wagging a mile a minute. Norah gave him a pat on the back, then pointed at me.

"Biscuit, you remember Walker. He's the one who gave you the belly rub. Be nice to him, he might be a keeper."

Again, she was kidding.

At least, that's what I thought.

Chapter Six

Biscuit waddled over and flopped down on the floor. I knew what he wanted and didn't dare disappoint. I squatted down and rubbed his fat belly. And kept rubbing until his back leg started kicking the air. That was the signal for me to stop.

Norah was shaking her head when I stood. "I sure wish someone would pay that kind of attention to me."

I smiled. "You want me to rub your belly? Is that what you're saying? Cause if that's what you want, I'll do it. Just lay down."

She grinned. "Maybe later. But first, let's get my water problem solved."

She walked over to the RV control panel and flipped on the water pump. It immediately rumbled to life. The low hum let us know the motor was working. The system had passed its first test.

Now on to the second.

"Norah, try the kitchen sink."

She turned on the faucet. The sound from the pump changed, but no water came out.

"Turn it off! It's sucking air."

"Sucking air? What does that mean?"

I took a deep breath. "It means air is getting into the system. The pump can't get a prime. Either the water line has a break in it, or the valve setting is wrong. I'm betting it's the valve.

"Let's go out and check."

I went out first and Norah followed. She didn't bother locking the door behind her. Biscuit stayed inside.

We walked to the back of the RV. Then made the turn to get to the utility compartment on the other side. Our path was blocked by an older Ford Focus hooked up to the RV's back bumper.

It was a small four-door hatchback. The kind you used to see just about everywhere. Before SUVs took over. Nowadays, you mostly see them in 'Buy Here, Pay Here' car lots. Or being driven by people down on their luck.

These older hatchbacks are pretty reliable and get good gas mileage. They usually don't come with many extras, but they have everything you need. Small enough to be easy to park, yet still have enough room inside to carry just about anything you want.

Wasn't too long ago, everybody was driving them. But these days, people want a big SUV so they can sit high above the lowly hatchback. Of course, they have to pay a lot more to do that, but hey who's to judge?

Norah's little hatchback was different from most of them. The kind of different sure to be noticed by other drivers on the road.

Because Norah's little tow car was yellow. But not just yellow. It was bright sunshine yellow from bumper to bumper. Like a shiny banana on wheels.

I grinned. "It's yellow."

"Yes, it is. All over. But other than that, what do you think? Did I do good?"

The car looked to be in pretty good shape. No visible rust, no dents, and decent looking tires. The tow bar connecting it to the RV looked new. As did the safety chains.

It was the paint that demanded your attention though. Bright, bright yellow, with a high gloss shine that made the car impossible to miss. The bright yellow would help in traffic. No one could claim they didn't see you. And you wouldn't lose it in a parking lot either.

I nodded my approval. "I like it. I think you made out on the deal. How'd it do when you towed it down from Tennessee? Any problems?"

"No, not really. I kept worrying it would come loose. But it didn't. In fact, I almost forgot it was behind me. Until I pulled into a gas station came close to hitting a pump

"Other than that, it was easy towing it behind the RV. Little Buttercup followed me everywhere I went."

"Buttercup?"

"Yeah, Buttercup. That's what they named her. I think it fits, don't you?"

"Yeah, I guess it does."

Norah stepped around the car and headed to the other side. "Come on, let's get the toilet fixed."

Over at the RV's utility compartment, she pointed to the water panel. "Show me what I did wrong."

I looked, and as I suspected, the input valve was the problem.

"Norah, see the way the arrow on that valve is pointing? Most of the time it should be pointing to 'City Fill'. If you forget to set it that way, the valve stays open and the pump will suck air instead of water."

She nodded as if she understood. Then said, "You seem to be using the word 'suck' a lot. Is that something I should be worried about?"

I laughed. "No, it's just that "sucking' best describes the problem. Go ahead and turn the valve to 'City Fill.'"

She did.

"So, this should stop all the sucking?"

"It should. Let's go inside and check."

I followed as she went back to the RV's side entrance. She hadn't locked the door so we went right in.

She went straight to the kitchen sink and turned on the faucet. No water came out.

Clearly disappointed, she shook her head. "That didn't work. What now?"

I smiled. "Try turning on the water pump."

She had turned it off before we went out. She turned it back on and tried the sink a second time.

This time, the pump rumbled to life and after a few seconds, air hissed out of the spigot. Followed by a steady stream of water.

"It worked! I've got water! I'm going to try the toilet. You stay here."

She hurried into the bathroom, flushed the toilet, and came back out smiling. "It's working! I don't have to use Taco Bell anymore."

She came over and gave me a hug. "I was so afraid I'd have to take the RV somewhere and get it worked on. Me and Biscuit would have to live on the streets until they got it fixed because we wouldn't have a place to stay with a toilet.

"But not now, because you fixed it. And you showed me what to do if it happens again. I can't thank you enough."

She came over and hugged me again. This time holding on a bit longer than before. When she finally let me go, I stepped back and said, "Always happy to help. If you run into any other problems, just let me know. I'll be back in my RV if you need me."

I didn't want to leave but couldn't think of a good reason to stay, so I headed for the door.

Before I got to it, Norah said, "Don't go. Not yet. You still owe me a belly rub."

Chapter Seven

"So, that belly rub you promised? We'll get to that later. But right now, there's something else that needs your attention."

I was thinking my day was about to get a lot more interesting.

Unfortunately, I was wrong.

Instead of wanting a belly or any other kind of rub, she wanted me to take a look at another problem in her RV.

"Something's wrong with my TV. I can't get any channels using the antenna. I cranked it up and did a channel scan, but all I get is static. That can't be right, can it? What about the TV in your RV? You getting any local channels?"

I was a little sad that the talk of belly rubs had given way to TV problems, but it was my own fault. I had offered to help her with her RV, and that's what she was asking me to do.

I did my best to smile. "If your antenna is up and you did the channel scan, you should be getting at least a few channels. I'm getting more than 30 over at my place. Mostly from Orlando and Daytona. A few local ones too. You should be able to get the same ones."

She frowned. "But I'm not. All I get is static. What am I doing wrong?"

I already knew the answer. But asked a question just to be sure.

"Did you press the antenna booster button?"

"The what?"

"The antenna booster button. Did you press it?"

"I don't know. I pressed all the buttons on the remote. Is that where it is?"

"No, it's not on the remote. It's in the media cabinet to the right of the TV. A little black button on the side wall. If you press it, a red light comes on. That's when you use the remote to run the channel scan. After you press the button and the light comes on."

She looked like she didn't understand a word I said.

I pointed to the media cabinet. "The button's in there. Open the cabinet door and you'll find it. Against the wall on the right."

I wasn't sure she'd be able to get the cabinet door open. In RV's, most doors are designed so that when you close them, they'll stay closed while going down the road. More often than not, if it's been a while since the door has been used, it can take a pretty good pull to get it open.

Since she was a nurse, and was used to lifting patients all day, she probably had more than enough arm strength to get the door open. But just in case, I stayed close.

She squeezed in between me and the wall of the RV. Rubbing up against me as she did. Making no effort to pull away. It was almost like she was teasing me.

Again.

Whether she was, or not, I wasn't going to complain. I liked it.

Still up against me, she grabbed the door knob and with almost no effort, pulled it open, revealing a large canvas tote that filled most of the space in the compartment.

I was surprised to see it crammed into the small space.

"What's that? Your bag of toys?"

"No, I keep those in the bedroom. Maybe you'll get to see them one of these days. That bag up there is my go-bag. It has everything in it I need when I travel. My keys, credit cards, glasses, pills, a change of clothes, and a lot of other stuff you don't need to know about.

"I figured the cabinet was a good place to keep it. Near the door and easy to get to. But I'm guessing you think it's in the way?"

"Yeah, it's in the way if you want to get to the antenna button. Maybe it'd be better to keep the bag in the cubby behind the driver's seat. It won't be in the way there and it'll be easy to get to."

She wasn't so sure. "I like it where it is, but if you think I need to move it, I will. Hand it to me."

I grabbed the bag, which turned out to be a lot heavier than I expected, and handed it over. She carefully placed it behind the driver's seat. And then squeezed back in next to me.

Pointing into the media cabinet, I said, "You can get to the button now. Press it and see if the light comes on."

She reached in, moved her hand along the cabinet wall, and found the button. When she pressed it, a tiny red light lit up next to it.

"That's cool. The light tells me it's working. That's good to know."

She stepped away from me, picked up the remote, and pointed it at the TV. "I'm supposed to scan the channels now, right? Using the remote?"

"Yep, that's how it works. Make sure the input on the remote is set to antenna. Then press the menu button and start the channel scan."

It took her less than a minute to get the scan started. Three minutes later, it finished, showing it had found 28 digital channels.

Norah was all smiles. "I can't believe it. It really works. You saved the day again."

She leaned in and gave me a quick hug. Then scrolled through the channels until she found the NASA station. The screen had a live feed from the launch site, showing the rocket on the pad. But other than a scrolling message at the bottom of the display, it didn't look like much was happening.

The message explained why. "Today's Space X launch has been rescheduled for 6:15 AM EST tomorrow." No details, just that the launch had been rescheduled.

Norah shook her head. "Well, that's not good. I was hoping they'd do it today. I really wanted to see it take off. But it looks like it's not going to happen.

"I guess that means I'll have to stick around til tomorrow. "What about you?"

"I'm staying too. I came to see the launch and I'm not leaving until I do."

She smiled. "That means we have the rest of the day off. You want to grab lunch?"

"Sure. As long as it's not from Taco Bell."

She laughed. "What? You don't like tacos? Or are you just a Taco Bell snob?"

"No. It's not that. I like tacos. Even the ones from Taco Bell. It's just that I've eaten there three days in a row and I'm kind of taco'd out. But if that's where you want to go, I'll go with you. They probably know you there by name now. What with all your visits to the john."

She gave me a playful punch on the shoulder. "Hey, we're

not talking about that anymore."

Then, "Let's take Buttercup and get something on the way to the beach."

"The beach? I thought it was just lunch. Now you're talking about taking me to the beach? What's up with that?"

She had a quick answer. "This is my cheat week. One of the things I wanted to do was put my toes in the sand before heading off to my next job. There is a beach close by, I want to go there. But I don't want to go alone.

"If I show up there by myself, guys will be hitting on me until I leave. I don't want that. But if you go with me, they'll see I'm with you, and they'll leave me alone.

"So how about it? Will you go play in the sand with me?"

I probably should have said 'no'.

But didn't.

Chapter Eight

"The beach, huh?"

"Yeah, Walker. Let's go to the beach. It'll be a lot more fun than hanging around here, doing nothing. I'll even buy you lunch on the way. We won't have to stay long. I just want to walk on the sand, test the water, then come back here.

"It'll be fun. What do you say?"

I didn't answer right away because I didn't want to seem too eager. But she was right. Going to the beach with her would be a lot more fun than sitting around in the Taco Bell parking lot.

Still, I shrugged, and acted like going would be a pain. Then, said, "Yeah, I guess I'll go with you. But before we leave, you have to tell me about this 'cheat week' thing you mentioned."

She smiled, probably because she'd gotten me to go to the beach with her. Then said, "So you want to know about my cheat week?

"It's like this. Working at the hospital means I come in contact with a lot of people who are in pain, are busted up, or are dying from something. I'm around them all day long, helping them the best I can. Some are screaming in agony, others are soiling their britches, and almost none are happy about being in the hospital.

"They didn't plan to get hurt, or get sick or do something that would put them in a hospital bed. They want to be back home, and not strapped down on a hard medical bunk, with tubes stuck in their bodies and machines beeping in the background.

"When they are in pain, or upset, or need to have their butts wiped, nurses are the ones that have to deal with it. But, we can't prescribe drugs to make their pain go away or magically make them well. When they want to see a doctor, we can't just make one appear. They have their own schedules and often are overworked, understaffed, and dead tired.

"On top of that, we are often restricted with what we can do by insurance, hospital policies, and government rules. So obviously, there's a lot of stress involved – for the staff as well as the patients.

"When my shift is over and I go home at the end of the day, I'm too tired to go out. Too tired to do anything except to eat and go to bed, knowing that I'll be facing the same thing when I go back in the next day."

"That's why so many doctors and nurses burn out. The stress of the job. So much of what we do is life or death, where even a small mistake can have deadly consequences. While I'm on duty, I have to take things very seriously and concentrate on my work. I can't play around, can't slack off, can't let my mind wander. And it wears on me.

"But, when the job ends and I get a couple of weeks off, I treat them as my 'cheat weeks'.

"That's when I can sleep late. And eat whatever I want. And go wherever I want, and be with whomever I want to be with.

"That's why we'll be eating junk food for lunch today. And why I might be wearing a tiny bikini at the beach. And why I chose you to keep me company. Because it's my cheat week and I get to do anything I want. Even get a bit wild, if I get the urge."

She took a deep breath, then continued. "So, yeah, we're going to the beach. Go back to your place and get ready. I'll pick you up in about fifteen minutes. Bring a towel if you have one."

She ushered me out the door.

As I headed back to my RV, I decided I liked the idea of her cheat week. Especially the part about the tiny bikini.

Bob was still napping when I got back to the RV. His food and water bowls looked like they hadn't been touched since I'd topped them off earlier. His litter box was starting to fill and would need to be changed soon.

I had a plan for that. I'd wait until Taco Bell closed, bag up the litter, and dump it into one of their outdoor trash cans. I was pretty sure they wouldn't mind.

Norah said to get ready for the beach. To me that meant, bringing something to swim in, a tube of sunscreen, and a towel.

I hadn't owned a swimsuit since I was a kid, preferring to wear cutoffs. I had a closet full of cargo shorts, but those weren't really suited for swimming. When they got wet, they'd get heavy, and at the beach, the pockets would fill with sand and weigh you down.

Since I didn't have a swimsuit or cutoffs, I grabbed the next best thing – a pair of colorful boxers shorts – the kind I wear under my pants every day. They're comfortable and look enough like swim trunks that most people wouldn't be able to tell the difference. And if they could, who cares.

I didn't have a beach towel either. But I did have a white bath towel hanging over the shower door. It was slightly damp but would have to do.

Grabbing a tube of sunscreen from the medicine cabinet, I headed up front. With my sunglasses, hat, phone, wallet, and keys, and a cold bottle of water in hand, I called myself ready to go.

Norah showed up three minutes later. In Buttercup.

With a smile, she asked, "You know how to drive a stick?"

"Yeah."

"Good. You can drive."

She moved over to the passenger side and I took my place behind the wheel.

As soon as we were buckled in, she pointed ahead, "Turn right when you get to the road. There's a Krystal about four miles south. Take me there."

She hadn't asked if I wanted to eat Krystal burgers for lunch, which was a good thing, because it wouldn't have been my first choice. But since it was her cheat week, it was her choice. If she wanted Krystal burgers, that was what we'd be having.

Chapter Nine

We pulled into the drive-through at Krystal. Ordered six burgers, two medium fries, two Cokes.

It sounded like a lot of food, but wasn't. Krystal burgers are tiny. That's what they are famous for. Tiny square burgers.

Not much taste to them, but they get them to you quickly and they don't cost much.

We finished eating before leaving the parking lot. After tossing our empties in a nearby trash can, I asked, "Where to next?"

Norah had a quick answer. "The beach! Take me to the beach!"

I was ready to go. But her little car didn't have GPS and I wasn't familiar with the area.

"I'll take you to the beach. Just tell me how to get there from here."

She had apparently checked the map before we left and knew the way.

"Pull out and turn left. Turn right when you get to the bridge. Then follow the signs to Playalinda."

It took us about fifteen minutes to get to the Playalinda Ranger Station. I paid the twenty-dollar entry fee and passed through the gate heading toward the beach.

I was about to pull into the first beach side parking lot, when Norah said, "No. Not here. Google says the best beach is at parking area thirteen. That's where I want to go. Area thirteen. It's at the end of the road."

I didn't really care which beach we went to. I was just along to keep her company. If she wanted to go to area thirteen, that was fine with me.

According to the sign at the gate, it was six miles ahead. If I kept to the posted twelve-mile-per-hour speed limit, it'd be a thirty-minute drive. Since there was no reason to speed, I didn't.

But most of the cars coming toward us did. A long line of them going well over the limit. So many, in fact, it looked like they were evacuating the area.

I started to wonder if maybe we should turn around and join them. I decided to mention it to Norah.

"See all the cars coming our way? They seem to be in a hurry to get away from where we're going. Maybe the beach is closed up ahead. Think we should turn around and leave with them?"

She shook her head. "No, I looked it up before we left. Supposedly, parking area thirteen is one of the best places to watch a rocket take off. It's right across from the pad. On launch day, people come out here early to get a prime viewing spot.

"But since this morning's launch was scrubbed, all those people are heading home now. That's why there's so many cars leaving."

Her explanation made sense.

But the official-looking sign just ahead, didn't. It warned that we might encounter nude sunbathers at parking area thirteen.

"Norah, did you see that sign? It says we're going to a nude beach. Is that where you're taking me? To a nude beach? Is that your plan? To get me naked and take advantage of me?"

She laughed. "No, that was not part of my plan. I just wanted to go to the beach. I didn't know there'd be naked people. But hey, being on a nude beach with you might make the day a bit more interesting. Unless you're chicken."

"Me, chicken? Just say the word and I'll drop my pants right here."

I was bluffing. I wouldn't be dropping my pants in the middle of the road. Unless she dropped hers first.

Then I might.

"Walker don't worry. I was joking. You can keep your clothes on. At least until we get to the beach. Then we'll see what happens."

Three minutes later we reached area thirteen. There was no parking lot. Just a row of painted white stripes on the side of the road. Enough room between each one for a car to pull in headfirst. There were plenty of cars already there. And a few open spaces left by early risers who'd gone back home.

I pulled into the first empty slot and parked.

Before getting out, I asked Norah if she had any valuables we needed to lock up.

"No. There's nothing valuable in here. Not even a radio worth stealing. The only thing I brought was sunscreen and a towel. I'm taking both with me."

She stepped out, opened the back door, grabbed a towel and a small tote. I figured it was where she kept her sunscreen. And maybe her bikini.

I got my towel and we both headed up the road toward what looked like the entrance to the beach. A wood-planked boardwalk going up over a sand dune.

Norah led the way.

From behind, I got my first look at what she was wearing. Loose-fitting, cream-colored beach pants. An unbuttoned light blue shirt. Dark blue sports bra peeking through. And sandals.

Classic beach wear.

I was wearing what I usually wear in Florida. Well-worn cargo shorts, a faded button-up fishing shirt, and lace-up tennis shoes.

I wouldn't win any fashion awards, but was comfortable.

As we headed toward the boardwalk, we passed a small block building with a men's sign on one side and a woman's on the other. We hadn't made any pit stops since eating, so it was nice to know bathrooms were nearby if needed.

Going up the boardwalk steps, we passed three men coming back from the beach. Oiled up with sunscreen, they were all smiles, and thankfully, fully clothed. One of them winked at me as he passed. Norah didn't notice.

When we reached the top of the boardwalk, we could finally see the beach and the blue-green waters of the Atlantic. The snow-white sand was peppered with colorful beach umbrellas flapping in the wind.

Gentle waves lapped the shore. Seagulls floated in the breezes above. No buildings, no condos, and no tourist attractions marred our view. Just the beach, the ocean, and the sea oats covering the dunes.

Norah reached out and squeezed my hand. "This is why I wanted to come out here. To see this."

She stood still for a few moments, taking it all in. Then pointed to a spot about fifty yards north of where we were. "That looks like a good place. Not many people around it. Let's go set up there."

She let go of my hand and headed down the steps.

The beach wasn't crowded. The few people there were mostly sitting in groups of three or four. A few singles as well. Almost all of the men were naked, the women topless.

I tried not to stare.

We made it halfway to the spot Norah had picked out when she turned to me and whispered, "It's mostly men out here. That's why I wanted you to come with me. So these guys wouldn't hit on me."

I squeezed her hand and whispered back. "I don't think a lot of these men are interested in women. Some seem to be checking me out more than you."

She laughed. "You wish."

I shook my head, "Nope. Not at all."

We kept walking and only stopped when Norah found a place that suited her. Away from the water, near the edge of the dune high enough to give us a bit of shade from the bright west-moving sun. There was no one nearby.

"Walker, does this work for you?"

"Yeah, if you like it, I like it."

She smiled at my answer, then unrolled her towel and spread it out on the sand. I did the same, putting my short bath towel up against her much larger beach towel.

I expected her to say something about my poor excuse for a towel, but she didn't. Instead, she stepped out of her pants. There was no tiny bikini underneath. Just dark blue running shorts.

Not what I was expecting, but still nice. They showcased her long legs and firm butt.

While I was admiring her lower half, she pulled off her shirt.

The sports bra she was wearing, hid more than it showed but hinted at toned abs and firm breasts.

I must have smiled, because she asked, "Like what you see?"

I knew there was only one answer.

"Yes, I do. I definitely do."

Chapter Ten

We were sitting on our towels at Playalinda Beach watching the waves roll in. Norah handed me a tube of sunscreen.

"Do me. Start with my back."

She turned away from me and lowered the straps of her sports bra. There were two nickel-sized scars just below her right shoulder. Bullet wounds. Sometime in the past, she'd been shot.

I had questions but didn't ask them. Instead, I squirted sunscreen onto my palm and got ready to do her.

Beginning at the base of her neck, I gently rubbed the cream in. Taking my time as I made my way down. The warmth of her skin against my hands awakened a desire within me. One that I hadn't felt in a long time.

I squirted more sunscreen onto my palm and kept working her back. When I reached the first scar, I hesitated, not knowing if I should touch it or not.

She noticed. "Don't stop. Keep doing what you're doing. Cover everything. I don't want to burn."

I kept going. Gingerly rubbing the cream over her scars, then continuing on down. Paying careful attention to her spine.

I stopped when I reached the top of her running shorts and sat back to admire my work.

Sensing my movement away from her, she said, "You're not done yet. You still have to do my legs."

I decided then and there if there was such a thing as a professional sunscreen applier, I'd be up for the job, but would only offer my services to women.

Squirting another dollop of sunscreen onto my palm, I got ready to work on her legs. Starting just below the hem of her running shorts, I massaged the cream slowly onto her inner thighs, being careful not to touch her private parts.

As I was massaging the soft skin near the hem of her shorts, she whispered, "Oh God, that feels so good," followed by "Yeah, that's the spot."

The words of encouragement kept coming until they evolved into a soft cooing sound. Apparently, she was enjoying what I was doing as much as I was.

I kept going, massaging the cream onto her lower thighs, the back of her knees, her lower legs, and finally, her ankles. I stopped at her feet, sat back, and took a deep breath. It had been an enjoyable experience for me. So much so, that I need to take a short break.

But it wasn't to be.

She rolled over. "Do my front. Legs first. Start at my ankles and work your way up."

I held up my hand. "Give me a minute. I need to take a break."

She smiled. "What's the matter? Never touched a woman before?"

I shrugged. "It's been a while."

Still smiling, she said, "Well, don't worry. It felt like you knew what you were doing. I'd give it an eight out of ten."

She raised her knees and nodded toward the tube of sunscreen I was holding. Letting me know it was time to get back to it.

I started on her ankles. Massaging her skin as I worked my way up the front of her legs. Her shins and knees didn't need much attention. But when I moved to her thighs she said, "Slow down. Take your time. Do it right."

I wasn't sure what she meant by 'do it right', but I slowed and paid special attention to her upper thighs. Massaging the skin in a slow circular motion.

"That's better. Keep doing it that way."

I kept working the area until I reached the lower hem of her running shorts. When I stopped, she said. "Go a little higher. I don't want to burn there."

I took a deep breath and began massaging cream between her legs, getting dangerously close to her special parts, but deliberately not touching them.

Her breathing got deeper and deeper as my hands moved closer to her forbidden zone.

I was almost there, when she suddenly reached down and grabbed my hand. "Stop! That's enough. I need to get into the water."

She quickly stood, brushed the sand off her belly, and headed toward the shoreline.

I followed.

I needed to get in the water too.

Chapter Eleven

Without testing the temperature of the water, Norah waded into the waves and only stopped when the water reached just above her belly button. She crossed her arms and shivered, but didn't look back at me.

That was a good thing since I had a bit of a problem with the way my pants were fitting at the moment.

I was still wearing the same cargo shorts I had on when I started the day. I was in no hurry to get them wet since I didn't bring any to change into. But rubbing sunscreen on Norah's warm body had created a problem that even my cargo shorts couldn't hide.

The quickest cure was to soak the problem area in cold water.

Since it was a nude beach, and no one would probably care, I stepped out of my cargo shorts, dropping them on the sand behind me as I walked into the ocean wearing just my boxers. As luck would have it, I'd chosen to wear the ones with the Popeye print that morning. They were from a company called Crazy Boxer. After buying and wearing the first pair, I was so impressed with the fit and feel, I quickly bought eleven more, giving me an even dozen.

Each pair was imprinted with a cartoon character from a popular TV show or comic book. Popeye, Mighty Mouse, Mickey Mouse, Star Wars, Donald Duck, and a few others. I didn't buy them for the artwork. It was the soft fabric that sold me.

Wearing just my boxers, I waded into the water. And kept

going until it was up to my naval. Being late January, the Atlantic Ocean was still cold. That's what my body needed at the moment. Cold water. My guess, Norah needed the same.

It only took a few minutes of me standing out in it to feel it was safe to return to shore. Norah had already gone back in and was standing on the beach where I had dropped my cargo shorts, waiting for me to catch up with her.

While I was still belly deep in the water, she called out to me. "Walker, come closer, I want to see what you're wearing."

We were on a nude beach. Seeing that I had stripped out of my pants, she may have thought I had gone into the water naked. But if she was thinking that, she was going to be disappointed, as were the three men who had stopped to see what was going on.

I waded back to shore while pulling the cloth of my boxers away from my private parts.

Norah started applauding when she saw what I was wearing. "Popeye? Is that your secret identity?"

I smiled. "It is today. Might be someone else tomorrow."

When I got close, I could see that she was shivering and had goosebumps on her arms. We were both wet. The cool breezes coming off the Atlantic added to the chill.

I pointed to our towels. "Let's go dry off."

She shook her head. "No, let's not. Since you're already wet, let's see what you have under those shorts."

I smiled. "You first."

Without hesitation, she pulled off her sports bra revealing her breasts. They weren't large, but by no means small. They definitely got my attention.

She then slipped her fingers around the waistband of her bottoms and acted like she was going to pull them down.

But didn't.

Instead, she said, "Your turn."

I'm not bashful about taking my clothes off around a woman, but being on a public beach with a growing audience was different. The cold water had caused a bit of shrinkage and I didn't feel like showing the result to onlookers.

So instead of dropping my boxers, I said, "Maybe later. But right now I'm going to go dry off."

She smiled. "Later, huh? I might just hold you to that."

With her sports bra in hand, she followed me to our towels. After she dried off, she lay down, with her breasts exposed to the world.

I tried not to stare, but it was hard not to. Upon close inspection, I noticed two bullet holes just under her right breast, about an inch apart, matching the ones on her back. Completely healed, probably a few years old. I wanted to know how they came to be, but didn't ask. If she wanted me to know, she'd tell me. Maybe.

Norah, still topless, picked up the sunscreen and held it out to me.

"My front needs doing. You up for it?"

I shook my head. "No, I don't think so. My heart might not be able to take it. You'll have to do them yourself."

She laughed, squirted cream into her palm, and started massaging her breasts.

Seeing me watching, she smiled. "You sure you don't want to do this?"

I shook my head again. "Norah, I'm afraid it'd create a problem my boxers couldn't hide. So, reluctantly, I'm going to have to pass."

She nodded toward my shorts.

"It looks like you might already have a problem down there."

She was right. The bulge was unmistakable.

I needed to change the subject, so I asked, "How'd you get shot?"

Instead of answering right away, she picked up her sports bra and put it back on. Then crossed her arms and looked out at the water. She stayed that way for a while. Then finally said, "I was working. A guy came in with a gun. He started shooting. I got hit twice. It hurt like hell. But I lived."

She lay back down on her towel, turned her head away from me, and said nothing for the next hour.

The sun had moved far enough west so that we were mostly in the shade. Even though she wasn't speaking, it was nice to lay on the sand next to her, listening to the gentle sounds of the waves.

It would have been nicer had I not asked her about the scars. Or, as I later found out, if she had told me the truth about how they came to be.

Chapter Twelve

Neither of us had worn a watch or brought a phone, so we weren't able to keep track of time. But since we didn't have to be anywhere until the launch the following day, we stayed out on the beach, in no hurry to leave.

Norah, still on her back facing away from me, drifted off to sleep. Her soft snoring gave it away.

I was still wondering about the scars. She hadn't said much about them. Just that she'd been shot at work. I was sure there was a lot more to it than that.

I wasn't going to ask about them again. The first time, it seemed to upset her. I didn't want to do that a second time.

An hour or so later, she rolled over, opened her eyes, and took my hand. "I'm glad you came with me."

I smiled. "I'm glad you asked me to. It's been fun."

She lay there looking at me for a while, then closed her eyes and fell back to sleep.

Sometime later, she stirred again. "I'm hungry. Let's go back to town and see if we can find something to eat."

I was hungry too. The tiny burgers we'd had for lunch hadn't filled me up. We'd brought no food with us, so we missed out on an afternoon snack.

We gathered up our things, put on our clothes, and went back to the car. The parking area, which had been almost full when we first arrived, was now mostly empty. Buttercup looked lonely with no cars around her. But she was still there. No one had bothered to try to steal her, or break out her windows looking for things of value. One look told them it wouldn't be worth the effort.

After stowing our towels, we headed to town.

Twenty minutes later, as we were coming off the Max Brewer bridge onto the mainland, Norah pointed to a truck on the side of the road. A man standing near it was holding a hand-painted sign that said, "Fresh Oysters. $24 per dozen."

We were on the coast, it made sense that people might be selling freshly caught seafood from the back of their trucks. Had it been shrimp, I might have been interested. But not oysters. I don't eat them. The look and texture remind me too much of something that comes out of a child's nose during flu season.

Apparently, Norah felt differently. She wanted me to stop.

So of course, I did.

I pulled onto the side of the road and parked behind the truck. The older gentleman who had been holding the oyster sign set it on the ground and signaled for me to pull the car up closer.

I wasn't sure why, but I did, leaving enough room between the rear of his truck and Buttercup's front bumper so that if I needed to get back on the road quickly without having to put it in reverse, I could.

As soon as I got the car stopped, Norah reached into the glove compartment and pulled out a wad of cash. She'd said earlier there was nothing in the car worth stealing. Apparently, she'd forgotten about the money.

I didn't say anything. It was her car and her money. If it were stolen, it'd be her loss, not mine.

She tapped me on the shoulder. "Come on, let's go see what he has."

I already knew. He had oysters and I wasn't interested.

Without waiting to see if I was going to join her, she got out of the car and headed toward the truck.

Reluctantly, I followed.

Seeing us coming, the oyster man wiped his hands on his well-worn apron, walked over, and said, "That's the brightest yellow I've ever seen on a car. Did it come that way?"

Norah grinned. "Yep, that's what I was told. It's a factory option. Called grabber yellow."

He nodded his approval, then pointed to the camper shell on his truck. "I got a good deal on fresh oysters today. Twenty-four dollars a dozen. How many can I get you?"

Instead of answering his question, Norah asked one of her own. "Those oysters? They from around here?"

He nodded. "Yep, they sure are. Fresh harvested today. Been on ice ever since. I got a special price. A dozen for twenty-four dollars."

Norah looked at me. "What do you think?"

I shook my head. "I don't eat oysters. Don't get any for me."

The man, hearing my answer, said, "You're missing out. Oysters are good for your love life."

Norah chimed in. "Yeah, they're good for your love life, Walker. Might come in handy tonight. Let's get some."

I wasn't convinced.

The oyster man, fearing he might lose a sale, said, "Tell you what. It's the end of the day and I'm tired. How about a dozen for twenty? I'll throw in two lemons and a bottle of hot sauce. You won't find a better price anywhere. What do you say?"

Norah peeled off a twenty and handed it to him. "We'll take a dozen."

He grinned, took the bill, and stuffed it into his jeans.

"A dozen oysters coming right up."

He went into the back of his camper and quickly came out with a pie tin holding a dozen shucked oysters on ice.

He showed the plate to Norah, then quickly covered it with clear plastic cling wrap.

"You sure you only want a dozen? They're pretty tasty."

Norah didn't have to look at me to know the answer. "No thanks, those will be enough."

With the plate in hand, she headed to the car, saying, "We need to get these in the fridge before they spoil."

I figured the ice they were packed in would keep them cool, but seeing how I didn't know much about oysters, I could have been wrong.

With me driving and Norah giving directions, it took us less than ten minutes to get back to the Taco Bell lot and her RV. As soon as we parked, she grabbed the keys and said, "I'm going to put them in the fridge. Meet me back here in thirty minutes and we'll eat."

Before I could tell her I wasn't going to eat any of the slimy little creatures, she stepped out and headed to her RV. Once she was safely inside, I went back to my place.

Bob was waiting for me at the door, chirping, letting me know he was happy I was back. At least, that's what I thought he meant. It could have been something else.

I quickly stripped off my clothes and went to the bathroom. I needed to shower off the salt and sand from the beach. I moved Bob's litter box out of the stall, started the water, and after it warmed up, stepped in.

Six minutes later, I stepped out wondering if I had any clean clothes to wear on my dinner date with Norah. Except it wasn't officially a date, though. Just two new friends sharing a meal. But it might be more. She'd warned me that it was her cheat week and things could get wild.

I wanted to be presentable in case they did.

The choices in my closet were limited to what I call Florida casual. Cargo shorts, tees, and fishing shirts.

I did have a pair of long pants but they were heavy-duty camo and I only wore them when I needed to get under the RV to do some work. They were still dirty from the last time. I wouldn't be wearing them to Norah's.

I ended up putting on Mighty Mouse boxers, a clean pair of cargo shorts, and a light blue Columbia fishing shirt. My idea of dressing up.

Twenty minutes later, just before heading over, I remembered the unopened box of Chardonnay I had in the fridge. I'd gotten it at Publix a week earlier. Mainly because it was in a box, had a screw off top, and was on sale.

It wouldn't be the wine they'd be serving in a fancy restaurant, but it was better than not having any wine at all.

With the box in hand, I locked up and headed to Norah's.

Had I known how the night would end, I would have stayed in my own place and never left.

Chapter Thirteen

She was outside, sitting on the steps of her RV, waiting for me. Seeing the box of wine I was carrying, she smiled. "I like a man who only drinks the best."

There was no doubt she was kidding. Still, she invited me in.

Biscuit was laying under the dining table on a dog bed that she had put there for him. When he saw me, he stood, stretched, and waddled over. He smiled the way some dogs do, plopped down, rolled over onto his back, and lay there, belly up.

It was clear he wanted another rub, and I was happy to oblige him. I got down and rubbed his fat belly until he started kicking his right leg. It was clear I had found his sweet spot.

After a few minutes, he'd had enough. He rolled over, stood up, and waddled back to his bed, his little tail wagging all the way. He was a happy dog.

When I got up off the floor, Norah handed me a glass of wine and led me over to the sofa. After we sat, she raised her glass in a toast. "To being together tonight. May we both wake in the morning with smiles on our faces."

We clinked our glasses and took our first taste of the wine.

Surprisingly, it wasn't bad for box wine that was bought on sale at Publix. In fact, it went down smoother than a lot of the more expensive and pretentious wines I've tasted.

Norah must have felt the same way. She took a couple of

sips and didn't make a frowny face.

I considered it a win.

Smiling, she put down her glass. "Remember me telling you about cheat week?"

"Yeah, I remember. No way I could forget."

"Well, today was just an example of the things I get to do on cheat week. I get to eat junk food, go to new places, be with new people, and sometimes get a little bit wild.

"It rarely goes beyond that, though. Usually, not even that far. More often than not, I just stay in, read a book, take it easy."

She took another sip of wine. I did the same. Then she continued.

"Once in a great while though, I meet someone special during cheat week. Someone who makes me smile and feel good about myself. Someone willing to go to places I pick out, and do wild and crazy things when we get there.

"Like what we did today.

"But no matter what, you and I know that after this week, maybe even after the launch tomorrow, we'll go our separate ways, and probably never see each other again.

"That means tonight might be our first and only night together. And because of that, I intend to make it memorable.

She smiled and looked me in the eye. "But first, I need to ask you a couple of questions. Is that okay?"

"Sure, ask away."

She set her glass down and turned to me. "I know you're not married. At least that's what it said in the report I got today. Is that still the case?"

"Yeah, I'm still single."

"Good. What about a girlfriend? Is there someone back home who wouldn't be happy to know you are here with me tonight?"

I thought about the people in my circle of friends and couldn't come up with anyone who would consider my spending time with another woman as being unfaithful.

I didn't have a steady girlfriend or even a girlfriend in waiting. I had plenty of friends, as well as female companions who I'd spent time with in the past, but nothing within the last several months.

"Norah, there's no one waiting for me back home. In fact, most of my friends would be happy to know I was dining with someone other than just my cat."

Smiling, she reached out and patted my arm. "You poor thing. Eating alone with just your cat. We definitely have to change that tonight. Maybe, if you're really lucky, it'll be more than just a meal. Maybe a lot more."

She picked up her glass, finished off the wine, and stood. I watched as she walked to the fridge, reached in, and came out with the oysters. She brought them over to the dinner table, along with two plates and a box of saltines.

Pointing her finger in my direction, she signaled for me to come over and join her. I wasn't interested in the oysters, but I wasn't going to be rude and not sit at the table while she ate. I walked over and took a seat across from her.

After refilling our wine glasses, she said, "Let's eat and see where the evening takes us."

She picked up an oyster, squeezed lemon juice onto the meat, and brought the shell to her mouth. In one quick motion, she tipped it up and the gray blob slid down her throat. After taking a sip of wine, she put the empty shell back on the plate and said, "Your turn. "

I smiled while shaking my head. "Uh, No. No oysters for me. I'll just watch you eat. It'll be better that way."

She didn't agree.

"Walker, that's not the way it works. See, if I'm eating oysters, you have to eat them too. Else, later on, when we kiss, I'll be the only one with oyster breath. We wouldn't want that would we?"

I held firm.

"Norah, I'm telling you, I'm not eating any oysters. But you go ahead. It won't bother me."

She held her smile. "Walker, you need to try at least one."

"Nope. Not going to do it."

She wasn't giving up. "Walker, how about this? For each oyster you eat, I'll take off a piece of clothing. I've only got four things on, so you won't have to eat many to win the prize."

I knew then, that she was evil. She had come up with a way to make me eat oysters.

A way I couldn't resist.

Chapter Fourteen

"Okay, I'll try one. But I can't guarantee I'll be able to get it down."

"Don't worry, you'll like it. But since you've never eaten an oyster before, I'll dress it up with a little hot sauce so it'll go down easier."

Norah picked up one of the larger ones from the plate, covered the gray matter with a thin layer of hot sauce, and handed it to me. "Tip the shell up and let the meat slide into your mouth. Bite into it to get the full taste, then swallow."

I still didn't want to eat it, but when Norah grabbed the bottom of her shirt and teased me by pulling it up, revealing her belly button, I figured, what the hell, one can't hurt.

I tipped the shell up just like she said, and let the meat and juice slide into my mouth. Rather than chew, I bit into it, then swallowed it whole, almost gagging as it went down.

It wasn't a pleasant experience. Kind of like swallowing something that should have been blown into a tissue. There was a mild fishy taste which the hot sauce did a pretty good job of covering. But the consistency of the oyster meat, or lack of it, did nothing for me.

Frankly, after eating the first one, I couldn't figure out why anyone would voluntarily eat them, much less shell out good money to buy them. A good New York Strip at any restaurant would cost less than a dozen oysters and taste a lot better.

But, against my better judgment, I'd done it. Eaten an oyster. Norah rewarded me by pulling off her top, revealing a white lace bra that did little to hide her perky breasts.

She picked up another shell and downed the meat quickly. Then pointed at me. "Your turn. Take something off."

I realized then, for the first time, that we were both playing the game. Each time she ate one, I too was supposed to remove a piece of clothing. I didn't mind, as long as it meant I didn't have to eat another one. She could eat all she wanted and I'd take everything off.

I'd let her win the game as long as I didn't have to swallow another one of the slimy creatures.

But according to her, that wasn't the way the game was played. Each time she ate one, I had to eat one too. Whether I wanted to or not. Those were the rules of Strip Oyster. Once the game started, you had to keep playing until it was over.

So following the rules, which I was pretty sure she'd just made up on the spot, I unbuttoned my shirt and took it off.

And then, according to those same rules, it was my turn to eat another one.

I for sure, didn't want to. But if I wanted to see where the game was headed and what would happen when one of us, probably me, had no more clothes to take off, I had to eat another one of the gobs of phlegm.

So I did.

I picked out the smallest one on the plate, covered it with hot sauce, and quickly downed it. As before, I almost gagged as it slid down my throat.

But I'd gotten it down and Norah rewarded me by standing up and taking off her shorts, revealing white French lace panties that matched her top.

I nodded, showing my appreciation.

She frowned. "Walker, I'm not sure this is a fair game. I'm

down to two pieces of clothing. You've got at least four things left if we count your socks.

"So, here are the new rules. Socks and shoes don't count. That'll make us even. We both only have two things left. The next round is when it's going to get interesting."

She unexpectedly winced, touched her stomach, then said, "Maybe we should take a break. Want another glass of wine?"

"Sure, maybe wine will get the fishy taste out of my mouth."

The truth was, my stomach was starting to feel a bit weird. Probably from the oysters. Taking a break and drinking a bit of wine might give my gut a chance to deal with what I'd just put in it.

Norah filled our glasses, and we both took a sip. She winced again, like she was in pain, then said, "I'm not sure about those oysters."

About the same time, my stomach made a strange noise. A bubbling gurgle. I took a deep breath.

"What do you mean you're not sure about them?"

Norah, still wincing in pain, said, "The guy claimed the oysters were fresh, right off the boat. But now that I think about it, oysters sold in Florida come from Apalachicola, way on the other side of the state. The ones he was selling either had to be trucked in from over there, or were restaurant culls. Either way, I think they may have been well past their prime."

She grabbed her stomach. "I think we should call the game. I'm not feeling well. How are you doing?"

I barely got the words out.

"Not good."

Bad things were going on in my gut. It felt like someone with scissors was trying to cut their way out. Contractions were coming about every thirty seconds. If I were pregnant, the baby was due. Sweat was forming on my brow. My stomach was telling me I needed to get to a toilet, and soon.

I stood, quickly put my shirt back on, and said, "Norah, I need to get back to my place. I think those oysters are fighting to get out. I need to be somewhere they can."

She laughed, then winced again. "Walker, I think we're both going to be sick. You go on home. I'll catch up with you in the morning."

My stomach made a noise that sounded a lot like the last bit of water swirling down a bathtub drain. At the same time, I felt a mass moving toward the bottom of my belly. It was definitely time to go.

I headed for the door, hoping I could get home before it was too late.

Outside, walking as quickly as I could with clenched butt cheeks, I counted off each step as I got closer and closer to my RV, hoping that I could make it before the volcano erupted.

Remembering that the door was locked, and not wanting to be held up for any reason, I got the key out and had it ready as soon as I got close.

I was sweating the last few steps, almost sure I wouldn't make it.

But I did.

I got the door open and headed for the toilet. What happened next is something I'd rather not talk about.

Bob could tell you about it though. He came into the bathroom and kept me company most of the night. Sitting across from me, he cried as I sat on the porcelain throne in agony.

I least I think it was he who was crying.

It could have been me.

Chapter Fifteen

At some point during the early morning hours, I must have felt safe enough to go to bed. Because that's where I was, when I woke to someone pounding on my side door.

It wasn't the way I wanted to be woken, nor was it the time of day I wanted to get up. After the previous evening's toilet disaster, I needed sleep. Lots of it.

I also needed whoever was outside pounding on my door to go away.

But they didn't.

They kept pounding. Then a woman's voice said, "Walker, get up. I've got something to make you feel better."

It was Norah. She was the one making all the noise. Keeping me from going back to sleep, while trying to make me get up.

I wanted her to go away, to just leave me alone. That's what I would have told her, except for one thing.

She'd said she had something that would make me feel better. She was a nurse. So maybe there was a chance she did have some magical cure that would make my agony go away.

I doubted it.

My head hurt, my stomach was raw, and my butt cheeks were sore. There was no magic pill that would cure these ills.

What I needed was sleep. And time. Those were the only cures I could think of.

Then I remembered Norah had eaten more oysters than I had. When we parted ways, she too was feeling ill and probably spent the night as I had. On the toilet.

But now, the morning after our mutual bowel destruction, she apparently felt good enough to get out of her bed, get dressed and come over and pound on my door.

So maybe, she really did have a cure for what ailed us.

If there was any chance she did, I wanted to give it a try.

Reluctantly, I got out of bed, pulled on clean shorts and a tee, and went to the door.

She was standing outside. Smiling. In her left hand, a clear plastic bottle. No label. No identifying marks. Filled about halfway up with a green liquid.

If what was in the bottle was the cure and she had taken it, it hadn't worked for her. Her face was ashen, her hair a mess, and it looked like she had slept in her clothes.

I didn't say anything about how she looked, though. I figured I looked worse. I just nodded and invited her in.

Her first words were, "How do you feel?"

"Bad, real bad. And empty. There's nothing left in my stomach. I flushed it all away."

She winced. "Same here. But I brought you something that will make you feel better."

She handed me the bottle and a small pink pill. "Take this. Then drink the juice."

I should have asked what she was giving me. But I didn't. I didn't have the strength. I took the pill and a sip of the liquid. It tasted slightly metallic. And sweet. I put the bottle down after the first sip.

"Walker, you have to drink it all. It has electrolytes. It'll help re-balance your system."

Pointing to the door, she said, "The launch is still on. Lift-off is in thirty minutes. We're both going to be out there to watch it."

I wasn't so sure. I didn't feel like watching anything, especially if it meant I'd have to be more than ten feet from a toilet in case of a bowel relapse.

Before I could tell her that, she said, "I'll give you fifteen minutes to wash up and get ready. Then I'm coming back to get you. Don't you dare go back to bed. Fifteen minutes. Time for a quick shower. Be ready when I come back."

Chapter Sixteen

I didn't much care about the launch anymore. And I sure didn't want to go outside and stand around with a crowd of people. My head hurt too much, my stomach was raw, and I felt weak all over.

All I wanted to do was go back to bed.

But I didn't.

Because more than anything, I needed a shower to wash the night sweats off my body. And help wake me up.

Bob followed me to the bathroom. He had been in there with me most of the night and was in bed with me when I woke. I wasn't sure whether it was because he cared for me, or that I was his provider of food and water and he didn't want me to die.

Either way, it was good to have him nearby.

I took a quick shower, brushed my teeth, and rolled on some deodorant. Then headed to the bedroom to find clean clothes. Nothing fancy, just t-shirt, boxers, and cargo shorts. I added socks and shoes and checked the mirror to see what I looked like.

With my clothes on, almost normal.

I realized I was starting to feel a little better. Maybe the magic pill Norah had given me was starting to kick in.

I sure hoped so.

I was hungry and needed to put something in my stomach. I went to the kitchen, found a box of unfrosted strawberry Pop-Tarts, and took one out of the foil bag.

I didn't bother putting it in the toaster. I ate it cold and washed it down with water.

Then I took a seat on the sofa to see how my stomach would handle it. Bob joined me.

Five minutes later, Norah was at the door. I hadn't locked it since her last visit, so instead of getting up and opening it, I told her to come in. I stayed on the sofa. I needed to conserve my energy.

She stepped in and looked me over. "How do you feel?"

"A little better. What was in that pill?"

"Magic beans. Now get up and come watch the launch with me."

I shook my head. "No, I need to stay here. I'm still too weak."

She reached into her shirt pocket and came out with a vial filled with white powder. "Take this. Open the top and pour it down your throat."

She went to the fridge and came out with a bottle of water. "Go ahead, take it. Wash it down with this. I promise it'll make you feel better."

I was too weak to argue. I opened the vial and poured the powder down my throat. Then followed it with water.

There was no immediate effect. I didn't feel better, or worse. My stomach was doing okay though. It wasn't having a problem with the Pop Tart.

Definitely a good sign.

I hadn't had any bathroom urges since Norah's first visit. Maybe the pill she'd given me earlier was actually working. Whatever it was, I wanted to stock some in my medicine cabinet.

Before I could ask about it, she pointed outside. "We don't want to miss the launch. So, get up. We're going out there to see it, even if I have to drag your butt out the door."

I didn't feel like being dragged. So I stood, walked to the door, and bravely went outside with her.

Chapter Seventeen

The lot had filled up. Every parking space was taken. A large crowd had gathered at the side of the road to watch the launch. A few had radios tuned to the NASA channel with the volume turned up so everyone could hear what was going on.

The countdown hadn't started yet. According to the radio, it was ten minutes and holding.

Looking around, I saw that a few more motorhomes had pulled in overnight. Most had parked near the back of the lot, behind Norah's RV. An ambulance had parked a few spots behind Buttercup.

"Is that there for me? In case I got worse and you couldn't wake me?"

She shook her head. "Nope, it's not for you. But I'm glad they're here. No telling what might happen with all these people crowding each other to get a better view. Someone could get hurt."

She looked at the crowd. "There's no way we're going to be able to see over all these people. Maybe we should get up on your roof."

My RV, like a lot of others, has a ladder on the back making it easy to get on the roof. It's flat up there and stable enough to walk on. The six solar panels take up some space, but there's still plenty of room for two people to stand or sit.

"You're right. We'll have a better view from up there. Let's go see if I have the strength to get up the ladder."

She smiled. "You will. That powder I gave you should be

kicking in any minute. When it does, you'll feel plenty strong. I guarantee it."

She was right about the powder. I was already feeling it. My headache was gone and I'd almost forgotten about the soreness in my butt. It truly was a miracle drug. It made all my aches go away. It was something I needed to keep on hand. Or maybe not. At least not until I knew what it was.

"Norah, that powder. It's not illegal, is it?"

She laughed. "No, it's not. Just a mixture of aspirin, acetaminophen, and a heavy dose of caffeine."

"So, it's not meth or cocaine?"

"No Walker. Like I said, just aspirin, acetaminophen, and caffeine."

We went to the back of the RV to get to the ladder. Being a gentleman, I suggested Norah go up first.

She did and I enjoyed the view as she climbed. I went up next, surprised I could do it without any pain. The powder had definitely kicked in.

Up on top, we had a great view of the crowd below and the launch site in the distance. We hadn't thought to bring our phones, so we wouldn't be taking any pictures of the launch, but at least we'd be seeing it live.

We sat on the fiberglass roof and listened to the NASA radio feed from below. When the announcer said, 'a minute to go', the crowd pushed forward. Everyone's attention focused on the launch pad.

The final countdown began, and in unison, the crowd called out each second as it passed, getting closer and closer to lift off.

When the count reached zero, a huge white cloud blossomed out over the launch pad. In slow motion, the rocket moved skyward, leaving a fiery orange trail behind.

Moments later, the sound washed over us, quickly followed by shock waves from the mighty engines roaring to life. Norah and I had to hold on to each other to keep from being blown off the roof. The crowd cheered.

We watched the rocket gain speed and altitude as it headed toward the heavens, leaving a white plume behind.

Soon, it was too far away for us to see. The only evidence of the launch was a thick white contrail floating away in the breeze.

With the show over, we thought people would start leaving. A few did, but most didn't. They kept looking toward the launch pad as if they expected something else to happen.

And then it did.

First, a sonic boom, then out of the sky, the first stage of the rocket, with engines blazing, came back down toward the launch site. Slowing as it got closer to the ground. Then deploying tripod-like landing legs. And finally it settled down safely at what we later learned was Landing Zone 1.

When it stuck the landing, the crowd cheered, people applauded, and most seemed thrilled to have seen what had to be one of the most spectacular events on the planet. A rocket launching into space, then part of it returning to safely land on earth.

Norah and I were happy to have finally seen what we had come for. We hugged, traded smiles, and like just about everyone in the crowd, repeatedly said 'did you see that!'

We stayed up on the roof and watched as the crowd dispersed. Many folks were on their phones, posting photos, sending texts, or telling friends what they'd seen.

It took about fifteen minutes before most of the cars had

cleared out. The ambulance that had been parked at the back of the lot, left with them, without having to provide emergency services to anyone.

Seeing it go, Norah said, "The show's over. I guess we can climb back down now."

That's when I realized how much better I felt. Not only had I been outside for almost thirty minutes without needing to head to the bathroom, I felt good. Almost great.

The powder she had given me had worked. Along with the green juice and the magic pill.

Back on the ground, Norah gave me a hug. "I need to go check on Biscuit. The sonic boom probably scared him. I might need to let him out so he can do his business."

She started to walk away, but stopped and came back.

"You plan on leaving right away?"

I shook my head. "No, I'm going to let traffic die down before I head out. How about you?"

She thought for a moment, then said, "I don't know. Maybe I'll stick around another day or two. You should too. If you remember, we have some unfinished business to take care of."

She winked and walked away, leaving me wondering what she meant.

As long as it didn't involve oysters, I'd probably be game.

Chapter Eighteen

Back in my RV, I checked on Bob. He didn't like loud noises and I figured the sound of the rocket taking off, along with the sonic booms that followed, would send him into hiding.

And of course, it did.

He was tucked up in a corner under the bed. His favorite hidey hole.

The roar from the massive engines, the chest throbbing shock waves, and the ear-busting sonic booms could make a person think world war three had started. If they were smart, they'd be looking for a hidey hole just like Bob had.

Fortunately, the war hadn't started. At least not yet.

Bob's hiding place was in a tight cubby between the bed and the nightstand. No one could get to him there. Not even me.

I tried to talk him out.

"Bob, it's okay. There won't be any more noise, at least for a while. You can come out if you want. But if you want to stay in there, it's okay."

I went back up front, grabbed a bottle of water, sat on the sofa, and took a sip. My body was craving fluids, the water felt good going down. My stomach had quit hurting. My headache was gone. I was starting to feel normal.

But not for long.

Norah showed up a minute later. Frantic. Saying, "Someone broke into my RV! They took my bag. It has my phone, my keys, my wallet, my credit cards. Everything!

"Without the keys, I can't start or lock the RV. Same goes with Buttercup.

"No phone means I can't call for help. Even if I could, without credit cards, I can't pay for anything."

"What am I going to do?

I held up my hands, trying to calm her down.

"Norah, take a breath. Then tell me again what happened. This time slowly."

She looked around, then sat on the sofa. Holding back tears, she said, "Walker, someone broke into my RV. They took my go-bag. It was behind the driver's seat. Where you told me to put it. They found it there and took it."

I nodded.

"Okay. So you went back to your RV, and when you went in, you couldn't find your bag. Was anything else missing?"

"I don't know. But I do know someone got in and took it."

I nodded again.

"How'd they get in?"

She frowned. "I forgot to lock the door."

I could have said something about her not locking the door, but didn't. She was already feeling bad and there was no reason to make her feel worse.

Still, I needed to know more.

"You're sure your bag is missing? You looked everywhere,

right? Including in the cubby where it was before?"

"Yeah Walker. Of course I looked there. My bag is gone. Someone took it."

I took a deep breath. If she was positive that someone had broken in and taken her bag, we needed to do something, and soon. Especially since I was somewhat responsible for making the bag so easy to find.

I thought for a moment, then asked, "Your phone was in it?"

"Yeah, it was. And everything else. What am I going to do?"

"Norah, do you have a 'find my phone' app?"

She almost smiled when she realized why I was asking. "I do! Think we can use it to find my stuff?"

"Maybe. Let's give it a try."

I brought up the Chrome browser on my phone and handed it to her. "Log into your account. See if the app can show you where your phone is."

She entered the web address of the app. Then entered her password and phone number. After a few seconds, she pointed to the screen. "It works! It shows my phone is out on I-95, going north. We have to go after them. Right now! I need to get my things back!"

Knowing that we could track the location of her phone would make what we had to do a bit easier. We'd have to chase the thief down in my motorhome, which wasn't the best pursuit vehicle. But at the moment, it was all we had. And we couldn't leave without taking care of one very important thing.

"Norah, we'll go after them. But we can't leave Biscuit in your unlocked motorhome, he won't be safe. Go get him. Bring him back here. And hurry. We'll hit the road as soon as you get back."

She was out the door and back with her beagle in less than two minutes. Biscuit looked around, saw a spot he liked under the dinette, and settled in.

Bob was still in the back in his hidey hole. He didn't have much experience with dogs. I figured he would stay back there until the coast was clear.

But maybe not. If Biscuit got too close to his food bowl, he might come out and have a word with him.

I'd worry about that later. For the moment, my focus was on helping Norah get her bag back from the thieves.

Chapter Nineteen

The parking lot had been packed with cars and people right before the launch. A lot of them had left soon after, but there was still a line of cars trying to get out into traffic.

Normally, I would have waited until they were all gone before trying to get my big rig out. But not this time. We had to catch up with the thieves who had stolen Norah's go-bag.

We didn't have time to be polite. Or to wait our turn. We needed to go.

"Norah, get out and see if you can get one of the cars to stop so I can pull out."

She didn't hesitate. She jumped out of the RV, ran to the first car behind us, and waved her arms until it stopped. Going over to the driver's window, she said something to the man behind the wheel.

Whatever it was, it worked.

He flashed his headlights, which I took as a signal for me to pull out ahead of him. I eased into the tight space, gave him a wave of thanks, and nodded when Norah got back in the passenger seat.

"Good job. Now, when I get to the street, which way do I need to turn?"

She looked at the 'find my phone' app. "Turn right. It's the quickest way to get on I-95."

I made the turn. The car I had pulled out in front of wasn't too happy about it, but if the driver knew what was at stake, I'm sure he'd understand. Or maybe not.

He pulled out around us, honked his horn, and gave me a one-finger salute as he passed. Then quickly sped off.

I didn't take offense. I'd pulled out in front of him in heavy traffic. It was my bad.

Two stop lights later, a sign told us to take the next right to get on I-95. In less than three minutes we joined the high-speed traffic on the interstate going north.

The speed limit was seventy. Most drivers were doing that and more.

In the big RV, I like to keep it around sixty-five when I'm on the road. It weighs just over twelve thousand pounds and it takes it a lot longer to slow and get it stopped when you're going fast.

With cars all around you, you have to be careful. If traffic in front of you comes to a screeching halt, you could end up being a rolling car demolition machine. Something I wanted to avoid.

Holding to sixty-five wouldn't cut it this time. We were trying to chase down thieves who had a pretty good head-start on us. If they were doing seventy or more, I'd never catch up if I kept to sixty-five. I'd have to go at least as fast as they were going.

"Norah, does that app show their speed?"

"Yeah, they're doing just over seventy."

"Good, we're going to do the same. Maybe a little more."

The big Ford V10 under the hood of my RV had no problem getting up to seventy. It could do that easily. And more without much effort.

I quickly got us up to speed and checked the gauges. Fuel tank three-quarter full, oil pressure 80 psi, water temp two hundred. The tach showed twenty-eight hundred RPM. All within normal operating specs.

Norah was closely monitoring the 'find my phone' app. Keeping up with the progress of the car we were chasing. But we didn't know for sure if it was a car. It could have been anything. A car, truck, or motorcycle. Maybe even an RV.

Whatever it was, we knew it was ahead of us, doing seventy, going north on Florida's I-95.

We had been on the road about fifteen minutes when Norah said, "They just passed the Smyrna Beach exit. They didn't get off. They're still on I-95. About twelve miles ahead of us."

A minute later, she sounded frustrated. "Can't we go any faster? I don't want them to get away."

I didn't want that either, but I didn't want to kill us or anyone else if we got into a crash. Fortunately, traffic was light, and even though we were doing seventy, we were being passed by everyone. I stayed in the far right lane, giving the speeders plenty of room to get by.

But Norah didn't like seeing so many cars going around us. She repeated what she'd said earlier. "Can't we go any faster? They're going to get away."

Instead of answering, I pushed our speed up to seventy-five, then rechecked the gauges.

Oil pressure and water temp were still good. Fuel was down to just over half a tank. RPMs had jumped up to three thousand. The motor was louder, but everything was still within normal operating range.

As long as nothing went wrong, we could continue the chase for at least another two-hundred miles before we'd need to stop for fuel.

Sixteen miles later, I had to get hard on the brakes as traffic slowed near the intersection of I-4, the main artery coming from Orlando. Tourists leaving Disney World heading back north on I-95 were gumming up the works.

"Norah, did our guys get off at the Orlando exit?"

"No, they're still on I-95. And they're not so far ahead of us now."

That was good to hear, but the only way we could be gaining on them is if they were stuck in traffic going slower than we were. That wouldn't last long. The traffic jam they were in would eventually clear for them, and we would get caught up in it. Probably at the next exit, which went to Daytona Beach.

But I was wrong.

When we got to the Daytona exit, traffic was moving smoothly, there was nothing to slow us down. I pushed the RV back up to seventy-five.

Fourteen minutes later, just as we passed the Daytona Speedway exit, Norah said, "They got off! They took the exit!"

"Which one? Which one did they take?"

"244. It's six miles ahead of us."

"Good. We're going to catch up with them. They'll be sorry when we do."

I moved over into the right lane but didn't slow until I saw the exit sign. I lifted off the gas and let the RV burn off speed as we headed down the off-ramp.

Things were about to get exciting.

One way or another.

Chapter Twenty

"Which way did they turn?"

We had taken the same exit the thieves had, and followed the off-ramp down to a stop light. The light was red, but with traffic piling up behind me, I needed to know which way to go when it turned green.

Norah knew the answer.

"Turn right. That's the way the app says they went."

I was about halfway through the turn, when she said, "Wait! They've stopped. Just ahead of us. On the left. According to Google Maps, there's nothing there except a big empty field. Slow down. See if we can see them."

It didn't make sense that they'd stop in an empty field unless they broke down or maybe had a flat. Either way, if they were parked just ahead of us, it'd be easy to find them.

Or so I thought.

We traveled for about two hundred yards looking for the empty field that was supposed to be on our left. But we never saw it.

Instead, there was a Buc-ees where the field was supposed to be. It looked new, and apparently, had been built after Google had mapped the area.

I'd heard about Buc-ees. They were the largest gas stations in the state, most having at least a hundred gas pumps along with a Walmart-sized convenience store. The store itself was a major draw. Lots of food stations, serving up fresh sandwiches, barbecued meats, bakery treats, salads, candies, and ice cream. Their coolers were full of refreshing drinks, including beer and wine. The shelves packed with everything imaginable including Buc-ees merchandise and souvenirs.

It was the kind of place travelers went out of their way to stop and spend time at. If you were on the run and needed to top off your gas tank, grab some food, and use the facilities, Buc-ees would be the perfect place.

"Walker, I think they stopped there. Pull in."

I was already slowing to get behind the long line of cars making the turn into the Buc-ees entrance. When it was my time, I followed the leaders into the lot but avoided the line going to the row of gas pumps.

I didn't need to add fuel just yet and didn't want to get stuck behind the people waiting in line to fill up. I needed to park in a way that I could get out quickly if I had to.

That's why I smiled when I saw a sign directing me to the RV parking area. The arrow below it pointed to what appeared to be a big lot in the back, far away from the crowded pumps and store up front.

I followed the arrow and soon reached an almost empty lot with extra large parking spaces marked off, perfect for oversized vehicles like my RV. There were only three motorhomes in the entire lot, I planned to be the fourth.

The three RVs already there had backed into the sites they'd taken, with their windshields facing the store. That way, they'd be able to view all the action outside, without having to leave the comfort of their homes on wheels.

Each had left an open parking space between their rig and the one next to them. Presumably for privacy, and maybe to give them room to put out their awnings should they desire some shade.

There were six empty parking slots past the three RVs. Beyond those, lay what was left of the vacant field that had been shown on Google Maps.

A high curb marked the boundary between the field and the parking lot.

An ambulance was parked in the last spot, up against the field.

We parked three spots away from it, pulling straight in, with our passenger door facing the ambulance and the field. Our windshield faced away from the Buc-ees building, toward a narrow row of pines that created a semblance of green space between us and the road we had come in on.

After pulling into our slot, I killed the motor and turned to Norah. "So, what does the app show now?"

She'd been watching the phone while I'd been parking, and answered right away.

"They're still here. Not too far from us. Within fifty feet, give or take."

"Good. Let's get out and find them before they leave."

I unbuckled my belt and started to get out, but Norah stopped me with a question. "What are we going to do when we find them?"

It was a good question. But there was only one answer.

"We're going to get your stuff back. That's what we're going to do."

I was ready to go, but Norah who had been in a hurry just a few moments earlier, wasn't getting out just yet. She had another question.

"What if they have guns?"

It was another good question. One that I didn't answer right away. I needed to think.

Confronting armed thieves and trying to take back ill-gotten gains might not be a good idea. I had my own gun hidden away in the back of the RV, but I wasn't going to get it out. Pulling a gun is dangerous, and usually not necessary.

But doing it in a place like a Buc-ees parking lot where there could be thousands of witnesses is just plain asking for trouble. In more ways than one.

A lot of people in Florida pack their own heat, and some might want to join in once the shooting started.

So, no gun for me.

But that's not what I told Norah. Instead, I came up with something I hoped sounded good. And maybe even believable.

"Norah, most thieves don't carry guns. They know if they get caught with one, they'll go straight to jail. So don't worry, our guy won't be carrying."

She wasn't having it.

"Walker, you're wrong. They do have a gun. Mine. I keep it in my go-bag. And it's loaded. If they've looked in the bag, they have a gun."

I took a deep breath. The odds had changed. The people we were chasing could be armed. We weren't.

But still, I wasn't ready to get my pistol out. If I did, and pulled it on them, they'd probably pull theirs and someone might get shot. Maybe even Norah. Or me.

I didn't want to risk it.

So again, I tried to come up with something that sounded good.

"Norah, so maybe they have your gun. But maybe they don't. Either way, I don't think they'd use it here with all these people around. There are security cameras everywhere. Recording everything. The thieves wouldn't want to be caught on video shooting at us.

"So, I'm pretty sure they won't use a gun. But if, on the off chance, they do, we leave. We walk away. No heroics. Nothing in your bag is worth getting shot over."

I didn't wait for her to ask more questions or argue with what I'd just said.

I climbed out of the RV and started looking for suspicious vehicles. The kind a thief might be driving.

Unfortunately, 'suspicious' describes about half the vehicles on the road in Florida. Including quite a few parked in the Buc-ees lot.

Chapter Twenty-One

"Walker, wait up! I want to show you something."

Norah was pointing at the tracker app. "See that red dot? That's where my phone is. It's close. Within fifty feet of where we're standing right now."

We'd parked at the back of the lot, with only the Ambulance between us and the tall curb keeping cars from driving onto the nearby open field.

Three large Class A motorhomes were parked on the other side of us. The kind people with lots of money drive. Big, new, and expensive. With custom paintwork. They were also the kind of rigs an RV owner like me, would remember if they had seen them before.

They hadn't been in the Taco Bell parking lot. I was sure of that. They would have been hard to miss.

That didn't mean someone traveling in one of them wasn't the thief. They could have parked nearby, snuck in to do their dirty work, then hightailed it to Buc-ees.

It was possible, but not the most likely scenario. People traveling in million-dollar motorhomes aren't usually harboring petty thieves.

I wasn't going to rule them out, though. Not without first seeing what the tracker app had to say.

Trying not to look suspicious, I took Norah's hand and we walked toward the three RVs, pretending to be in love. Stopping in front of each rig, we admired the custom paint and other features that made each of the 'motels on wheels' stand out.

No one inside the three rigs had bothered to draw their privacy curtains. From our viewing angle, we could see the first one had adults and young children inside. Nora glanced at the app on her phone and shook her head.

"It's not this one."

I nodded and we kept walking.

The side door of the middle RV was open. Three men were standing outside talking, drinks in hand. Seeing us, they waved. We waved back and kept walking.

Nora glanced at the app. "It's not them either."

At the third one, a small dog was keeping watch on the dash. Seeing us, he stood and wagged his tail. Then barked three times, letting his people know that someone was outside. A woman came to the window to see what the dog was yapping about. Seeing us, she waved. Then picked up the dog and carried him away.

Norah looked at the app. "It's not them. We need to keep looking."

There were four empty parking spaces beyond the third RV. Then a row of parked cars. The nearest, an older Chevy van. White with dark tinted windows, sagging springs, and rust in the rear quarter panel.

It had definitely seen better days.

At first glance, it looked like the kind of vehicle a thief might drive. A nondescript white work van. The kind you see everywhere. The kind that no one notices.

This one had blackout curtains drawn over the windows. Maybe to keep the heat out. Or to keep prying eyes like ours from seeing what was going on inside. Three stubby antennas sprouted from the roof.

If it was a workman's van, they might be using a two-way

radio to communicate with their home-base while on the job. Maybe that's why they had the antennas.

But we didn't know whether it was a workman's van. It could be that someone was living in it full-time. A lot of people were doing that these days. Buying an old van, fixing it up, and making it their home.

Most of these road warriors weren't thieves, though. But a few were.

With curtains blocking our view, there was no way to know what was going on inside. Unless I went over, knocked on the door, and asked whoever answered if they had stolen Nora's bag.

But I wasn't going to do that. Not until I checked something else first. What I learned would help me decide whether a knock was needed or not.

I walked up to the van and put my hand on the engine cover. It was warm. Much warmer than just from the sun. The heat told me the engine had been running recently. The small puddle of antifreeze on the ground below the radiator told me more.

The van had very recently been driven hard, maybe at high speed. Like it would have been, if it had just made a trip from the Taco Bell parking lot in Titusville to the Buc-ees lot we were in.

If it had made that trip, the people inside could be the ones we were looking for. I wanted to bang on the door to get their attention. Then ask if they were the ones who'd stolen from Norah.

But I didn't. Instead, I turned to her. "What's it say? Is your bag in there?"

She shook her head. "No, not according to the app. In fact, it says the further we are from your RV, the further we're away from my phone."

I frowned. "That doesn't make sense. Are you sure?"

She tapped the screen. "Look for yourself. It shows that we are farther away from my phone now, than we were when we parked."

I looked. She was right. The app showed that instead of getting closer to the phone we were tracking, we were getting further away.

That couldn't be right. The white van fit the profile. Norah's things had to be in it. No other vehicle close to us seemed to fit. The only explanation was, the phone app wasn't accurate.

"Norah, something's gotta be wrong with the app. This van has to be it."

She looked at the screen again, then shook her head. "I don't know. It still says it's somewhere else. Not in the van.

"Let me try something else."

She dialed a number on my phone, then walked over to the van. With one hand cupped over her ear, she leaned in close. I walked over and did the same, not really understanding what we were doing.

There was a strong odor of marijuana, but it didn't sound like anyone was inside. It was all quiet. I kept listening just in case there was something I'd missed, but after almost a minute, I heard nothing, except traffic behind us.

Norah stepped back. "This is not it. I called my phone. If it was in there, we should have heard the ringtone. But we didn't. So it's not in there. Unless they turned it off. But they didn't, because the tracker would tell me that.

"The phone is still powered up. It's just not in that van."

She looked at the screen again.

"The app still says it's down there by your RV. Maybe in the field on the other side of the parking lot. The thieves could have thrown it out and left. Let's go look."

As we walked past the three big motorhomes, Norah rechecked the app. "Still shows it's down by your RV."

I was starting to wonder how accurate the app was. If it were off by fifty feet or more, the white van we just walked away from, could be what we were looking for. It was still the most likely candidate.

But since we didn't hear Norah's ringtone inside it, we had to rule the van out.

Maybe the tracker app was right. Maybe her phone was actually somewhere near my RV. Or out in the nearby field.

There was one other possibility, one that we hadn't considered.

Maybe Norah had left her phone in my rig when she came over to watch the launch. I didn't remember seeing it with her, but I was pretty much out of it at the time.

If she'd left it there, in my RV, it would mean we'd been chasing something that had been with us all the time.

Chapter Twenty-Two

"Norah. We need to check my RV. Your phone could be in there."

This stopped her. She thought about it for a moment, then said, "Walker, I didn't have it with me this morning. I didn't leave it in your RV. It was in my bag. The bag you told me to leave out in plain sight, making it easy for the thieves to find. It's your fault they took it."

I could have told her she was wrong. That it wasn't my fault. That it was hers because she hadn't locked up her RV. Had she locked the doors, we wouldn't be on a wild goose chase, looking for unknown thieves that were now armed with her gun.

But I didn't tell her that. She was already upset and there was no need for me to add fuel to the fire.

I nodded, pretending to accept blame for her loss. Then calmly said, "Let's go inside. We can check on Biscuit. Maybe rest for a minute. Then get back out and find your bag."

I went to the door, unlocked it, and went inside, hoping she'd follow.

She did.

Bob was sitting on the kitchen counter A place he knows he's not supposed to be. But he had a good excuse. There was a creature unknown to him, snoring under the dinette table across from him.

Bob had seen dogs before but hadn't spent much time up close and personal with one. And certainly had never been around one that snored as loud as Biscuit did.

"Bob, it's okay. He won't hurt you. He's just sleeping."

Norah went over to Biscuit and rubbed his back. The dog looked up, wagged his tail once, then laid his head down and went back to sleep.

I walked over to her. "Let me see the phone."

Without saying anything, she handed it to me. The app was still running. It showed that her phone was within thirty feet of where we were standing. Even though she was sure it wasn't in the RV, I had to check.

I punched redial and waited to see if we could hear her ringtone.

Standing behind me, shaking her head, she said, "My phone is not in here. There's no way it could be."

As it turned out, she was right.

Her phone was ringing, but we couldn't hear the ringtone in the RV. That meant it was somewhere else. If the app was right, somewhere close.

We went back outside, to see what we had missed.

There were no new cars parked nearby. Just the ambulance on the far side that had been there when we pulled in.

That got me to wondering.

"Norah, does that ambulance look like the one we saw back at Taco Bell? The one I pointed to this morning?"

She looked at it, then said, "Yeah, it kind of does. Same color and everything."

She looked closer. "There's something not quite right about it. On the side, it says, 'Emergency Rescue'. But it doesn't say what town or county it's out of. No hospital name either. They always have something on them that tells you where they're from. But not this one."

She continued. "See where it says 'Emergency Rescue'? The words above it have been painted over. Maybe that's were the name of the hospital was. Or a phone number."

I looked to where she was pointing. The words had definitely been painted over.

A few other things didn't look right. The overhead emergency lights had been removed. There was a crack in the windshield. The box truck it had been built on, looked a lot older than most ambulances you see on the roads these days.

Norah said it first. "Walker, it's not a real ambulance. It's been decommissioned. Someone has bought it and is using it for something else. Maybe they're living in it. Or maybe it's what we've been chasing all morning."

She looked at the phone app. "Look at this! It says my phone's in there. In the ambulance. We finally found it! Let's make sure."

Hitting redial on my phone, she called hers. Almost immediately, I heard the Good, the Bad, and Ugly movie theme song coming from inside the ambulance. Apparently, Norah's ringtone.

She heard it too. "It's in there! Let's get it."

She walked up to the driver's door and peeked in. Not seeing anyone inside, she knocked. "Open up. We need to talk!"

There was no response.

She knocked harder. "Open up! Last chance before we call the cops."

Again, no response.

She turned to me.

"No one's inside. They must be in Buc-ees."

"Good. We'll wait for them out here. Then we'll get your

stuff."

Norah wasn't having it.

"I'm not waiting for anyone. I'm getting my things now. You have a tire tool?"

"Yeah, I've got one. In the RV. But I'm not giving it to you."

"Why not? I need it to get inside the ambulance."

"Norah, you're not using my tire tool to break in. We don't know for sure how your phone got in there. Maybe they didn't steal it. Maybe someone gave it to them. Maybe they're trying to get it back to you.

"Whatever the reason, we're going to wait here until they come back. Then we're going to talk to them and straighten this out."

She sighed. Under her breath, I was pretty sure she called me a "Pussy."

She was mad, her phone was close, and she wanted to get it back. And I wouldn't let her. I couldn't blame her for calling me a name. I would have been surprised if she hadn't.

Then she surprised me. "Okay, Walker. We'll do it your way. We'll wait. But we're not going to wait out here unarmed, are we? Don't you think it'd be smart if we had something to defend ourselves just in case things get out of hand?"

She had a point.

We didn't know who we'd be dealing with. Could be just a wayward kid up to no good. If that were the case, we could handle it.

But if it were a gang of hardened criminals not willing to just hand over their stolen loot because we asked them to, it would be in our best interest to have something to convince them we meant business.

I had a gun hidden away in the RV, but there was no way I was going to get it out and wave it around in a parking lot. Too many witnesses. Too easy for things to get out of hand when guns are pulled.

I didn't want to get into a shootout over a few stolen goods. The gun was still a 'no go' for me.

But we did need something in case we had to defend ourselves.

I went with Norah's first suggestion. A tire tool. The RV had a big one, made of heavy duty hardened steel, strong enough to remove lug nuts from a six-ton motorhome.

Having it in hand would definitely give us an edge.

The RV was parked so that it blocked the view of anyone on the other side of it from seeing what was going on with the ambulance. It also kept hidden what I was doing on the passenger side as I opened the utility compartment to retrieve the tool.

I had to get down on my knees and use both hands to pull the heavy tire iron free from the brackets that held it firm. When it released, I lost my balance. To keep from falling over, I handed the tool to Norah. Then I closed and re-lock the compartment I'd taken it out of.

My mistake was thinking she'd wait for me before she did anything.

But I was wrong.

She didn't wait.

Chapter Twenty-Three

Norah walked over to the passenger side of the ambulance. She tried the door. It was locked. She pushed on the window, to see if it would give.

It didn't.

Unfazed, she stepped back, swung the heavy tire tool and slammed it into the glass. The tool bounced off, the glass didn't break.

She tried again. This time, it worked. The window shattered into a glass mat.

After dropping the tire iron, she pushed what was left of the broken glass out of the way, unlocked the door, and climbed into the front seat of the ambulance.

All this before I could get to her and tell her to stop, leaving me outside wondering how many laws she'd be breaking before we left the parking lot.

I leaned in through the broken window. "Norah, you can't be in there. If they come back and find you inside, things could get ugly. Come out."

She didn't.

Instead, she went through a small door between the seats, going into the back of the ambulance. I couldn't see what she was doing, but did hear the ringtone of her lost phone.

She must have called it again.

"Norah, get your bag and get out. We gotta go!"

"No, not yet. Meet me at the back door. You need to see this."

I hurried around to the back of the ambulance, hoping she she wanted to show me her bag, so we could leave.

But she wasn't ready to leave. There were things inside she wanted me to see.

She had opened the ambulance's back doors and was standing there with her bag in hand. She handed it to me. "Put this in your RV, then come back here. Hurry. You need to see this."

I didn't argue. I ran to the RV, put her bag in the front seat, and headed back to the ambulance.

Norah was still inside.

"Walker, you won't believe what they're doing in here. Take a look."

Reluctantly, I climbed in. All the gear typically found in an emergency vehicle had been stripped away and replaced with a single wooden workbench against the driver's side wall. An office chair was bolted to the floor in front of it.

On the left side of the bench, sat three medium size plastic storage tubs. Each one a different color.

The yellow one was filled with phones. The blue one next to it was stacked high with wallets and purses. The red one had cameras, radar detectors, and other electronic gear.

All presumably stolen.

Next to the tubs, in the middle of the desk, a laptop computer. Beside it, a stack of credit card blanks and SIM chips.

On the other side of the laptop, a credit card writer. And a stack of newly burned credit cards.

Norah pointed to the tubs, "You know what they're doing in here, right?"

"Yeah, they're stealing credit cards and cloning them. And they're copying SIMs and creating ghost phones. We need to get out of here and call the police."

She didn't move. "Walker, no way we're leaving this stuff. The crooks could get back before the police get here. Then drive off without being caught.

"The people whose phones and credit cards were stolen, will get hurt. We can't let that happen. We need to get these things back to them somehow"

We'd been in the ambulance for almost four minutes. Way too long. Sooner or later the thieves would return. They wouldn't be happy if they found us inside.

"Norah, we need to go. But you're right, we can't just leave this stuff. We'll take it with us. But before you touch anything else, use my phone to take pictures of everything inside. We can show them to the police when we turn this stuff in."

She nodded, and quickly snapped off several photos. Then started handing me tubs.

It took us less than two minutes to get everything moved to my motorhome. When we were done, I was ready to leave, but Norah wasn't.

"What about the laptop? If they've been cloning phones and credit cards, they might have already cloned mine. It might be stored on the laptop. We can't leave it."

I didn't think they'd had enough time to clone hers, but I didn't want to risk being wrong. I grabbed the laptop, the credit card blanks, the SIMs, the burners, and connecting cables.

When Norah was satisfied we had gotten everything, she closed the back doors hoping the ambulance wouldn't look like it had been broken into – at least until the thieves returned and saw the busted out passenger-side window.

Back in my RV, I put the things we'd taken in the back bedroom. Then started the motor and made my way out of the crowded Buc-ees parking lot.

Eight minutes later, we were out on I-95, heading south toward Titusville, where Norah's RV was still parked in the Taco Bell lot.

While I drove, she checked her go-bag and saw that everything that was supposed to be in it, still was, including her phone and pistol.

Setting the bag on the floor between her feet, she said, "I can't believe we did this. We broke in and got everything back. And more.

"I'd love to see their faces when they come back and see everything is gone."

I nodded, thinking we were lucky we weren't caught.

Three minutes after getting on the interstate, one of the phones we'd retrieved, started ringing.

Norah turned to me. "Should we answer it?"

"No, Just let it ring. It's probably someone calling their phone, to see if anyone would answer. Trying to get it back."

When another one rang, Norah asked again, "What do we do?"

"Don't answer. Not until we figure out how to get them back to their rightful owners."

I thought about it and came up with an idea. "We could take everything to the Titusville police station. They probably had a lot of stolen property reports this morning. We could drop off everything we found and let them take care of it."

Norah nodded. "Yeah, we could do that. But how do we explain how we got the stuff? We can't tell the cops we broke into an ambulance and stole everything in it. That might not sit well."

She was right. The police would definitely ask questions. Ones that we wouldn't want to answer.

I was just about to say something along those lines, when flashing blue lights showed up in my rear-view mirror.

My first thought was the people in the ambulance had caught up with us. If it was them, I wasn't going to stop. I'd keep going until we got to the Titusville police station.

When I checked the mirror again, I was relieved that the flashing blue lights didn't belong to the ambulance. They were fitted in the grill of a black SUV. There were three of them in a row behind us, all with flashing blue lights.

It reminded me of a presidential motorcade. Secret Service agents driving in SUVs escorting the president to an important meeting.

Thinking it was something like that, I switched on my blinker, letting them know I was going to move over so they could pass. Then slowed and pulled over onto the shoulder, still keeping my speed close to fifty.

The three black SUVs didn't go around. Instead, they pulled over behind me. Which meant they weren't part of a presidential motorcade. They were after me.

I should have stopped right then. But didn't.

There was too much traffic on the interstate, going way too fast. I wasn't going to park in the emergency lane and become a target for an inattentive driver.

Instead, I pulled back out onto the highway and led the parade of unmarked cars to the next exit. The first place with enough room for me to safely pull over and park was a Pilot travel stop. I pulled in, drove to the back of the lot, and parked.

The three SUVs followed me in. One went around me and

parked nose in on my front bumper. A second pulled up close to my rear bumper. The two cars effectively blocking me in. I wouldn't be going anywhere unless one of them moved.

The third SUV parked several feet behind the one on my rear bumper.

Not knowing why they stopped me, I reached for my door handle, planning to go out and talk.

Before I could get the door open, an amplified voice commanded, "Driver, stay in your vehicle. Turn off your engine. Roll down your window. Put both hands out where we can see them."

Chapter Twenty-Four

I'd watched enough cop shows to know the best thing to do when they tell you to raise your hands, is to do exactly that. Raise your hands.

Do it slowly, and don't start digging around under your seat or anywhere else that would make them think you're going for a gun.

If they think that, things are going to go badly for you.

So, after hearing the command coming from the SUV with the flashing blue lights parked behind me, I did exactly what I was told to do.

I killed the motor, rolled down the window, and put both hands out so they could see I was unarmed.

Immediately, another command was given. "Passenger, roll down your window. Put both hands out so we can see them."

Norah didn't hesitate. She did as she was told.

In the rear-view mirror, I watched two plainclothes officers, one male, one female, step out of the SUV that was on our rear bumper.

The female officer drew her gun and cautiously approached my open window. Stopping about five feet back, she said, "Slowly open your door and step out. No sudden moves unless you want to get shot."

I knew from personal experience, that when you get shot, it hurts, so I very carefully opened the door and slowly stepped out, raising my hands above my head as soon as my feet were on the ground.

The female with the gun said, "Face your vehicle, put your hands behind your back. Lace your fingers like you are praying."

Again, I did as commanded.

With a loaded gun pointed in my direction, I didn't want to give her any excuse to use it.

While I waited for her next command, I heard a male officer giving the same commands to Norah.

Not hearing a gunshot from her side of the RV, I figured she had complied without hesitation.

From behind me, the female officer said, "I'm going to place you in handcuffs. If you struggle, I'll shoot you."

I stood perfectly still as she snapped the cuffs on my wrists, locking my hands together.

When she was done, she stepped back and said, "Turn around. Face me."

When I did, her face lit up with a smile. "Mr. Walker. We meet again. I've been waiting for this day. Please do something stupid so I have a reason to taze you."

She looked familiar, but I couldn't place her.

"Do I know you?"

"Yes, we've met. Last year. I was riding with you in your RV. You stopped at a rest area. And left me behind. Remember?"

I thought for a moment, then it came to me. She was working undercover, which I didn't know at the time. Pretending to be a battered woman trying to escape an abusive boyfriend. She had approached me at a diner and begged a ride. I fell for her story and gave her a lift.

Ecstasy. That's what she said her name was. She had hinted she was a part-time hooker. And suggested that we could have some fun together.

We had been on the road for less than an hour when I got suspicious.

It started with her shoes. They were cop shoes. No hooker wears cop shoes. And then there were her teeth. Perfect with no sign of neglect. Her hair was clean, her eyes clear. She spoke perfect English. Not what you expect from a street hooker.

What clinched it though, were the questions she was asking. Trying to get information from me about a person involved in a case she was working on.

I knew then that she had to be a federal agent. So, soon after, we pulled into a rest area. I suggested she get out and stretch. When she did, I drove away without her.

"Yeah, I remember you. Ecstasy. That's what you said your name was. I'm guessing that's not really it."

"You're right. I'm Special Agent O'Connor. And unlike our first meeting, I'm not working undercover. I'm letting you know right up front that I'm with the FBI. And this time, you won't be running off without me. Today, you're going to jail."

Without saying another word, she marched me back to the SUV parked furthest behind my RV. She put me in the back seat and read me my rights. And locked me inside.

She then walked toward the agent dealing with Norah.

He had pulled her out of the RV and brought her back to the car parked directly in front of the one I was in. He put her in the back seat, locked the doors, and turned to speak with Agent O'Connor.

After a few words, O'Connor returned to me and asked, "Anyone else in the RV?"

"Yeah, there's two of them. Bob and Biscuit."

She frowned. "Two? Are they armed?"

"No, neither one has a gun. But you better watch out for Biscuit, he might lick you to death. And Bob, well you know how cats are. He'll want a little petting."

She shook her head. "Mr. Walker, this is not a game. Don't pretend it is. I don't want to get shot because you're playing around. So tell me, are there any people in the RV?"

"No, there are no other humans in there. Just Bob and Biscuit."

"So they're pets, right?"

"Yeah, they're pets. Biscuit is a dog. Bob is a cat. You figured that out without even looking. I guess that makes you a pretty good detective."

She shook her head again, then changed the subject. "How long have you known this Norah woman?"

"I met her yesterday."

"It figures. Do you know her last name?"

"Uh, no, I don't."

She looked at me in disgust. Then said, "Let me get this straight. You met this woman yesterday. You spent the night with her last night. And this morning, the two of you decide to drive up here, break into a truck and steal thousands of dollars of property. Is that pretty much it?"

I sighed, not wanting to admit to breaking into the truck. Or telling her why we did it. Instead, I said, "You're wrong. I didn't spend last night with her. But if I had, would you be jealous?"

"Jealous? Of you? Give me a break."

She pointed to the car Norah was in. "I'm going to ask you again. Do you know her last name?"

Sadly, I didn't.

"No, I hadn't got around to asking her. But I was planning to."

"Right. You were planning to. Maybe after the two of you broke into the truck?"

Before I could come up with an answer, her radio buzzed. "O'Connor, come over here. We may have a problem."

She turned to me, smiled, and sarcastically said, "Don't go anywhere." Then she closed the SUV's door, making sure I was locked in.

With her hand on her holster, she walked toward the other agent leaving me wondering exactly what kind of problem he had run into, that would require two agents with guns to surround Norah.

Chapter Twenty-Five

Fifteen minutes after O'Connor had locked me in her car and left to talk to the other agent, they were still talking. He was standing beside Norah, who was still in cuffs, nodding his head as he spoke. He pointed to the RV, then back at me. Then the three of them went inside. I was pretty sure they weren't going in to check on Bob and Biscuit.

Everything we'd taken from the ambulance was in my bedroom in plain sight. Three tubs filled with stolen phones, cameras, and purses. Credit card blanks, programmable SIMs, and a computer to make copies. All the evidence they needed to immediately charge us with felony theft.

Even if we explained that we had good intentions and planned to get everything back to the original owners, I doubted they would care.

I was pretty sure the Agents wouldn't see what we'd done as a good deed. To them, it was an open and shut case. We had broken into a vehicle and stolen thousands of dollars worth of merchandise. We'd done it in clear daylight with no effort to hide or wipe our fingerprints from the scene.

I expected that before long, one or more patrol cars would roll up to take us away.

But that never happened.

Instead, O'Connor stepped out of the RV with Norah following close behind. Her cuffs had been removed. She was smiling. Agent O'Connor, who was heading in my direction, wasn't.

When the two of them got to me, O'Connor unlocked

my door and had me get out. Norah took my place in the backseat of the SUV. Before leaving, O'Connor asked if she was comfortable or if she needed anything. Norah said she was fine but asked if it was okay to roll down the window.

O'Connor smiled. "Sure, no problem. I'll do it for you."

She rolled the window halfway down, then led me away, but not before telling Norah she wouldn't be locking the door. If she wanted to get out at any time, she could.

This was a surprise. O'Connor had treated me like a common criminal. Locking me in and not asking if I needed anything. But with Norah, it was different. She was acting like she actually cared whether Norah was comfortable or not.

I wondered about it as I walked back to the RV, hands still cuffed behind me.

O'Connor had to help me get up the steps to go in. Once inside, I was surprised to find someone I knew, Special Agent Mike Harris, of Homeland Security, was sitting on my sofa, with Bob in his lap.

I'd met him three years earlier when our paths crossed. He was investigating a weapons smuggling operation on Florida's west coast. I was working in the same area, trying to recover a stolen dog for a friend.

The people who had taken the dog were the ones moving the weapons. I didn't know it at the time and had almost wrecked his investigation when I confronted one of the smugglers.

He had me taken off the streets to cool my heels. Then, convinced me to help run a sting on the gun runners. It didn't go as planned. I was almost shot. But in the end, both cases were resolved favorably. He got the bad guys and I got the dog.

Seeing me walk in, he smiled. "Walker, we meet again. This time though, under less than pleasant circumstances."

He pointed to the seat across from him. "Sit. I'll bring you up to speed."

With my hands still cuffed, I sat and listened as he told me the mess Norah and I had created.

"Walker, we've been chasing a ring of thieves who have been breaking into cars. Normally this would be a local police matter. It wouldn't involve Homeland Security or the FBI. Except in this case, it does.

"These thieves are part of a nationwide organized ring. The proceeds from the thefts fund terrorists here and abroad. That's why we're involved.

"The ring's m.o. is to show up at large events where victims will be out of their cars, with their attention focused elsewhere.

"Like a concert, a football game, or in this morning's case, a rocket launch.

"While the victims are distracted, the thieves break in, stealing mostly phones, purses, wallets, and credit cards.

"They then go back to their base of operation, clone the phones and cards and use them to clean out the bank accounts of their victims. Often before they even know it's happening.

"The proceeds are then sent on to the leaders of the ring. We're talking about millions of dollars here.

"That's why the FBI and Homeland Security have gotten involved. We're trying to take the ring down, jail their leaders, and stop the flow of money to terrorists.

"But it hasn't been easy. The low-level thieves work in isolated cells. We don't know in advance which events they'll hit. We didn't know how they managed to stay invisible doing their dirty deeds.

"Only recently did we learn they use decommissioned ambulances to hide in plain sight. They can go to any major event and hardly anyone will take notice. The ambulances look real, not at all out of place at these events.

"Usually, there is a team of three working inside each one. Two of them, often a man and a woman, do the stealing. The third stays in the rig, in the back, working at a computer.

"While the thieves are out doing their thing, the guy inside sets up a free Wi-Fi hot-spot. When unsuspecting people in the crowd connect to it, he steals their personal information and uses it to drain their bank accounts.

"In a matter of hours, one of these ambulance crews can take in tens of thousands of dollars, sometimes a lot more, from bank accounts before the victims even know. The phones and wallets they steal make it easy to create fake identities.

"Because these ambulances are mobile, and are widespread, it's been hard to identify and capture one in the act along with the evidence of the crimes they've committed.

"Shutting down this operation has become a top priority. To that end, a joint effort teaming the FBI and Homeland Security was put together with Agent O'Connor in charge. For her, it's a pretty big deal. Her reputation and standing within both agencies hangs in the balance.

"She's been working on it for three months, and until recently, wasn't making much headway. The thieves aren't leaving much of a trail. With them being mobile, it's hard to know where they will hit next. They change the markings on their ambulances often. You never know which one is real or not.

"But one of the crews got sloppy. Security cameras recorded them in action in the parking lot of a Stones concert. They left before they were caught, but they didn't bother changing the markings of the ambulance they were in.

"Using those unique markings, the agency was able to track

their movements. O'Connor and her team were on site when they hit again.

"That was this morning. In the Taco Bell parking lot. Her team recorded everything. Then followed them hoping to see them give the goods to higher-ups. It would have been a major break in the investigation.

"But it won't be now. Because of you and Norah.

"The ambulance you went after is the one O'Connor was tracking. When you broke in, you destroyed her case. You've tainted the evidence.

"You obtained it illegally, which means she can't use it. All the time and money she put into tracking them down has been for naught, because of your actions.

"That means we have a big problem. As do you.

"We've got you on tape breaking in. We also have the items you stole. It's a clear-cut case of felony theft involving a weapon."

I started to say the only weapon we had was the tire iron, but then remembered that by admitting to using it, I was also admitting our guilt to the crimes he had mentioned.

I decided to say nothing.

Agent Harris continued. "So we have you on tape committing a felony. Also interfering with a federal investigation. We could file charges right now and hold you both in federal prison for as long as we wanted.

"Or, we could go another way. One that could make all the charges disappear. Before we talk about that, though, let's talk about your friend, Norah."

Chapter Twenty-Six

"According to what you told Agent O'Connor, you just met the woman calling herself Norah, yesterday. Is that correct?"

I nodded. "Yeah, that's right. We met in the parking lot next to Taco Bell. We were both there in our RVs to watch the launch."

"So, you didn't know about her before then? About her past? Things she may have done?"

"No, like I said, I just met her. She told me she's a nurse and that she just bought the RV she's in. And that she traveled to Florida from Tennessee. That's pretty much it."

Agent Harris nodded. "Did you notice anything unusual about her when you were on the beach yesterday?"

Before I could answer, he added, "We know you and her went to the beach. She told us. So, did you notice anything unusual about her?"

I smiled, thinking about how she had pulled off her top. That was kind of unusual. But not worth mentioning. Then I remembered the scars on her chest and back. The ones that looked like she'd been shot.

When I asked her about them, she clammed up. Said she didn't want to talk about them. That could be what Harris was asking me about.

I wasn't going to say anything about the scars. Instead, I said, "I did notice something unusual. Her car. She calls it Buttercup. It's bright yellow. Really stands out."

Harris shook his head. "Walker, forget about the car. I'm

not asking about that. What I want to know is, did you see anything on her body, that made you wonder about her past?"

I shook my head, still not wanting to say anything about the scars. "Why are you asking? Is she some kind of criminal?"

He didn't answer my question. Instead, he said, "We have her on video. In fact, just about every law enforcement agency in the country has seen it. Many of them, including the FBI, now use it in their training exercises.

"What it shows has changed the way police respond to active mass shooter situations.

"Are you sure she didn't say anything about this?"

I shook my head. "I have no idea what you are talking about."

He smiled again. "You told Agent O'Connor you didn't know Norah's last name. Maybe you should have asked. It's Shepard. Norah Shepard. Does that ring a bell?"

"No. Should it?"

He frowned. "You don't watch much TV, do you?"

"No, not much. For the past three years, I've been pretty much off grid. I don't keep up with the news. Is Norah Shepard some kind of criminal?"

He shook his head, reached into his pocket, and pulled out his phone. After tapping the screen, he held it so I could see.

"Walker, this is a video showing what Norah did. Watch it closely. It's only twenty-seven seconds long."

He pressed 'play'.

The screen showed a wide hallway with lockers on both walls. It reminded me of my high school.

A kid, probably in his mid-teens, walked into the hallway, a pistol in his right hand. It looked like a Glock. The kind favored by TV gang bangers.

He pointed the gun at something off-camera and fired three rounds. Bang, bang, bang. No way to tell what he was shooting at or if he hit it. The camera was focused on him. Not where the gun was pointed.

Then he turned toward the camera, pointing the gun at a woman who suddenly walked into the scene. She was speaking in a calm voice, asking the kid to put the gun down.

He shook his head, smiled, and said something that the camera didn't pick up. Then, he waved the gun in a way that looked like he was telling her to get out of his way.

She didn't.

Instead, she took four steps toward him, then dove into his chest, taking him to the ground. He fired twice as she made her move. Shooting at her from close range. It would have been hard for him to miss.

She crashed into him full force. Both landed hard on the floor. She was on top. He struggled to get out from under her, but she kept him pinned down. When he continued to struggle, she head-butted him. Twice.

Then grabbed his gun hand and twisted it in a way that made him drop the weapon.

Seconds later, four police officers rushed in, helped the woman get up, and cuffed the gunman. It was only then that the woman turned to face the camera.

It was Norah. Blood was spreading across the white shirt she was wearing.

She'd been shot.

Agent Harris stopped the video.

"You didn't know?"

I didn't answer right away. I couldn't. What I'd seen was so unexpected.

All of it. The kid with the gun. Norah trying to talk him down. Her rushing him and getting shot.

I was still thinking about this when Harris repeated his question. "You sure you didn't know about this?"

This time I answered. "No, I didn't. I can't believe she did that. That's when she got shot?"

"Yes, she took two bullets. Close range. Both on her right side, barely missing her lung. She lost a lot of blood before they could get her to the hospital. They weren't sure she was going to make it.

"But she did. Just barely.

"Unfortunately for her, the media got their hands on the video before she got out. It was played over and over on every news station. Local, national, and worldwide. It quickly became one of the most-watched videos on YouTube and Instagram.

Norah was being hailed as a hero.

Instead of following standard school protocol which was to run and hide from a gunman, she confronted him and took him down.

"It was later learned the gun was loaded with fifteen rounds. The kid had two extra mags, each with another fifteen. He had entered the school seven minutes before the halls would have been full of students. Had Norah not stopped him, he could have killed a lot of kids."

Harris paused, then continued. "Not many people would have done what she did that day. She wasn't even supposed to be there. The normal school nurse had gotten ill a few days earlier. Norah had volunteered to step in – even though it was, as she called it, her 'cheat week'.

"When she eventually left the hospital, she was interviewed by the FBI and local police. She told them everything they wanted to know. But refused to speak to the media. She turned down interview requests from all the major networks. She even declined to go to the White House to receive the Presidential Medal of Freedom.

"Norah didn't want to be famous. All she wanted was to get back to the life she had been living before the shooter got involved."

"That's the woman you've been spending time with. Norah Shepard. A real-life American hero."

Agent O'Connor had been standing nearby while Harris was telling me the story. When he finished, she had me stand up and turn around. From behind, she removed my cuffs. Then had me sit back down.

Looking me squarely in the eye, she said, "We have a situation here. You guys interfered with an ongoing investigation, broke into a private vehicle, and stole thousands of dollars of electronics.

"We have it all on video. There's no disputing what you did. It shows everything. Starting with Norah breaking the glass.

"It would be bad for both of you if that video ever sees the light of day. Especially for Norah.

"But we can make it disappear. If you're willing to help us."

Chapter Twenty-Seven

It'd been four hours since we'd left the Taco Bell lot.

Normally, it would have been just me and Bob traveling together in the RV, like we'd been doing for the past three years. It was my home. And Bob's. Where he felt safe. The place he ate, slept, and used his litter box.

Almost always without strangers lurking about.

But now it was different.

Instead of it just being me in the RV, Norah, Norah's dog Biscuit, FBI Special Agent O'Connor, and Homeland Security Senior Agent Harris were all in there with us.

At the moment, Bob was somewhere in the back, probably hiding under the bed, waiting for the strangers to leave.

But it didn't look like they were going to leave us anytime soon.

When Agent O'Connor returned from her car with Norah, Biscuit, who had been sleeping under the dinette, came out to see what was going on. Seeing all the people, he made a noise that sounded like a muted bark.

Norah understood what it meant. She reached down, gave him a pet and said, "Biscuit needs to go out and potty. Who's going with me?"

I immediately raised my hand. "I'll go."

Before I could get up off the couch, Special Agent O'Connor, the woman whom I had met months earlier when she was undercover and I had abandoned at a Florida rest area, stopped me. "Hold on there, Buckaroo. You're not going anywhere. Not now, and not later. Consider yourself under house arrest until we tell you otherwise. I'll go with Norah and the dog."

Three minutes later, they returned. Biscuit came in first, stepping a bit more lively than he had before his potty break. Norah was smiling. Agent O'Connor wasn't.

The dog moseyed back to the bathroom where I kept Bob's food and water bowls. We could hear him lapping up water, then crunching down on Bob's kibble. After a few bites, he rejoined us up front and plopped down under the dinette.

It didn't bother me that he had gotten into Bob's food. There was plenty to go around. Even if he ate it all, there were two unopened bags in the pantry. Bob had taught me to never let him run out. I'd only let it happen once. He made me pay. By pooping in one of my shoes.

From that point on, I made sure his food bowl was never empty.

The only other thing in the bathroom that might interest Biscuit were the little dumplings in Bob's litter box. I wouldn't have been surprised if he had come up front with one of the little turds in his mouth.

Fortunately, he hadn't.

When the two women returned from their potty walk, Norah took a seat beside me on the couch. Agent O'Connor didn't sit. She stood guard by the door, probably to make sure I didn't try to run off. Which of course I wouldn't, since the RV was the only place I could run to.

After asking if we wanted something to drink, Agent Harris nodded toward the tubs filled with phones we had taken from the ambulance. They'd been ringing off and on, ever since we'd brought them into the RV.

It was likely their owners had been calling trying to get them back. I would have done the same.

So far, we've not answered any of the calls.

Harris took a deep breath and started in.

"We have at least two problems.

"The first, is all the things that were stolen this morning. By the thieves. And then by you.

"We have to do something with them. Either destroy them or return them to their owners. We'll figure that out later.

"The second, is what happens next.

"O'Connor's plan was to catch this morning's crew red-handed with the stolen goods. She could then threaten them with federal charges and long jail terms. Then suggest if they would tell her who their bosses were, she might drop the charges.

"But she didn't get the chance. Because you interfered. You broke in and tainted the evidence she planned to use against them.

"Because of that, no judge in the country would allow the charges to proceed. Everything you touched would be considered fruit of a poisoned tree.

"So legally, we can't charge the Mango crew with anything. All we can do is charge you."

I interrupted him. "You called them the Mango crew? How you'd come up with that?"

He smiled. "Agent O'Connor learned the ambulance they're using was retired out of Mango, Florida. A small town just north of Tampa. So we refer to them as the Mango Crew.

"Now, if you don't mind, no more questions until I finish."

He continued.

"Agent O'Connor has spent months tracking these different crews trying to find out who's calling the shots. If she could find a phone or laptop or some other device they used to communicate with, it could be a major breakthrough.

"There was probably something like that in the Mango truck. Had you two not broken in, she likely would have found it. It could have been a key piece of evidence that would eventually lead to the capture of the ringleaders.

"But she didn't get a chance to look.

"Now, she's going to have to start over. Unless you two have any ideas on how we can salvage the mess you created."

He stopped talking, waiting for one of us to say something.

Norah spoke first. "It was all my fault. Walker had nothing to do with it. I was the one who forgot to lock up my RV. I was the one who convinced Walker to chase the thieves. And I was the one who broke into their truck and took what was inside.

"So blame me for everything. Charge me, not Walker. He's totally innocent."

Agent Harris smiled and looked over at Agent O'Connor, who was still standing by the door. "I told you she was something special. No one else would voluntarily take the blame for this. But she did.

"Of course, what she said is pretty much true. If we were to charge them both, Walker would likely walk. His involvement is minimal.

Agent O'Connor shook her head. "No. I blame it on him. He obviously led the poor girl astray."

Harris laughed, then said, "O'Connor there's no need for you to stand there and guard the door. Walker's not going anywhere. Why don't you sit?"

She crossed her arms. "I'm fine right where I am."

Agent Harris tried again. "Come on, sit."

She shook her head. "I don't mind standing."

Harris looked at me, then back at O'Connor. "Why don't you want to sit?"

She frowned. "Cat hair. It's everywhere in here. I don't want to get it on my clothes. So I'll just stand."

She was wearing dark blue slacks, a white shirt, and a dark blue blazer. Pretty much the standard outfit for FBI field agents. Bob's orange hair would definitely show up on her outfit. In fact, it had already started.

Harris laughed. "You might as well get used to cat hair. We're going to be here for a while. So sit."

Reluctantly, she did. At the dinette table next to the sofa.

Agent Harris turned his attention back to Norah and me. "Do you two have any thoughts about the mess you've created?"

I had a few ideas, but before mentioning them, I waited to see if Norah had anything to say.

She did.

"I think we should start answering the phones when they ring. We tell the callers we found their phones and will be turning them over to the Titusville Police Department. Same goes with the wallets and purses. We tell them they can pick them up there."

"If anyone says they don't want us to give their phone to the police, that they'd rather get it from us in person, we arrange a meetup. Because anyone who doesn't want their phone to go to the police, could be someone Agent O'Connor might want to talk to."

Harris nodded. "Okay, sounds good. I'm with you so far.

Anything else?"

Norah looked at me, giving me a chance to talk.

I pointed to the computer we'd taken from the truck. "We have the laptop they were using to clone credit cards and phones. We might be able to use it to get the people behind this, to come to us. The same way we found their truck. With a tracking app.

"To keep that from happening right away though, we should put the laptop in the microwave."

O'Connor stopped me. "Why there?"

I smiled. It was the first time she'd said anything to me since telling me I was under house arrest. I took it as a win.

"The microwave's metal frame works like a Faraday cage. No signals can get in, none can get out. They won't be able to track the laptop if it's in there."

She nodded. "Okay, do it. Put it in there."

I got up from the sofa and put the laptop away. Then instead of returning to my seat, I said, "Norah shot a few photos while we were inside the ambulance. I think you'll find them interesting."

Chapter Twenty-Eight

The TV in my RV was mounted up high, between the two cabinets above the driver's seat. I had upgraded it several months earlier with a forty-inch flat screen with all the latest features. One was the ability to receive media from my Android phone. Anything on the phone's screen could be cast to the TV.

It took me a minute to get everything set up. Then I posted the first picture Norah had taken. She had been standing inside the ambulance, near the back door. The camera had been pointed at the workbench and the three tubs of stolen gear.

Viewing the photo on the big screen made it easy to see the details.

Agents Harris and O'Connor could see for the first time, what the inside of the truck they had been tailing for months, looked like.

Harris spoke first. "That's a pretty sophisticated setup."

Agent O'Connor nodded. "Yeah, if these two goofs hadn't gotten involved, I could be in there serving warrants right now."

I ignored her comment and brought up the second photo. It showed the laptop. Next to it, a card duplicator and a stack of credit card blanks. On the other side, a SIM card reader.

I pointed to the TV. "They're cloning credit cards and phone SIMs. And that's not all."

There was a small white box connected to the back of the

laptop. I pointed to it.

"That's a Fonera router. It's used to create public Wi-Fi hotspots. Anyone nearby with a phone set to automatically connect to Wi-Fi can be hacked."

I paused to see if either of the agents had questions. Neither did. I continued pointing out things in the photo.

"See that phone? The one sitting on a charger next to the laptop? All the stolen phones were still in the tub when we got there. But that one wasn't. It was being charged. Like it might belong to one of the guys in the crew.

"If it does, maybe we should put it in the microwave with the laptop. So it can't be used to track us."

Norah didn't wait to hear what the two Agents thought. She stood, quickly found the mystery phone and put it in the microwave.

Harris pointed at the TV. "Show us the next picture."

I brought it up on the screen.

Norah had taken it after we'd gotten almost all the stolen gear out of the truck. It showed what the workbench looked like without anything on it. At first glance, it didn't add much to the story.

But then I noticed something we had missed.

I pointed to the upper left corner of the photo. "See that? It looks like a security camera. We might have been recorded while we were in there.

"If we were, they'll know what we look like. If they have other cameras, maybe even one on the outside, they could know what we were driving."

I let that sink in.

No one spoke for a few moments, then Agent Harris stood.

"We'll look at the rest of the photos later. But right now, we need to make sure you're both safe. If the thieves know you're in this RV, and they've tracked your location, they could be coming for you right now. So we need to get moving.

"Let's start by going back to the Taco Bell lot and getting Norah's RV. Then we'll move both of you to a safe location.

"I'll stay here in the RV and ride with you and Norah. Agent O'Connor can follow in her car.

"While we're on the road, we'll answer the phones that ring. We'll let the callers know they'll be able to pick them up at the Titusville police station. If anyone says they don't want to go there, we'll tell them to call back around noon and we'll give them a time and place they can meet up with us.

"Who knows? We might get lucky. Maybe the thieves will call wanting their phone back and will agree to meet us somewhere.

Harris looked at Agent O'Connor. "Is there anything you want to add?"

She shook her head. "No, let's get this over with."

As she walked past on the way to the door, I could see cat hair on the back of her pants. She wouldn't be happy knowing it was there. I didn't say anything about it, but had to smile.

Eight minutes later, I was back behind the wheel of the RV, going south on I-95, heading toward Titusville.

Agent Harris and Norah were behind me on the sofa, answering calls as they came in. The callers were told the phones and purses had been recovered and could be picked up at the Titusville PD as long as they could provide proof they were the owners

Everything was going smoothly, until it wasn't.

One caller was giving Norah a hard time. She put it on

speaker so we could hear what was being said.

The man didn't want his phone handed over to the police. He wanted to pick it up in person.

When Norah said that wasn't possible, he said, "Yeah it is. You're going to give me my phone back, or I'm going to come after you and take it. So what's it going to be?"

Norah didn't answer. Instead, she hung up.

"He'll call back. Just wait and see."

Two minutes later, the same phone rang with an incoming call. As before, Norah answered. But this time, before she could get a word out, the man said, "Don't you ever hang up on me again. If you do, you'll be sorry. I want my . . ."

Norah ended the call as soon as the man made the threat.

She was playing with him. He didn't know we were traveling with federal agents. If he threatened violence and tried to follow through, it wouldn't end well for him.

A minute later, the phone rang again. This time, she let it ring five times before she answered.

When she did, she spoke before the caller had a chance to say anything. "Listen up. No threats, no foul language, or this phone goes straight to the Police. If you're tracking me, you can see that's where I'm heading right now."

The phone was still on speaker, we could hear him when he said, "Look, I apologize for getting upset. It's just that I need my phone and I don't have time to deal with the police. I'm working undercover with the FBI. The phone has evidence from the case I'm working on. I need to get it back before it falls into the wrong hands.

"So, I'll pay you five hundred dollars cash for it. We can meet where ever you want. If you're heading to Titusville, we can meet there. How about it?"

Norah smiled. "That's a very generous offer. But five hundred is not enough. A thousand is more like it. And before you get your phone back, you have to prove it's really yours."

The man spoke. "What do you mean I have to prove the phone is mine? I told you it was mine. That should be enough. That plus the grand you're getting."

Nora paused for a moment, then said, "You say you're FBI and the phone has important evidence on it. That might be true, but what if it's not? What if you are the one the FBI is after, and you are trying to get the phone because it has evidence against you?"

The man started to say something, but Norah stopped him. "Don't interrupt me if you ever want to see this phone again."

She continued, "If you can prove the phone is yours and show up with a grand, you'll get it back. Otherwise, it's going to the police. Understand?"

The man waited to make sure Norah was through talking before he answered. Then, "Yes, I understand. But how? How do I prove the phone is mine?"

Norah had the answer. "Give me the unlock code. You should know what it is if the phone is really yours."

We waited to hear what he would say.

Twenty-Nine

We were about thirty miles from the Taco Bell in Titusville. The man who called wanting his phone back was still on the line. We were waiting to see if he'd come up with the unlock code.

Thirty seconds had passed. He had said nothing. Norah figured it was time to push him a little. "I guess your silence means the phone really isn't yours. I'll drop it off at the police station."

She ended the call.

The man immediately called back. "I'll give you the code, but don't look at my private files. Promise me that."

Norah smiled. "The only thing I'll promise is, if the code works and you show up with a thousand dollars, you can have the phone back. Otherwise, it goes to the police."

"No, no need to get the cops involved. My unlock code is nine, one, nine, one, pound."

I could hear Norah punching it in. Then, "It worked. Meet me at Taco Bell in Titusville. Around five this afternoon."

"I'll be there. How will I recognize you?"

Norah was quick to answer. "I'll be wearing a red ball cap. If you don't see me, call the phone. And bring cash."

Without waiting for a reply, she ended the call. Then went to the microwave and put the phone inside.

Agent Harris was waiting when she came back up front. "You handled that well. Maybe you should be working for us. But you're not going to be the one meeting him at Taco Bell. It's too dangerous."

He pulled out his phone and called Agent O'Connor. I couldn't hear everything, but did hear him say, "Bring your overnight kit. You're going to be on a stakeout for a few days."

When he ended the call, he turned to Norah. "What's on the guy's phone."

I was driving and couldn't see without looking back over my shoulder. I wanted to look, but I needed to keep my eyes on the road. Too dangerous to try to look at the phone while at the wheel of a twelve ton RV. Still, I could at least hear what they were saying.

For a few moments, Norah said nothing as she scrolled through the unlocked phone. Then, "This is bad. Real bad. I don't want to look at this."

I couldn't tell for sure, but I think she handed the phone over to Agent Harris. He was quiet for maybe a minute. Then he used his own phone to make a call.

"O'Connor, we're pulling over and stopping at the next exit. Stop with us. I have something here you need to see."

We were just twenty miles from Titusville, but if Harris wanted me to stop, I would. The next exit was for Mims. I took the exit ramp and pulled into the Loves Travel Stop. Agent O'Connor, in her dark unmarked cruiser, pulled up next to us.

Without waiting for her to come to the RV, Agent Harris went out to talk.

Neither Norah nor I knew what they were saying, but we assumed it was about the phone. Norah had seen something bad on it. I wanted to know what it was.

"Tell me."

"You don't want to know."

"I do. What'd you see?"

She took a deep breath. "Photos of an older man with a young girl. Too young to be doing what she was doing. There were others, too. Different men, with young girls."

She paused, then said, "They need to put the guy in jail, along with all his friends."

I didn't ask any more about the photos. If they were as bad as she said, I didn't want to know the details. But I did agree with her that the people involved should be put in jail. For a long, long time.

Harris came back into the RV and said, "They'll be waiting for him at five when he gets there."

We got back on the road. Twenty minutes later, I pulled into the Taco Bell lot. Norah's RV and Buttercup were still there, where they'd been when we'd left. I parked close and killed the motor.

Agent O'Connor pulled up behind me in her SUV, blocking me in. It was her way of letting me know she was still mad for what I'd done months earlier. I guess I couldn't blame her. It never feels good when someone ditches you in the boonies.

Agent Harris waved at her to join us in the RV. When she stepped inside, he looked at the three of us and said, "You're not going to like what I'm about to tell you."

Chapter Thirty

"I want you to forget about the phone and the pictures on it. Other agents will handle it. Just be assured the people involved will not walk free.

"Our priority continues to be shutting down the theft ring and capturing those who head it. Agent O'Connor is the lead on that. I will be assisting her."

He looked directly at us.

"Unfortunately, things have gotten a lot more complicated since the two of you interfered this morning. Not only did you blow our chance to gather valuable intel, we now have civilians to worry about.

"When the three individuals who were traveling in the ambulance, came back out of Buc-ees and saw that it had been broken into, they made at least one phone call. Then they left in the ambulance, heading north on I-95. One of our agents followed them for a hundred miles. But since he had no reason to stop them, the agent was told to return to base.

"As we now know, there was at least one security camera in the ambulance. There could have been another on the outside. That means there's a good chance the bad guys know what the two of you look like. They might even know what you are driving.

"Chances are good they'll come after you to get their laptop back. In fact, I'd be surprised if they haven't already started looking for you.

"For that and other reasons, we need to get both of you

out of this lot and go somewhere safer.

"To that end, I want Agent O'Connor to stay with Walker in his RV, for the next few days. I'll be staying in Norah's with her. That way, if the bad guys do find you, there will be an agent on board to protect you."

I started to say I didn't need any protection and didn't want Agent O'Connor staying with me. But before I could, O'Connor made her own feelings known.

"Agent Harris, wouldn't it be better if I stayed with Norah. And you stayed with Walker? I mean the optics of you staying with a female and me with a male, might come back to haunt us."

Harris smiled. "I'm not worrying about the optics. I'm worried about their safety. You will be staying with Walker. I'll stay with Norah, unless she objects."

He turned to her. "If you would rather O'Connor stay with you, I'll understand."

Norah smiled. "Sure, you can stay with me. There's plenty of room. Of course, you'll have to sleep on the couch. And cook for me."

Agent Harris grinned. "No problem. I'll be glad to cook."

I turned to O'Connor. "How about it? You going to cook for me?"

She started to say something, but stopped. Maybe she knew it was a lost cause. Agent Harris had made it clear. She'd be staying with me for the duration.

There was no doubt she didn't like the arrangement, but at the moment, there was nothing she could do about it.

That kind of worried me.

How would she handle living under the same roof with Bob and me. It was a tight space and I already knew she didn't like me. She carried a gun and handcuffs. What if I got on her nerves? Would she be using them on me?

I would soon find out.

After telling us about our new sleeping arrangements, Harris went to the back of the RV and made a quick phone call.

When he came back up front, he said, "Time to get on the road. We need to be gone before things start happening here."

He turned to O'Connor. "We're going to KARS. You know how to get there?"

Apparently, she did.

"It's on Merit Island, right? The campground there?"

"Yep, that's it. The guard at the gate knows we're coming. He'll let us in."

Harris turned to me. "KARS is a private campground managed by NASA. It's right on the river, across from the launch pad. Not open to the public. Just to NASA employees and retired military. And in our case, FBI and Homeland Security agents.

"Norah and I will leave here first. You and Agent O'Connor will follow twenty minutes later.

"Any questions?"

I had one.

"When do we eat? Norah and I haven't had anything since early this morning. It'd be nice to get something in our stomachs before we set up camp."

Harris thought for a moment. "Agent O'Connor's car is in the parking lot. Get her to take you to get food. Get enough for all of us. Then come back here, load up the RV, and head to KARS."

Turning to O'Connor, he said, "One of the other agents will

pick up your car later on. Leave the keys under the mat."

Without waiting to see if there were any other questions, he led Norah and Biscuit out to her RV, leaving me and O'Connor alone to sort things out.

Three minutes later, Norah's RV pulled out of the parking lot with Buttercup trailing behind.

O'Connor watched as they left, shaking her head. It was clear she didn't like the situation she'd been put in.

After they disappeared into traffic, she turned to me.

"This is your fault. Every bit of it. If you were a normal person, living in a house instead of in this gypsy wagon, I wouldn't be stuck here with you.

"I would have never met you and you wouldn't have made me the laughing stock of the agency six months ago when you dumped me at the rest area. All the guys got a good laugh at my expense.

"Then today, on the most important assignment of my career, you stumble in and wreck the case I've been working on for months.

"If, because of you, we don't catch these guys, it'll be my head on the chopping block. I'll be assigned to desk duty, or worse."

She paused, took a breath, then continued.

"Just so you know, I don't want to be here with you. I don't want to have to live in this hippy wagon on wheels for the next few days. I'm not happy about it and I'm going to make sure you know.

"I won't be fun to be around and if you give me a good enough reason, I'm going to shoot you."

She crossed her arms, leaned back, and waited for me to say something.

I couldn't help but smile. Bob had come up from the back and was rubbing up against her ankles, trying to calm her down.

She looked down at him, then back up at me. "You're an ass. You know that, don't you?"

"Yes ma'am, I do. But I'm your ass for the next few days. Enjoy it while you can."

She shook her head and pointed to the door. "Get out, before I shoot you."

I was pretty sure she was kidding, but in case she wasn't, I went out.

Chapter Thirty-One

Unlike the last time, O'Connor didn't lock me in the back seat of her SUV. She let me get in front with her. Without waiting for me to buckle in, she pulled out of the parking lot and turned right, squealing her tires as she made the turn.

A mile down the road, she pulled into the drive-through at Chipotle. Without looking at the menu she ordered three beef taco salads and one vegetarian, She paid with what looked like a government issue credit card.

While we waited for our order to be filled, I could have told her that I'd been parked next to a Taco Bell for three days and had had my fill of Mexican food. But knowing that she wasn't in a good mood, I stayed quiet. No need to further rile her up.

When our food was ready at the pickup window, she handed me the bags without saying anything, then pulled back out onto US-1, going north. A mile later, we were back at the parking lot next to Taco Bell.

She pulled up close to my RV and parked. Before getting out, she put her car keys under the floor mat and grabbed a small gym bag from under the back seat. Probably the overnight bag Agent Harris had told her to bring. With it in hand, she headed to my RV, not waiting for me. I followed behind, fumbling with the food bags, being careful not to spill anything.

The RV's door was locked and it didn't open when she tried it. But what did she expect? That I'd leave it unlocked right after Norah's had been broken into?

She turned and looked at me. "Well? Are you going to unlock it?"

Instead of answering, I tapped the unlock button on my remote. After hearing the click, she opened the door and went in. Not bothering to shut it behind her.

If Bob had been waiting for our return, the open door would have given him the chance to head out and explore new territory. It's not something he does regularly, but you never know when he might decide to go for a walkabout.

I got to the door quickly and closed it behind me. Bob was nowhere to be seen. Probably in the back sleeping.

I'd have to make it clear to O'Connor not to leave the door open. I didn't Bob to getting out.

I put the bags of warm food from Chipotle into the kitchen sink and took my place in the driver's seat. As soon as O'Connor was buckled in, I started the engine and said, "Which way?"

Before she could answer, Bob came trotting up from the back. He usually does whenever he hears me start the motor. He likes riding shotgun when we first start out on a trip.

But this time, he couldn't. O'Connor was sitting in his seat. He didn't like it. He looked up at her and said, 'Murrrf?' Probably wondering why this stranger was in his place by the window.

She should have at least looked down and acknowledged his presence when he spoke to her. But she didn't. She ignored him.

That was a mistake. Bob doesn't like to be ignored.

He did the one thing I hoped he wouldn't do.

He launched himself off the floor and landed in her lap, knowing that would get her attention.

And of course, it did.

He's a big cat. Twenty-five pounds of muscle and fur. When he landed, she sat back, then quickly scooped him up and put him down on the floor, saying, "Cat, if you know what's good for you, you'll stay away from me."

When he didn't run away, she held up her hands in the form of claws and hissed in his direction.

That's all it took.

He turned and ran toward the back. He didn't like the way she acted and neither did I.

"You're going to regret that."

"Why? You going to do something about it?"

"No. Not me. But Bob is pretty good about getting revenge."

She smiled. "I'm big, he's little, and I've got a gun. What could he possibly do?"

I shrugged. "Probably nothing, at least while you're awake. But you have to sleep sometime."

I pointed to the back. "I suggest you make nice with him before you go to bed. Else you'll want to sleep with your shoes on."

She didn't ask why. And I didn't explain.

Instead, she brushed cat hair off her lap, and said, "What are you waiting for? We need to go."

I put the RV in gear and headed toward the street. Before pulling out into traffic, I asked the same question I'd asked before.

"Which way?"

"Right. Turn right. When we get to the NASA bridge, take a left and stay on the road until I tell you to turn. Try not to wreck us."

153

I took a deep breath and drove.

Moments later, I noticed that she kept glancing over her shoulder back to where Bob had gone. She was either worried he might sneak up and attack her, or was wondering what she could do to make nice with him.

Either way, it pleased me that she now took him a little more seriously than before.

I let her do that for a few minutes, then figured I needed to clear the air. I started by saying, "Look, I know I messed up with the ambulance. I'm really sorry about that. I didn't mean to cause you any trouble. I was just trying to help Norah get her bag back.

"If I'd known we were stumbling into your investigation, I would have done things differently. But I didn't know, and again I'm sorry for the problems I caused.

"I'm also sorry you're being forced to babysit me for the next few days. I'm sure that wasn't part of your plan when you got up this morning.

"But since it looks like we're going to be stuck with each other, let's call a truce. I promise to try my best to not get on your nerves."

I took a breath and continued.

"You're probably going to get tired of me calling you Agent O'Connor. Especially if we get out in public where you may not want people to know you're FBI. When we first met, you said your name was Ecstasy. If it is, I'll call you that.

"But if it's something else, let me know. Whatever it is, it'll be easier than always addressing you as Special Agent O'Connor. Okay?"

At first, she didn't respond. It was like she didn't hear me.

But then, she said, "Walker, you're a screw-up. I know it,

and you know it. What you did this morning proves it beyond any doubt. Your actions nullified months of research and cost my team a huge part of our budget. So forget about the apologies. They're meaningless.

"And don't think that just because I have to babysit you, you're going to somehow win me over. It's not going to happen. We're not friends now, and we're not going to be friends later. I'm a federal agent and I'm only here to do my job.

"As for how you should address me, it's always going to be Agent O'Connor."

When it was apparent she'd had her say, I nodded, as if I accepted it as being the final words on the matter. But in my mind, they weren't.

In fact, I took it as more of a challenge.

She didn't think we'd ever be friends. I'd try to prove her wrong. And instead of calling her Agent O'Connor, I'd somehow find out her first name, and start calling her that.

Surely, that would win her over.

Chapter Thirty-Two

After crossing the NASA bridge, we rode in silence, each of us probably thinking about what O'Connor had said about me being a screw-up and the two of us never becoming friends. It was harsh to hear her words, but I got over it pretty quickly. Especially since I had a plan in place to make her change her mind.

When she finally broke the silence, I figured she was going to apologize for her words.

But I was wrong.

Instead of an apology, she pointed ahead. "Take a left at the Circle K."

It put us on a narrow road with no shoulders. My lane was just barely wide enough to keep the tires of the RV on the pavement. Not wanting to slide off into the ditch, I took it slow until we came to a sign with the word 'KARS' painted in black on a white background.

Below the sign, a red arrow pointed to the left.

I tapped the brakes and looked at O'Connor for directions. She looked at me like I was a fool. "What are you waiting for? Turn in. That's where we're going."

The turn took us down a short driveway and ended at a closed gate next to a guard shack. I pulled up and stopped.

Almost immediately, an armed guard carrying a clipboard came out and walked toward us. I rolled down my window so I could hear what he was going to say.

His first question was, "Do you have a reservation?"

Before I could answer, O'Connor leaned across me and flashed her badge. "FBI. Check your list."

The guard looked at her badge, then at his clipboard. After a few seconds, he handed me a sheet of paper that had a map on one side and campground information on the other. "Your party is already here. They're in site nine. You're in ten. If you need anything, call the number on the back."

He went to his shack and slowly raised the gate so we could get through. While waiting for it to get all the way up, I glanced at the map.

Our campsite was about two hundred yards straight ahead. On the way to it, we'd pass a road on our left that would take us to the campground dump station.

After the painful oyster voiding event of the night before, I knew the RV's holding tanks would be pretty full of noxious material. The organic matter would soon fill the RV with the kind of stench you'd want to avoid, especially when an unhappy guest with a gun was staying with you.

So, instead of going straight to our assigned campsite, I took the loop road on the left. To the dump station.

O'Connor, who had taken the map away from me after we'd gone through the gate, immediately said, "That's the wrong way. You were supposed to go straight. You screwed up again. Unless you think this is a sightseeing tour, which it definitely isn't, get this thing turned around and back on the right road."

I acted like I didn't hear her. I just kept following the loop road. She was not amused.

"Walker, don't make me shoot you. Turn this thing around, now."

I slowed, as if I was about to stop so I could turn around. But instead of coming to a full stop, I coasted to the dump station and aligned the side of the motorhome to the sewer inlet.

After killing the motor, I turned to O'Connor. "Our dump tanks are full. That means you won't be able to use the toilet. If you do, poo will start backing up into the shower stall. I don't think you'll like that.

"So, if it's okay with you, I'm going to get out and dump the tanks. Unless you shoot me first."

It took her a moment to fully understand what I was saying. That she wouldn't be able to pee or poo unless I dumped the tanks. When she finally got it, she said, "Go ahead. Do it. And wash your hands before you come back in."

She crossed her arms and watched as I went outside to do the dirty deed. I pulled on the rubber gloves I keep near the sewer hose and got to work.

I pulled out the sewer hose, connected one end to the RV's tank and the other to the campground dump station. Then dumped the black tank, followed by the gray. With both tanks empty, I disconnected the sewer hose, capped off the tank connections, and put everything away.

Pulling off the rubber gloves, I said, "All done."

I don't know if she heard me or not, but it was something I always say when I finished dumping the tanks without getting splashed with black water.

Before going back inside, I washed my hands with the RV's outside water hose. Then I got back in and drove to our assigned campsite.

Unlike most campgrounds, the site at KARS was not paved. It was just a strip of grass, running parallel to the road. About twenty feet wide. Bordered on one side by open water with a clear view of the NASA launch complex in the distance. Our spot was marked by a pedestal with the number ten painted on it.

I pulled in, making sure the RV's utility compartment was lined up with the power pedestal. As soon as I killed the motor, O'Connor was up out of her seat. She grabbed the Chipotle bags and headed for the door.

Norah's RV was already parked in her site in front of ours. She and Agent Harris were outside sitting at a picnic table. O'Connor joined them.

I didn't.

Instead, I checked on Bob's food and water bowls, then made sure nothing had fallen while we were on the road. I ran the slide room out, and then went out and hooked us up to shore power and campground water.

With that done, I went over and joined the others at the picnic table.

Chapter Thirty-Three

Seeing me coming, Agent O'Connor pointed at the food bags. "You drew the short straw. You get the vegetarian one."

As far as I was concerned, Taco salad is supposed to have meat in it. Either ground beef, chicken, or pork, the kinds of meat they use in actual tacos. Making it without meat and calling it a taco salad should be illegal. It should be called what it really is. Bean and lettuce salad without meat.

I was hungry and ate it anyway. It turned out to be pretty good. I wouldn't say that out loud for fear of being banned by the meat eaters club, but it was a close second to the real thing.

When O'Connor bought the food, she hadn't ordered drinks. That could have been a problem if Norah hadn't had a six-pack of orange soda in her fridge. The kind you see being sold at roadside taco stands.

It was weird she had them with her, but they went well with the Tex-Mex food on our table. Still, I wondered. Who in their right mind pulls over on the side of the road and buys a six-pack of bottled south-of-the-border soda?

It was a mystery.

I was going to ask about it, but before I could get the words out, she told us the story.

With a bottle of the orange drink in hand, she said, "So there was this little taco stand across the street from the RV park I stayed at. It was late in the day and I didn't have much food with me. Even if I would of, I was too tired to fix anything on my own. So I walked over to the taco stand to check it out.

"I wasn't sure what I wanted, but I knew I was hungry. They had the standard fare. Tacos, burritos, tortas, enchiladas, even hand rolled tamales.

"I was hungry and went with the dinner plate special. It had rice, black beans, guacamole, and beef enchiladas.

"The woman running the place asked what I wanted to drink. When I shrugged, she pointed to a bottle of Jarritos Orange soda. I was too hungry to be choosy, so I got it and took the food back to my RV.

"Everything was delicious. Especially the orange soda. The next morning I went back and got a breakfast burrito. As an afterthought, I got a six-pack of orange soda. I don't know why, but I'm glad I did."

Agent Harris raised his bottle in a toast. "To Norah, our hero."

We were just finishing up our meal when two Titusville police cruisers rolled up. One in full dress, the other unmarked. Neither had their flashing blue lights on.

A detective wearing street clothes got out of the unmarked car and walked toward our table. An officer in uniform stepped out of the second car but didn't head our way.

Agent Harris got up and quickly walked over to the detective.

We were too far away to hear what was being said. But it seemed to be a cordial meeting. No cuffs were brought out, no guns were unholstered.

After a short discussion, Harris came back to our table and looked at me. "They're here to pick up the phones and other things you recovered this morning. We need to go into your RV to get them. You need to go with us."

Leaning in close, he whispered, "You are not to say anything to the detective. He may ask you some questions. If he does, don't answer them. Just shrug, like you don't know anything. Even if he doesn't ask, don't say anything. Don't ask how his day is going, don't tell him why you're here or who's with you. And Walker, whatever you do, don't make any jokes.

"Just keep quiet. Think you can do that?"

I nodded, as proof that I could.

"Good. You and Agent O'Connor are going to go in first. As soon as you get inside, lock your cat up. We don't want him getting in the way or getting out.

"I'll come in with the detective and we'll get the three tubs and carry them outside. Don't tell them how they ended up in your RV. And don't say anything about the phone or laptop in the microwave. There's no need for them to know about them.

"After we take the tubs outside, they'll do a quick inventory of everything we are turning over. While they are doing this, stay inside. Do not come out. Stay in there until they leave. Got it?"

I nodded.

He turned to Norah. "If you don't mind, I would appreciate it if you would go into your RV and stay there. We don't want to take a chance that they might recognize you or start asking questions.

"So, please, go into your RV and wait until I tell you the coast is clear. Will you do that for me?"

She smiled and nodded an okay.

I noticed he was being a lot nicer with her than he had been with me. He had given me orders. But with her, he made it sound like a polite suggestion.

Of course, she was a national hero and a nice-looking

woman. That probably had a lot to do with it.

Without any objection, she went to her RV and waited.

Agent O'Connor and I walked over to my place. As soon as we were inside, she said, "Don't screw this up. Don't say anything, don't do anything, just stay out of our way. Understand?"

I smiled. "Yes dear. Whatever you say."

She pointed to the back bedroom. "Go put your cat up, smart ass."

"Yes dear. Whatever you say."

Chapter Thirty-Four

The Titusville detective spent less than three minutes inside my RV. Agent Harris showed him the tubs filled with the recovered items and said they were found during a classified operation. Because it involved Homeland Security, he couldn't say how the items ended up in the RV.

I stood near the back staying out of the way. As instructed, I kept my mouth shut, even when the detective asked if the RV was mine and did I live in it full-time.

Instead of answering, I shook my head, hoping he'd take it as a no.

It seemed to work. He didn't ask any more questions.

Agents Harris and O'Connor took the recovered items outside. Since I was told not to go out until I was given the okay, I stayed in.

With nothing else to do, I decided that since O'Connor would be living with me for a few days, I should probably do a little house cleaning. Starting with the bathroom.

Bob and I had left it in a bit of a mess the night before.

I cleaned the sink, scrubbed the toilet, wiped down the vanity and mirror, and put out a fresh roll of toilet paper. To make it extra nice, I cleaned Bob's litter box which I keep in the shower stall. He'd appreciate it. As would anyone else who walked into the bathroom.

Going up front, I wiped down the kitchen counters, cleaned the sink, and almost opened the microwave to clean away the food spatter on its metal walls. But I stopped when I remembered that's where we were storing the laptop and phone.

Opening the microwave, even for a few seconds, might let someone ping the devices and know where we were staying. We didn't want that.

Not yet, anyway.

After cleaning the kitchen, I picked up around the living area and made sure there was nothing in the bin above the sofa bed that might embarrass me, should Agent O'Connor get curious. The only things up there were sheets and a well-used pillow, sans case.

Nothing out of the ordinary.

After spending ten minutes cleaning and picking up, I thought the place looked pretty good. At least to me. Of course, when you live full-time with a cat, it's hard to keep it clean for long. They tend to shed, leaving cat hair everywhere. And the occasional hairball.

I'd gotten used to finding Bob's hair on just about everything. But I was pretty sure Agent O'Connor wouldn't be a fan.

Remembering that Bob was locked in the back bedroom, I went to check on him, opening the door quietly, in case he was sleeping. And, of course, he was. His head was on my pillow, a paw over his eye, shading the light streaming in through the side window.

Not wanting to bother him, I went back up front and settled in on the couch. From that vantage point, I could see Harris and the Titusville detective having a conversation just outside my door. I ducked down so they wouldn't see me.

Due to a lack of sleep the night before, I dozed off.

I woke to Harris's voice outside my door.

"Walker, you can come out now. They're gone."

Outside, the others had convened again at the picnic table. Norah had brought out a bottle of wine and glasses for all. Only one was being used. Hers.

Agents Harris and O'Connor weren't drinking.

Not wanting to see the wine go to waste, I had her pour me a glass.

"Walker, I'm glad someone decided to drink with me. These two claimed to be on duty. Said they couldn't partake. I told them it was my cheat week and I was going to drink if I wanted to."

She took a sip from her glass, then continued. "I think the real reason Agent O'Connor isn't drinking, is she knows she'll be sleeping in your RV tonight. She's afraid if she gets a little tipsy, she might make a move on you."

I laughed. O'Connor didn't. She shook her head. "There's not enough alcohol in Florida to get me drunk enough to make a move on him."

I smiled. "I'm glad to hear that. But just in case, I'm locking my bedroom door."

O'Connor shook her head again. Something she seemed to be doing a lot when she was around me.

I finished my glass and stood. "I think I'll take a walk. There's a fishing pier I want to check out. Norah, you want to go with me?"

She held up her glass. "No, not really. I'm still enjoying my wine. You go ahead."

When I started to leave, O'Connor stood. "I'll go."

"Really? You want to walk with me? Can we hold hands?"

She was not amused. "No, we're not holding hands. And no, I don't want to walk with you. But I have to. I'm your babysitter. I'm not supposed to let you out of my sight. So if you go for a walk, I'm going. Even if I'd rather not."

I smiled. "Yeah, you keep saying you don't want to be around me. But I think we all know what's going on. I'm starting to grow on you."

She shivered. "Gross. Just walk. I'll be a few steps behind."

Earlier, while driving in, I'd noticed the park had a fishing pier which stretched out over the river. I didn't have any fishing gear with me, but still wanted to walk out on the pier to take a look.

O'Connor stayed about ten steps behind as I walked. Grumbling about how I had messed up her life. I decided to slow down and let her catch up so I could better hear what she was saying.

But my plan was flawed. When I slowed, she slowed. Always staying ten steps back.

At the pier, without waiting for her to catch up, I headed out over its weather-worn deck. The rubber soles of my sneakers made no sound as I walked, but Agent O'Connor's FBI-issued hard-sole shoes made a clumping sound with each step she took.

It sounded like I was being followed by someone riding a Pogo stick.

Chapter Thirty-Five

A sign near the middle of the pier got my attention. In bright red letters on a white background, were the words, 'Danger. Alligators and Snakes in Area.'

For those who couldn't read, a drawing of a toothy gator with its mouth open and a coiled snake in strike mode delivered the same warning.

If you travel much in Florida, you'll see similar signs near almost every body of water. But this one was unusual. Instead of being on the shore discouraging visitors from getting into the water, this one was midway down a four-hundred-foot pier. Well beyond the shoreline.

At first glance, the sign seemed to suggest gators and snakes could be up on the pier. That would not be good.

I didn't see how that could be possible though. They'd have to get up on the pier the same way I did. By taking the wooden ramp at the shoreline. If they were doing that, that's where the warning sign should be. At the pier entrance.

But there wasn't one there, which led me to believe the sign was warning that gators or snakes could be in the water below, not up where we were walking. Still, in case I was wrong, I pointed the sign out so O'Connor wouldn't miss it.

I kept walking, heading toward the end of the pier, ready to high-step it in case I came up on a snake or gator.

Fortunately, I didn't see either.

At the end of the pier, I looked out over the river toward the NASA launch complex on the other side of the river. Much of it was obscured by fog rising up off the water, but the aircraft warning lights on the main launch tower were clearly visible. On a clear day, the end of the pier would be a great place to watch a launch.

Hearing a splash nearby, I turned to see if Agent O'Connor had fallen in. She hadn't, at least not yet. She was leaning over the handrail, looking down at something.

I went over to see what it was.

When I got close, she pointed to the water below. "Maybe that's what the sign was warning us about."

Looking down, I could see a five-foot-long alligator gar, swimming in circles, snapping up small fish as it moved. Its long serrated snout resembled the barbs on a chainsaw.

As we watched, other gar swam into view. They seemed to be working as a pack, clearing out the schools of pin-fish living under the pier. The little fish didn't have a chance. Nor would a human if the pod of gar attacked them with the same viciousness.

It was interesting to watch, but after a few minutes, I'd had enough. It was getting dark and neither of us had brought a flashlight. Having read the warning sign about snakes, I didn't want to be walking around at night without one.

I didn't tell O'Connor I was heading back. I just walked away. She followed. A lot closer than she had before. At one point she was close enough that we could have touched. Or held hands.

But we didn't.

When we got back to the picnic table at our campsite, Norah's wine bottle was empty. Next to it, a lit citronella candle in a metal pot. The flame was supposed to ward off mosquitoes and other flying pests.

But it was having the opposite effect.

Swarms of small insects flew near and occasionally dive-bombed the flame.

Seeing us, Norah swatted at the bugs, and asked, "How was your walk?"

With a smile, I said, "It was nice. Almost romantic. Agent O'Connor wanted to hold hands, but I don't do that on a first date."

Norah laughed. Agent Harris smiled. O'Connor didn't say anything. She just shook her head while swatting away small insects that seemed to be attracted to her.

Harris stood and pointed to Norah's RV. "There are too many bugs out here. Let's go inside. There's something we need to talk about."

Norah was already heading to her door, not waiting for the rest of us. Harris blew out the candle and waved us over. "Follow me."

His words sounded more like an order than an invitation. Maybe one that Agent O'Connor had to obey. But not me. I was a civilian and could go anywhere I wanted. There was no rule that said I had to go with them if I didn't want to.

I could go back to my place and spend the evening with Bob. But if I did that, I'd miss out on whatever Harris and O'Connor wanted to talk about. And it might be important.

So I followed them in.

Norah's RV wasn't as big as mine. Hers was a few feet shorter, making it a little tight inside with four people and Biscuit.

But we made do.

Norah and I sat on the sofa, while Agent Harris and O'Connor stood across from us.

Harris spoke first. "I hope you two have enjoyed your time

here at the park. Because it's over. We're moving to a different place tomorrow.

"O'Connor has come up with a plan that she hopes will get her investigation back on track. It involves both of you."

He turned to her. "You want to tell them?"

She nodded.

"Tomorrow we're going to use the phone and laptop you stole from the thieves, as bait. We'll turn them on so they can track their location. Hopefully, they'll want to retrieve at least the laptop and come after it. When they show up, we'll arrest them.

"Since there is a good chance they know you were the ones who broke in, and what you and your RV looks like, we'll need to keep both of you around. Your presence will help sell the illusion that they're tracking us, instead of it really being us, tracking them.

"Of course, we'll be doing our best to keep both of you safe. As long as you do what we say and don't do something stupid, it should go smoothly."

She looked directly at me. "That means you, Walker. You have to do what we tell you to do. You don't get to improvise. This isn't a game. Understand?"

I nodded. "Yeah, I understand. You're using us as bait."

She smiled. "You're right. We are."

Chapter Thirty-Six

After our meeting in Norah's RV, O'Connor said it was time to go back to my place, where we'd both be spending the night.

Before we left, I asked Norah, "Do you have something O'Connor can wear? She's been in that fed suit all day. If she doesn't want to look like a cop, she needs to be wearing something more tropical. And something to sleep in tonight. A sexy teddy would do."

Norah smiled at my teddy joke. Agent O'Connor didn't. She just shook her head. Again.

Harris backed me up. "He's right. We don't need to look like cops while we're working on this. It could blow our cover. We need to look more like tourists. Shorts and tees. Maybe even flip flops."

He looked at O'Connor. "Did you bring anything like that?"

"No. Just a clean shirt to go with what I'm wearing now. Nothing tropical. Maybe Norah has something I can borrow."

Norah shook her head. "Sorry, most of the clothes I have are for work. Nurses' uniforms and scrubs. I don't think that's what you're looking for. But maybe Walker has something in his closet you could wear. Might be a little big for you, but that's the style these days.

"If we're moving tomorrow, we could stop somewhere along the way and get some clothes. I vote we do that. In the meantime, I do have a teddy you can wear. Red with matching panties. Walker would probably approve."

I nodded. "Yeah, that sounds good to me. What do you think O'Connor? You brave enough to wear a teddy?"

She tapped the Glock in her holster. "Sure, I'll take the teddy. If Walker comes after me while I'm wearing it, it'll give me an excuse to shoot him."

I was pretty sure she was kidding, again, but decided not to test it. "Norah, keep the teddy. I've got a tee shirt O'Connor can wear. I think it'll be safer for both of us if she sleeps in that."

With nothing else to say on the subject of sleepwear, we said our good-nights. O'Connor and I headed to my RV.

Bob was waiting for us at the door. Seeing O'Connor, he took a few steps back and growled. Then turned and ran to the safety of my bedroom.

O'Connor laughed. "He's not very brave, is he?"

I smiled. "It may not look like it, but he is when he needs to be. You should see him when he's up against a lizard or a mouse. He's a real tiger."

"Wait, you have lizards and mice in here?"

"Yeah, sometimes they sneak in. But they don't last long. Not with Bob around. If he kills one tonight, he'll bring it over and show you."

Hearing me say his name, he came back up front, skirted around O'Connor, and leaned up against my leg, purring. He was showing her he wasn't afraid. At least, not when I was around.

To further prove it, he moved over and rubbed against her pants leg. She didn't bother pushing him away, she even let him twine between her ankles for a few seconds.

When he got tired of doing that and trotted away, I saw

that he'd left a layer of fine cat hair on the hem of her suit pants. O'Connor didn't seem to notice. Or maybe she'd given up caring.

It'd been a long day and she was probably as tired as I was.

She sighed. "Where do I sleep?"

"The sofa. It folds out into a bed. Sheets and a pillow are in the cabinet above. There's a blanket if you need it."

"The bathroom's in the back next to my bedroom. Clean towels and washcloths in the closet. If you use the toilet, use the foot pedal to flush."

She crossed her arms. "I won't be using your toilet. The campground bathhouse is across the street. I'll use that instead."

I smiled. "You do remember what the sign on the pier said, right? Snakes and gators in the area. You sure you want to go over there at night? The doors are wide open. No telling what's crawled in there. Could be anything. Usually it's just spiders, but sometimes it'll be a snake. Or gator.

"I'm pretty sure it'll be safer in here. But do what you want."

She thought about it for a moment, then pointed to the back. "You have a tee shirt I can put on? Maybe some shorts?"

She was about four inches shorter than me and had a smaller waistline. My clothes would be baggy on her. But they'd be more comfortable than trying to sleep in the suit she was wearing.

"Yeah, I'll get you something."

I went to my bedroom, rummaged through the closet, and found a tee shirt I'd bought at the Florida Swamp Ape headquarters. It had a drawing of a large ape-like creature on the back. I figured O'Connor would like the artwork.

To go with the shirt, I pulled out the cleanest pair of cargo shorts I could find. Since her waist was a lot smaller than mine, I got out a belt she could use to hold the pants up.

She was waiting for me on the sofa when I returned and gave her the clothes. She took them without comment. Then asked, "Does the bathroom door lock?"

I nodded.

Apparently, she had decided going outside to the bathhouse in the middle of the night, might not be such a good idea. My bathroom would have to do.

While she was in there doing whatever women do to get ready for bed, I folded the sofa out and put a clean fitted sheet over the cushions. I put a second one at the foot of the bed along with a pillow.

I closed all the blinds, locked the doors, and got two bottles of water out of the fridge. One for me and one for her.

When she came back up front, I handed her the water, told her the doors were locked, and showed her how to unlock them if she needed to get out quickly.

She nodded, sat down on the sofa-bed, and waited for me to leave.

Instead of leaving though, I pointed to the back. "Just so you know, Bob will be roaming through the RV most of the night. If he starts crying, he's letting you know he is going to use the litter box, which I keep in the bathroom. He won't use it while you're in there, but he'll want you to leave the door open so he can go in when he needs to.

"There's also a good chance he'll join you on the couch sometime during the night. If he does, just ignore him and he'll eventually go away. Whatever you do though, don't wiggle your toes when he's around. If you do, he'll attack them. You won't like it."

She shrugged. "I can handle your cat. It's you I'm worried

about. If you come out here and try to get in bed with me, you'll learn firsthand what it feels like to be tazed in your private parts. I guarantee it'll hurt a lot more than having Bob bite your toes."

I smiled. "Well, I guess that means I won't be coming out to visit you during the night. Your loss."

After saying goodnight, I headed to the back to take care of my bathroom business and prepare for bed. Bob liked me to leave the bedroom door open so he could come and go as he made his rounds during the night. If I forgot and closed it, he'd scratch on it until I opened it for him.

After the first few times of him scratching, I'd learned to leave the door open. But with a female guest sleeping on the sofa, I decided it'd be best to leave it mostly closed.

Before getting under the sheets, I remembered I wanted to learn Agent O'Connor's first name. So I pulled out my laptop and did a Google search for 'FBI Agent O'Connor'.

There were two pages of results. Mostly from court cases where her name had been mentioned. Only one included her full name. Madison J. O'Connor.

Using that name, I did a people search. The results showed she was living in Orlando and employed by the FBI. Thirty-two, single with no children, and had only lived at her current address for four months.

That was all I needed to know. Her first name, age, and marital status. I could definitely work with that.

I put my laptop away, turned off the light, and got under the sheets. Before falling asleep, I started wondering what she would look like wearing the red teddy Norah had mentioned.

I was pretty sure Agent O'Connor, who I would soon be calling Maddie, would have shot me if she'd known what I was thinking.

Chapter Thirty-Seven

I didn't hear her when she first got up and started moving around in the morning. But I did hear her when she knocked on my door and asked, "Where do you keep the coffee?"

I was half asleep. Before I could answer, she said, "Walker, I need coffee. Where do you keep it?"

Then, "Walker, tell me where the coffee is."

And finally, "Coffeeee! Where is it?"

She was starting to sound desperate. And I knew she wasn't going to like my answer. Still, I had to tell her. "There's no coffee. But there's soda's in the fridge."

"Soda? What are you talking about? I don't want a soda. I need coffee. Where do you keep it?"

I could hear her opening and closing cabinet doors in the kitchen. Looking for coffee, which as I told her before, we didn't have.

Thinking maybe it was hidden away in a place she hadn't looked, she came to my door again. "Walker, get up. You can't sleep all day."

She was right, I couldn't sleep. Not with her banging on my door and yelling at me.

Knowing that she wasn't going to give up, I rolled out of bed wearing just my boxers.

I could have pulled on a pair of pants, and maybe a tee shirt but didn't bother. If she was in such a dang hurry to talk, I'd go out and talk to her. Wearing only my undershorts.

They were clean. And colorful, what with the Superman logo on the front.

When I stepped out to see what she wanted, she looked surprised. Then laughed and said, "Walker, nobody wants to see that. Go put some clothes on. Don't come out until you do."

I gave her a thumbs up. "Sure thing, Maddie."

Back in my bedroom, I quickly closed the door, thinking she might throw something at me after hearing me call her Maddie. But she didn't, so I got dressed and went back out to see what she wanted.

Seeing that I'd put on some clothes, she smiled. "That's better. Now tell me where the coffee is."

She still didn't believe me.

"Maddie, I already told you, I don't have any coffee. I don't drink it. If you need caffeine, try one of the Mountain Dews in the fridge. They have more caffeine than two cups of coffee."

She shook her head. "I don't want Mountain Dew. I want coffee. And don't call me Maddie. Not before I have my coffee."

She pointed out the window to Norah's RV. "You think she has any over there?"

"She might."

"Good. Put some shoes on. We're going to go and see."

O'Connor was still wearing the cargo pants and swamp ape tee-shirt I'd loaned her the night before. She wasn't wearing any makeup and her hair was tangled from sleeping on the sofa. She looked far different than the suit-wearing strait-laced federal agent that I had faced the day before.

She was starting to look normal. Like the rest of us. It was a good look for her.

Outside we were greeted with blue skies, mild temps, and a cool breeze coming off the river. Another perfect day in Florida. Maddie hardly noticed.

She marched over to Norah's, knocked on the door, and asked, "You guys up?"

From inside, Agent Harris answered. "Yeah, we're up. Come on in."

The smell of fresh coffee was strong. A cup was quickly poured, and Maddie gladly accepted it. I was offered the same, but declined, saying I preferred the bubbly burn of a Mountain Dew in the morning.

Looking around for a place to sit, I noticed the sofa didn't look like it had been slept on. There were no sheets or pillows anywhere to be seen.

Back in my place, the sofa was still folded out into a bed. The tangle of sheets left no doubt that Maddie, and probably Bob, had spent the night on it. But at Norah's, things looked different. No sign the sofa had even been folded out into a bed.

Maybe she and Harris both slept in the back in her bed. It would have been a lot more comfortable for him than being on the sofa. But most likely, he didn't sleep back there with her. He probably sleep on the sofa, got up early, and put everything away.

Or maybe not.

Harris and Norah both looked happy and seemed to be getting along well. A far cry from how things were going with me and Maddie. She was tense around me. Always threatening to shoot me. Claiming we would never be friends.

I was working on a plan to change that.

Agent Harris had an atlas spread out on the table in front of him. He put his finger halfway down the Florida page. "We're moving today. To the Ortona Locks Campground. A Corp of Engineers park under federal control.

"What I like about the place is there's only one way in, and one way out. A seven-mile-long road that doesn't go anywhere except to the campground. It'll be easy for our agents to keep track of anyone heading toward us once we set up there.

"All the sites are bordered by the Okeechobee waterway. That greatly limits possible escape routes. If you come in by car, you can only leave by car. Unless you have a river-going boat – which I doubt the people we are looking for, have.

"I called the campground this morning and was able to get two side-by-side sites near the back. No one will be camping near us. We'll be able to see anyone coming, long before they get close.

"It's about two hundred miles from here. A five-hour drive. We'll be going south on I-95 until we get to Fort Pierce. Then we'll follow seventy to Okeechobee, and finally, we'll take seventy-eight to the park."

He looked up. "Any questions?"

I had one.

"What about gas? I'm almost empty."

Harris nodded. "Fill up before you get on the interstate. There's a Walmart Super Center right before the on-ramp. Get your gas there."

He paused, then said, "We don't want to draw any attention to what we're doing or where we're going, so we won't be traveling as a convoy. We'll stay a few miles apart until we get there."

He turned to O'Connor. "Tell us about the timing of your plan."

She stood. "We won't turn their laptop or phone on until

we get to Ortona. That way, the thieves won't be tracking us while we move. That's assuming the microwave actually works like Walker said and blocks their signal.

"But he could be wrong. Maybe they still can track us. So if anything looks suspicious while we're on the road, we'll join up and take them on together."

"If we get to Ortona without any problems, we'll turn both of the devices on and hope the thieves will either call or start tracking us. If they call, I'll tell them we bought the phone from a guy at a rest area. I'll agree to sell it back if they'll meet up with us in the campground.

"If they don't call or make contact with us today, we'll stay in the campground until they do.

"Any questions?"

No one had any. Except Harris.

He looked at O'Connor. "So how was your night?"

She made a frowny face. "I didn't sleep much. The sofa is lumpy and that damn cat kept wanting to sleep on top of me. When I pushed him off, he would wait until I got back to sleep and then get back on."

O'Connor saw me holding back laughter.

She shook her head. "Walker, how about this? Tonight, you sleep on the sofa. I'll sleep in your bed. We'll see how you feel in the morning."

I nodded. "I do like the idea of you in my bed. But you know what sounds even better? We both sleep there together. There's plenty of room."

Harris and Norah smiled but said nothing. O'Connor stood and headed for the door. "Let's go. I need to get something to eat and clothes that fit."

I followed her out.

Ten minutes later, we were on the road. O'Connor in the passenger seat with Bob on her lap.

She didn't bother to shoo him away this time. Instead, she started stroking his back and rubbing his ears. Something he very much enjoyed.

Chapter Thirty-Eight

It didn't take us long to get to Walmart. There wasn't much traffic with it being so early in the morning. I pulled up to the fuel island and filled the RV with just over three hundred dollars of gas. A year earlier, when we had a different president, it would have cost half as much. Same with most other things we paid for.

With the gas tank full, I parked the RV at the far side of the lot and followed Maddie into the store. She grabbed a cart and headed to the woman's clothing department. On the way there, she made it clear that I wasn't to run off. I was to stay close to her so she could keep an eye on me.

Standing around in woman's wear while she shopped for clothes was about the last thing I wanted to do. But if I had no other choice, I'd do it.

And I'd make it a little more interesting.

Maddie found some Florida tee shirts on sale and put four of them in the cart I was pushing. She added four pairs of granny panties and the same number of white ankle socks.

After picking out three different sizes of shorts, she pointed to the dressing room. "I'm going to try these on. Wait here until I come back out."

I nodded. "Yes, dear. I'll stay right here."

But, of course, I didn't stay.

As soon as she disappeared into the dressing room, I removed the granny panties from the cart and replaced them with four pairs of lacy panties of the same size. I added two thongs, a white lace top with matching sleep shorts, three sports bras, and two sleeveless halter tops. And a pair of white panties with the words, 'Tonight's the Night' in red.

I carefully hid these at the bottom of the cart, under the tees she'd picked out earlier. I wanted them to be a surprise when she got to the checkout station.

Looking around, I found a few more things to add to her new wardrobe. A white bikini bra, two pairs of skin-hugging bike shorts, and a pair of black yoga pants.

I had just finished hiding these latest finds when Maddie came out of the dressing room.

"So you've been staying out of trouble, right?"

"Yes ma'am. I've been a good boy. Just standing here doing nothing."

Of course, that wasn't quite true as she would later learn. But until then, I was going to keep quiet about what I had done.

Of the three shorts she'd tried on in the dressing room, only one got her approval. She put the other two back on the sales rack and grabbed three of the same size and color that fit her best.

When she put them in the cart, she didn't notice that the pile of clothes in it had grown noticeably larger while she was away.

Satisfied that she had gotten all the clothes she needed, she led me to Walmart's grocery area and grabbed a package of Starbucks Instant Coffee. "Do you have coffee cups in your RV?"

I did, but they were kind of old, and likely not up to her standards. "Maybe you should get a new one."

She made a face, then went to the household department and picked out two coffee cups. From there, we made a quick trip to the produce department. She picked out four bananas, four apples, four pears, and four kiwis. Based on the quantity, it looked like she wasn't planning on sharing.

That didn't hurt my feelings. I had all the food I needed. Mostly frozen. Not knowing how long I was going to be on the road when I headed to Titusville, I had stocked up before leaving. I wasn't planning on going hungry. Or sharing. She could live off her fruit and I'd stick with the TV dinners.

But then she surprised me.

She headed over to the frozen food aisle and picked out four Healthy Choice frozen dinners. Chicken and rice, chicken and pasta, chicken noodle, and chicken and pineapple.

Apparently, she had a thing for chicken.

Leaving the grocery section behind, we headed to the front of the store to check out. I knew that if we went through self-check, she'd discover the clothing I'd added to the cart and would make me take everything back. But if I could find a line with a live person doing the checking, I might have a better chance of getting away with it.

I steered the cart to the first live checker we came to. There were four people in line in front of us. The checker was doing a good job of moving things along. It would soon be our turn.

My plan was to not unload our cart until the last moment while trying to distract Maddie when the clothes came out.

As it turned out, I didn't need to worry about her discovering what I had done.

She was behind me in the line, browsing the magazines on display. Just as the woman in front of us was leaving, Maddie tapped me on the shoulder. "I forgot a couple of things. I'll be right back."

She handed me her government credit card. "I don't want to

hold up the line, so go ahead and check out. Wait for me at the front of the store."

I took her card, knowing then, I was home free.

I got everything checked out and bagged before she returned. She came back carrying sandals, a lint roller, toothbrush and toothpaste, body wash, and an assortment of oils and lotions that I didn't recognize, and wouldn't be asking about.

I gave her back the credit card. She checked out and we were on our way.

Chapter Thirty-Nine

Back in the RV, I was worried Maddie would go through the Walmart bags and discover the clothes switch. If that happened while we were still in the parking lot, she could go back in the store and return them. Since I wanted to see her wearing the clothes I'd picked out, I suggested that after we put the food away, we not waste time unpacking the other bags. She could leave them until we got to our new campsite. There'd be plenty of time to sort through her new clothes there.

She thought it was a good idea. Without giving her a chance to change her mind, I started the RV and pulled out of the Walmart lot. Two minutes later we were back on I-95 heading south.

After getting up to speed, I set the cruise control to sixty-five and settled in for the drive. Maddie leaned back in the passenger seat, closed her eyes, and soon the monotonous sounds of the road, helped her drift off to sleep.

About twenty minutes later, Bob came up from the back. Maddie was in his seat again and he hadn't given her permission. She had taken his seat without asking.

He stared at her for a moment, then reached up and tapped her arm with his paw. There was no reaction. He did it a second time, and as with the first tap, Maddie did nothing.

Deciding there was no reason not to, he eased himself into her lap and settled in between her legs. Maddie let out a short moan, reached down, and put her hand on his back. Then went back to sleep.

Bob soon joined her in slumber.

They stayed that way for two hours until I switched on the turn signal letting the cars behind me know that I was taking the exit to Fort Pierce. The click-click sound of the blinker woke them both.

Maddie rubbed her eyes and looked up. "Are we there already?"

"No. Not quite. According to the GPS, we still have another two hours before we get to Ortona."

She nodded, then looked down at Bob, who was still in her lap. "How long has he been there?"

"About two hours. He got up there right after we left Walmart. You didn't seem to mind. I think he's starting to like you."

She licked her dry lips. "I'm going to get a water out of the fridge. You want one?"

"Yeah."

She gently lifted Bob and put him down on the floor, but not before saying, "I hate to disturb you, but I need something to drink. I've got to get up, but I'll be right back, okay?"

Bob rubbed her ankle, stretched, and said, "Murrph."

Kind of like he understood what she was saying.

But maybe not, because when she returned with the two waters, he had taken her seat.

It didn't seem to bother her though. She picked him up, sat down where he had been sitting, and put him back in her lap. "Bob, you can go back to sleep now."

After taking a few sips of water, she put the bottle away and started rubbing his back.

He purred, knowing that he'd won her over. In less than a

day.

I was hoping to do the same. Win her over.

For the next hour and a half, we rode in silence, listening to the GPS as it told me how to get to Okeechobee. It would be the last town of any size we'd go through before getting to our campsite at Ortona.

Agent Harris had said there'd be no stores after we left Okeechobee. If we wanted to stop to get anything, that would be our last chance.

We were just getting into town when Maddie broke the silence.

"You hungry?"

"I am. You going to make me something to eat?"

She laughed. "Yeah, I'm going to make you stop at a burger joint and buy me lunch."

"Sounds good to me. But you'll have to find a place with enough room to park the RV."

She pulled out her phone, tapped the screen for a few seconds, then said, "How about Dairy Queen? There's one just outside of town, on ninety-eight. It has truck parking. Will that work?"

"Yeah."

"Good. When we get there, pull in and park in the lot around the back. I'll go in and get the food while you and Bob wait outside."

Ten minutes later, I pulled into the Dairy Queen lot. The parking spaces near the front were mostly taken by pickups and work vans. Always a good sign. It usually means the food is good. Or, in a small town, there is no other place to eat.

I headed past the rows of parked trucks until I reached the

large lot in the back. Finding a place in the shade, I parked.

Maddie unbuckled her belt. "What do you want?"

I'd been thinking about it ever since she said we were going to Dairy Queen. Their burgers were famous. I already knew I wanted one.

"Get me a double cheeseburger, onion rings, and a large Coke. I can go in and get it if you want me to. That way I can pay."

"No way you're going in. You're staying out here with Bob. I'll get the food. And don't worry about who's paying. I'm on duty. Everything goes on the government card.

"Just promise me that while I'm inside, you won't drive off and leave me. Like you did last time."

I smiled. Because there was no way I was going to drive off without her. Not without first seeing her face when she discovered the wardrobe switch I'd made.

"Maddie, I won't leave you this time, I promise."

She leaned over toward me. As she got closer, I thought she was coming in for a kiss.

But I was wrong.

Instead of a kiss, she reached over the steering wheel and pulled the keys out of the ignition. "It's not that I don't trust you, Walker. But you did abandon me in a parking lot the last time we rode together. I'm making sure it doesn't happen again."

She returned eight minutes later with our food. We sat at the dinette table and ate, while she told me about the people she saw inside.

According to her, they were the kind of down-home folks she'd grown up around. Hard-working, church-going, polite, and happy. At least, that's the way they seemed to her in the few minutes she was inside.

Since she'd brought it up, I could have asked about her childhood. And maybe learned more about her background. But I didn't. I had a double cheeseburger and onion rings in front of me and wanted to eat them before they got cold.

She didn't seem to mind because she was well into her own burger. It would have been impolite for me to ask her questions when her mouth was full.

Later on, I learned there were things in her past that had I known about, I wouldn't have made the clothes switch.

It was something I would come to regret in the coming days.

Chapter Forty

It took us another twenty minutes to get to the Ortona campground after leaving the Dairy Queen in Okeechobee. The volunteer at the gate asked if we had reservations. According to Agent Harris, we did. But we didn't know whose name they were in.

Maddie pulled out her phone and called Harris, figuring he and Norah had already arrived and were in their site. Even if they weren't, Harris would know about the reservations.

Unfortunately, the call went directly to voice mail. Maddie tried again, and as before, it went to voice mail.

"Either his phone is turned off, or they're in a dead zone. Walker, try calling Norah. See if she answers."

Norah had given me her number the day we'd met. I pulled it up on my phone and hit dial. It connected almost immediately. But just like the call to Harris, no one answered. It went to voice mail. I tried two more times, with the same result. No answer. Just voice mail.

I ended up leaving a message, asking her to call me back.

The gate guard had waited patiently while we made the calls, but when another camper pulled up behind us, he said, "Sorry folks, unless you have a reservation, I can't let you in."

Maddie sighed, pulled out her FBI ID, and showed it to him. "Two sites were reserved this morning. Agent Harris of Homeland Security would have been the caller. He would have paid with a government credit card."

The guard looked at Maddie's ID, then at the clipboard he was holding. After a few seconds, he nodded. "Yeah, here they are. Two sites. Next to each other. At the back of the park. Reserved for the next four days."

After looking at Maddie's ID a second time, he checked us in and gave us a campground map with directions to our sites. As promised, they were at the far end of the park, with a water view over the Ortona Canal.

Relieved that we didn't have to wait at the front gate any longer, we followed the directions on the map and headed to our site. Along the way, we passed a sign pointing to the RV dump station. It wasn't a place we needed to visit right away, but if we stayed the full four days, we'd have to go there and empty our tanks.

Fifty yards beyond, we crossed a narrow bridge over a fast-flowing creek. Next to it, a short fishing pier extended out over the water. I made a mental note to check it out later.

When we passed the campground bathhouse, I pointed it out to Maddie. "If you want to shower, that's where you'll have to go. You can't do it in the motorhome. It uses too much water. It'll fill our tanks too quickly.

"So you have to use the bathhouse. Unless we conserve water by showering together in the RV."

She groaned. "Don't get your hopes up. We're not showering together. Ever."

I wondered if she was at least thinking about it. Even if she wasn't, I was.

The campground road ended in a loop that headed back the way we'd come. Our sites were on the water side of the loop. Far enough off the road to give us a bit of privacy. Both were level, paved, and had a nearby picnic table under a metal roof.

The closest neighbor was a good distance away. The tropical foliage between their campsite and ours would give us even more privacy. Something that might be important if Maddie's plan to lure the owners of the laptop to our site actually worked.

Since we'd arrived before Norah and Agent Harris, we had our choice of the two sites. Site twenty-one had the most privacy and the best view. It was also larger.

The site next to it, site twenty-two, was smaller, a little harder to get into, but closer to the bathhouse. Everything considered, site twenty-one was the better choice. Even so, I opted for site twenty-two. I figured that since Norah was an RV newbie, letting her have the site that was easier to get into was the right thing to do.

I pulled past site twenty-two's driveway, put the RV in reverse, and carefully backed onto the parking pad, using the side mirrors and backup camera to make sure I didn't hit anything. I kept backing until the rear tires reached the block at the back of the site. Rechecking the mirrors, I saw that I had lined the RV up perfectly on the pad.

Satisfied with my parking job, I killed the motor and turned to Maddie. "Impressed?"

She looked confused. "About what? Did I miss something?"

"Yeah, you missed my great parking job. I got this big boy backed in perfectly on the first try."

Still confused, she asked, "So how many tries does it usually take?"

I didn't answer. Because sometimes, depending on the obstacles around a site, it might take me a few tries to get it right. I didn't want her to know that. So, I said, "Never mind."

I unbuckled my belt and stood. "I'm going outside to hook up to shore power. You want to join me?"

"No. You go ahead. I'll stay in here and put away my new

clothes. Might even try some on. Knock before you come back in."

"Yes, dear. I'll be sure to do that."

I headed out the door, thinking that when she unpacked her clothes, I wouldn't need to knock.

I'd need to run.

Chapter Forty-One

It took me less than three minutes to hook the RV up to shore power and water. When I was finished, I could have gone back in to see Maddie, but didn't. I knew what was coming, and figured being outside was safer than being in with her and her new clothes.

So instead of going in and facing the music, I went over to the covered picnic table and sat facing the water. I had the map the campground host had given us, and looked at it to see what it had to say about the place.

According to it, the Ortona lock was just one of many locks on the Okeechobee Waterway, a man-made canal that stretched from the Gulf of Mexico on the west coast of Florida all the way to the Atlantic Ocean on the east coast. It had been dug by the Corp of Engineers to create a way for boaters to cross Florida without having to go all the way around the keys.

Using the crossing would save several days and avoid the possibility of a boater running into heavy seas that they might, if they had to go the long way around.

The canal open to all kinds of craft, but with an average water depth of just ten feet, it was used primarily by pleasure boats and barges. It was way too shallow for cruise ships.

After learning the story of the Canal, I put the map away and looked out over the water just in time to see a forty-foot yacht approach the lock. According to what I'd just read, the boat would enter and tie off to a cleat. Then the gates behind it would close. The water level in the closed lock would be lowered or raised to match the level on the other side. Then the far gate would open, and the boat would go on its way.

And that's exactly what happened.

The process took about ten minutes from start to finish. During that time, I didn't hear a word from Maddie. Which surprised me. I expected as soon as she went through the bags from Walmart, she'd be yelling my name.

But she hadn't. At least not yet.

The yacht that had just gone through the locks was slowly motoring past our campsite. An older man was at the inside helm, a woman who I presume was his wife, stood near him. A yellow lab lay on the deck just outside the pilothouse.

I waved at the couple. They waved back.

A few minutes later, a second vessel, a single-masted sailboat, approached the lock from the east. It entered as the previous boat had, and was waiting for the water level in the lock to match the level on the other side.

Since it was a sailboat, I wanted to see how it would come out of the lock. Whether it would be under motor power or sail.

I didn't get the chance to find out, because from inside the RV, I heard, "Walker, you idiot!"

I smiled. Maddie had apparently found the panties and other goodies I had picked out for her. Her reaction was pretty much what I expected.

Anger.

Which I hoped would soon turn to amusement.

Because it was funny. At least to me.

But maybe not to her.

She stayed quiet for a few seconds, then in a very calm voice, said, "Walker, come in here. There's something I want to show you."

Thinking that maybe she had tried on and liked some of the things in her new wardrobe, I headed to the door. Remembering what she had said when I went out, I politely knocked before going in.

"It's okay, Walker. Come on in."

I opened the door and cautiously stepped in. Maddie was standing in the kitchen, holding a pair of scissors in one hand, and my last three pairs of clean boxers, in the other.

With a smile, she said, "I couldn't find the panties I picked out at the store, so I went back to your closet to see if maybe somehow they had ended up in there.

"They hadn't, but I did find some that belonged to you. I hoped that maybe they'd fit me, but they didn't. My waist is a bit smaller than yours."

She held up the scissors. "I thought I could alter your boxers so they would fit."

She used the scissors to cut one of the boxers in half, letting the pieces drop to the floor.

"Oops. Didn't mean to do that. I'll try again."

She held up another pair, the one with the Batman imprint. One of my favorites.

Smiling, she used the scissors to cut out the crotch area. She held it up so I could see what was left. She shook her head. "No, that won't work either." She let what was left of them drop to the floor.

There was only one pair left. The Tony the Tiger pair. Another one of my favorites.

Still smiling, she said, "Before I start cutting this one up, if someone were to tell me where to find the clothes I picked out at Walmart, I might be able to let these live."

She snapped the scissors making sure she had my attention. "Do you know where I might find my clothes?"

I didn't answer.

I knew that the granny panties she'd picked out were not in the RV. They were still at Walmart. She would not want to hear that. And that meant my favorite pair of boxers were about to be scissored in half.

I tried to talk her out of it. "Maddie, don't do it. That's my last pair. I won't have anything else to wear."

She smiled. "That would be such a shame. You'd have to wear what you've got on for at least the next four days. But maybe I can help you out.

"I'd be happy to loan you some of the new ones you picked out for me. How about a thong? Will that work for you?"

Even though it pained me, I smiled because the thought of me wearing any of her newly bought panties was kind of funny. It wasn't something I'd ever be doing, but still, it was funny.

For a second time, I tried to save my boxers. "Maddie, if you cut those up, I won't have anything to wear. I'll have to go commando. You know what that means, don't you?"

That drew an immediate response. "Ugh. I don't want to even think about you walking around without underwear. Here. Take them."

She tossed them in my direction.

Then, still holding the scissors, she said, "I'm warning you. Never mess with my clothes again. Don't touch them, don't sniff them, and don't dare think about what I'm wearing under them. Understand?"

I nodded. "Yes ma'am. I understand."

I thought the discussion was over, but it wasn't. She had

more to say.

"As punishment for what you did, I'm taking over your bedroom. I'll be sleeping in there until this thing is over. You'll be sleeping out here on the sofa. Alone."

I started to say something, but she pointed the scissors at me and shook her head.

I knew I'd lost the battle.

But maybe not the war.

Chapter Forty-Two

Maddie had claimed my bedroom. She'd made it clear that she would be sleeping there and I would be spending the night on the couch. Alone.

It was my punishment for swapping out her clothes at Walmart.

I probably deserved it, but still thought it was funny. And anyway, I'd get to see her in the clothes I picked out for her. She had no other choice. The only other option was what she'd been wearing when she first stopped me. A dark blue sports coat, matching blue pants, a white button-up shirt, and black dress shoes. Her FBI outfit.

Not the kind of thing you wear when you're undercover and trying to fit in with the Florida tourist crowd.

As for the new sleeping arrangements, I didn't think they'd stick. She was supposed to be protecting me from the bad guys and it would make a lot more sense for her to sleep up front, near the doors, than in the bedroom at the back.

My guess was, she also knew this and would cede the bedroom back to me when it was time to sleep.

I didn't mention it, though. She was pretty steamed and was still holding scissors.

We were still inside the RV. The remnants of my boxers were on the floor, at her feet. She pointed at them. "Pick them up and take them outside with you. Stay out there until I tell you otherwise.

"But don't go far. If I have to come looking for you, it won't end well."

I nodded. "Yes dear, I'll stay close. Can I at least get my Kindle out of the bedroom? It'll give me something to read while I wait for you to cool down."

As soon as I said the words 'cool down', I knew I shouldn't have. It only made her madder. She pointed to the door.

"Out!"

I didn't wait for her to tell me again. I opened the door, dropped the remains of my undies in the nearby trash barrel, and headed to the picnic table to sit.

Maddie was mad. And surprisingly, I was starting to feel a little guilty about the situation with her clothes. Not super guilty, though. It wasn't like I'd replaced the items she'd picked out with things she couldn't use. She might not want to wear the tight biking shorts or the sports bras, but they'd be comfortable and wouldn't make her look like a fed.

If she thought they showed too much skin, she could always cover up with one of the tee shirts she'd gotten.

I could have mentioned this while I was still inside but didn't. I figured my best course of action was to keep my mouth shut and stay out of her way. And to say absolutely nothing about whatever she chose to wear.

Since she wouldn't let me get my Kindle before sending me out, I didn't have anything to read. All I could do was sit at the picnic table and watch the boats go by. Or take a walk, maybe down to the fishing pier and back.

But taking a walk was probably one of the things she didn't want me to do. She said to stay close.

So I opted to just sit at the picnic table.

For the next twenty minutes, I sat and watched as mostly pleasure boats passed by. In most cases, the people aboard looked happy and relaxed. Some had drinks in hand, others were out on the deck getting sunshine, while still others were napping in the shade.

The more I watched, the more I was convinced that maybe I should be doing what the boaters were doing. Which was pretty much nothing. They weren't being bullied around by the FBI or wondering if Homeland Security was going to charge them with a crime and put them away in a jail cell. They were just enjoying the sun and water and being chill.

Eventually, I got tired of watching the boats go by, and started wondering why Norah and Agent Harris hadn't shown up yet. They left before us and should have gotten to Ortona long before we did. We'd already been at the campground for more than an hour. Maybe they ran into a problem.

Hoping that Maddie had time to cool off, I decided to go in and ask if she had heard from them.

Leaving the picnic table, I went to the RV. Instead of barging in, I tapped on the door to let her know I was outside. I didn't want to walk in on her if she was trying on clothes or cleaning her gun. She wouldn't be happy and I might get shot.

Fortunately, she was doing neither. She opened the door and said I could come in. She was wearing a pair of bike shorts and one of the tee shirts from Walmart. I didn't ask what she had on under the shirt.

But I did wonder.

Crossing her arms, she asked, "What do you want?"

I gave her my most friendly smile. "I was wondering why Agent Harris and Norah haven't shown up yet. Have you heard from them?"

"No. I called but it went to voice mail. I'll try again."

With her phone close to her ear, she made the call.

Apparently, someone answered.

"Agent Harris, is everything okay?"

I couldn't hear his answer but could hear Maddie's response.

"Yeah, we're here."

"So far, no problems."

"We were wondering what was holding you up."

"Really? The governor?"

"Norah didn't mind?"

"That's a surprise."

Then, after a long pause, "We'll do that. I'll let him know."

"See you in a few minutes."

She ended the call and turned to me.

"Everything is fine. They stopped in Vero Beach and ran into the Governor. He and Harris are friends from way back. The Governor was there to speak at an educator's summit and when he learned that Norah was with Harris, he wanted to talk to her.

"That's why they are running late. They are about twenty minutes out."

"Good to know. Is there anything you want me to do?"

She pointed to the microwave. "Get the laptop and phone out. It's time to see if the bad guys are smart enough to track their location."

I went to the microwave and got both devices and put them on the dinette table. When I powered them up, both showed they needed to be charged.

Fortunately, they charged via USB and didn't need special cables. Using two of the spare cables I keep in the RV, I hooked them up and let them charge.

After waiting a few minutes, I tried the power button on the laptop. Surprisingly, it powered right up, going straight to the Windows home screen. No password required.

I guess the thieves were trusting that no one would ever get their hands on their equipment. That was a mistake on their part.

The status bar on the Windows screen showed the laptop had automatically scanned for and connected to an active Wi-Fi source. Since the campground didn't have Wi-Fi and I didn't have Wi-Fi active in the RV, I wondered what it had connected to.

To find out, I clicked the little Wi-Fi icon in the Windows taskbar. A small window opened, telling me the laptop had connected to the 'Samsung Galaxy S22-610240' network.

This meant it was getting its Wi-Fi via a phone hotspot. Probably from the phone we had taken from inside the ambulance and had just pulled out of the microwave.

This actually made sense. For someone on the move, having their laptop tethered to their phone meant as long as the phone had a signal, the laptop would have access to the Internet.

Apparently, when I powered up the phone, the laptop saw that it was live and used it to connect to the Internet.

This meant the location of both could easily be tracked by someone using a 'find me' app.

I was just about to let Maddie know, when the phone rang with an incoming call.

Without hesitation, she answered.

Chapter Forty-Three

Picking up the thief's phone, Maddie said, 'Hello'. Then she turned away from me so I couldn't hear what was being said. I tried to get closer, but she wasn't having it. She pushed me back with an open palm to my chest.

I got the message. She didn't want me listening in.

When the call ended, she put the phone back on the table where it had been charging and said, "They're coming. Tomorrow. To get the laptop. And the phone."

She started to say more, but before she could, I wrapped my arms around her and kissed her on the lips. I could tell she was surprised and trying to pull away, but I held firm.

Leaning in close to her ear, I whispered, "The laptop camera just came on. They can see and hear everything we do. Play along."

I kissed her again, then released my embrace. "You sold the phone? That's great! What'd you get for it?"

She held up three fingers. "Three hundred dollars."

"Wow! You did good. We can sure use the money. When are they coming?"

"Sometime tomorrow. They said they'd call when they got close."

"Great! We need to celebrate. But first, let's put the phone away so nothing happens to it before they get here."

I powered the phone down. Then took it to the microwave and put it inside.

Walking back to Maddie, I glanced at the laptop. The

camera light was off. Losing the tethered connection to the phone ended its ability to see what we were doing or hear what we were saying.

Just to be safe though, I powered the laptop down and put it in the microwave with the phone.

When I came back, Maddie was shaking her head. "You made that up, didn't you? No one was really watching. You just wanted to kiss me. Admit it."

I smiled.

"Maddie, you have to believe me. Someone remotely turned on the laptop camera. Whoever it was, they were watching and listening to us. It was probably the thieves or their bosses, trying to see if we had their laptop. Since I didn't want them to think you were FBI, I did what I had to do to make it look like we were a loving couple. So I kissed you. Twice."

I paused, and after smiling, continued. "But I'm not sure we convinced them. The kisses didn't feel real. At least to me. That means we probably need to practice until we get it right. That way, when they call back, we'll be able to put on a show they'll believe.

"They'll see us kissing and know we're a real couple. So, yeah, we need to practice. Maybe tonight is a good time to start."

Maddie crossed her arms. "Walker, we're not going to practice anything. Not now, not ever. You got away with those two kisses. But you're not going to get another chance, even if they are watching. We're not putting on a show for them. There won't be any kissing or hugging. Don't even try, unless you want them to see you get slapped."

I made a frowny face.

"You're no fun."

She shrugged as if she didn't care if she was fun or not.

I changed the subject. "Tell me about the call. What'd they say?"

With arms still crossed, she said, "This is FBI business. You don't need to know."

I was pretty sure I did.

"Maddie, what if when they get here tomorrow, they ask me about something you said during the call. It'll look suspicious if I don't know what they're talking about. So tell me what they said."

She thought for a moment. "Okay, I'll tell you.

"When I answered, a woman, who sounded like she was middle age, said someone had stolen her phone and wondered how I ended up with it.

"I told her we were traveling in our RV, heading to Key West. We had stopped at a rest area, and a guy came up and offered to sell us a phone and laptop. He said they both belonged to him, and he was selling because he needed gas money.

"We wanted to help him out, so we agreed to buy them."

"The woman said the phone and laptop were stolen from her car, and she needed to get them both back. She wanted to know what I'd sell them for.

"I told her three hundred. Not surprisingly, she agreed and said she'd bring us the money. I told her we'd be at the Ortona campground near Okeechobee for the next two days. If she showed up with the cash before we left, we'd sell her the phone and laptop.

"She said she was about eight hours away and wanted to know if she could come tomorrow. I told her 'yeah', as long as she brought the money. I didn't tell her what site we were in or what we were driving. I just said to call when she got to the gate and I'd meet her there."

I nodded. Maddie had handled the call well. But something about it was bothering me.

"What if she's not really eight hours away? What if she and whoever she's with, are a lot closer and show up before we are ready?"

Maddie thought for a moment. "You said they were tracking us using the laptop. Can you do the reverse? Can you use it to track them?"

Chapter Forty-Four

Could I track the thieves the same way they could track us? Using their phone?

It was a good question. One that I should have come up with on my own.

I knew that if the thief had a Google product on his phone, whether it was Chrome, YouTube, Maps, Gmail, or any of the other apps that the giant company controls, his location was always being tracked and stored in the cloud. Whether he knew it or not.

Due to privacy concerns, Google provides a way for account holders to see how their movements are tracked. To do that, they have to visit timeline.google.com. When they get there, they'll see a map showing every place they've traveled to, stopped, or spent any time at, for every month the account has been active. The timeline also shows their current location.

Since almost everyone uses at least one Google product, almost everyone is being tracked. Which meant there was a pretty good chance that if we could log into the Google Tracks timeline on the thief's laptop, we might be able to see their movements.

I let Maddie know.

"Yeah, there might be a way I can track them. It'll only take me a few minutes to find out."

I got the laptop back out of the microwave and brought it to the kitchen table. Because I didn't want their phone to automatically connect to it like it had earlier, I left it where it was. In the microwave.

I powered up the laptop and checked to see if it was connected to the Internet. It wasn't.

Which was good. For the moment.

But I'd have to connect it to the web if I wanted to log into their tracked timeline. But first, because I didn't want anyone to watch or listen in on what I was doing, I turned off the laptop's camera and microphone. Then I powered up my own VPN-protected Wi-Fi hot-spot. It's what I use when I want a secure connection to the Internet.

Once it was up and running, I connected the laptop, started the Chrome browser, and entered the Google Tracks web address.

Because Google knows the information on the page is sensitive, it requires a password to get in. So I was surprised when the 'password required' prompt didn't show up. Instead, the timeline screen appeared. Apparently, the last person to use the laptop had checked the 'remember me' box on the login screen. A very stupid thing to do.

But lucky for us, they had.

The Timeline page had a US map peppered with red dots. Each represented a place that the phone had traveled to. By mousing over a dot, we could see the exact location, the date and time they had visited, and how long they had stayed.

The map showed the phone had traveled mostly between Florida and Georgia, with a lot of stopovers in between.

That was the good news. We were actually able to track the movement of one of their phones.

The bad news was, we didn't know whose phone we were tracking. It could have been the one currently stored in our microwave. Or another phone we didn't know about, or the one that had been used to call Norah asking about the laptop. If we were lucky, it would be that one.

To find out, we first needed to rule out the phone in the microwave. If the track showed the current location of the phone as being in Ortona, where we were, it would mean the track map was for the phone we had in our possession. That wouldn't do us much good but might help the FBI later on.

But if the track showed the phone was not currently in Ortona, it might mean it belonged to the person who had just called. So, we were happy when we saw that the last known location of the phone being tracked, was an address in Savannah, Georgia.

Maddie had been watching over my shoulder as I worked through the map's timeline. She had been quiet until I pointed to the Savannah location.

"Walker, that could be the caller's phone. She said she was eight hours away. That's about how far Savannah is by car from here.

"If it is her phone, and she's coming to see us, we can track her location and know exactly when to expect her."

She put her hand on my shoulder. "Good job."

It was the first time she'd said something nice to me. I was hoping it wouldn't be the last.

Either way, things were about to get interesting.

Chapter Forty-Five

I didn't want the thieves to listen in, or watch us as we went about our day, so I powered down the laptop and put it back in the microwave. I'd get it out later when we wanted to check their travel progress.

Hearing tire noise outside, we saw Norah's RV pull into the site next to ours. Agent Harris was driving. Norah wasn't with him. Buttercup, Norah's little car, wasn't with the RV either.

A minute later, Norah showed up in Buttercup, with Biscuit at her side. She pulled up behind her RV and parked. As soon as she got out, Harris walked over to her and said something that made them both smile.

He was still smiling when Maddie and I approached. As was Norah.

Both seemed surprisingly upbeat. Not what you'd expect from two people who'd spent eight hours on the road on what should have been a five-hour trip.

I started to ask Harris why it took them so long, but before I could, he reached out, as if to shake hands. I responded by reaching out as well. When I did, he dropped the keys to Norah's RV into my open palm, and said, "Walker, if you don't mind, would you and Norah stay out here while I meet up with Agent O'Connor? There are a few things we need to talk about. In private."

The message was clear. He didn't want us to hear what he and Maddie were going to say.

I figured it would be about the case and saw no reason to

not let them discuss it in private. So I said, "Sure, no problem."

He started to walk away, but Maddie, aka Agent O'Connor, hung back. She turned to me. "Try to stay out of trouble while we're gone. Think you can do that?"

I smiled. "Me? Get into trouble? Never."

She shook her head, turned, and walked away.

We watched as the two Agents went into my RV, closing the door behind them. As soon as they were out of sight, Norah, who was standing behind me, asked, "What do you think they're going to talk about?"

I shrugged. "Could be anything, but most likely it'll be about the case."

She nodded, then asked a question I wasn't expecting.

"Is Agent Harris married?"

I'd only been around him a few times, and never socially. Usually, he was either threatening to arrest me or convincing someone else to let me go.

Instead of getting into this, I said, "I don't know if he's married or not. But he's never mentioned having a wife around me. Why do you ask?"

"No reason. Just wondering."

Yeah, sure. When a woman asks if a man is married, there's always a reason.

She quickly changed the subject. "I need to hook up to shore power. You want to help?"

"Sure."

Harris hadn't bothered to back the RV into the site, which meant the front end was overlooking the canal and the back side was at the edge of the road. This put the RV's utility compartment on the opposite side of the site's power pedestal.

To hook up to shore power without re-parking, we'd need an extra long water hose and power cord.

Fortunately, we found both in the RV's utility compartment. The previous owners had left them there when they sold the unit to Norah.

After pulling them under the RV and across the site, I was able to get both hooked up.

When I stood to wipe my hands, Norah pointed to my RV. "They're still in there. Wonder what they're talking about. Should we go see?"

"No. We shouldn't bother them. They wanted to talk in private. So let's let them. Okay?"

She sighed. "I guess. But I sure wish I knew what they were saying."

She changed the subject.

"So how was your day?"

I shrugged. "Pretty uneventful. We drove, we ate, and we got here. Not much else happened. Except Maddie spoke with the thieves. They're coming here tomorrow to pick up their phone and laptop."

"Maddie? Who's Maddie?"

I realized Norah didn't know Agent O'Connor's first name.

I filled her in.

"Agent O'Connor. Her first name is Madison. I've been calling her Maddie. She doesn't like it when I do, but it didn't make sense to call her Agent O'Connor since she's supposed to be working undercover."

Norah nodded. "So, you and Maddie, huh? Spending a lot of time together in the motorhome? How's that working out?"

I smiled, thinking about the clothes swap and the stolen

kisses during the phone call. I was making some headway with Maddie but wasn't going to tell Norah. Instead, I said, "She hasn't shot me yet, so I guess that means we're doing okay.

"What about you and Agent Harris? How are you two doing?"

"Oh, we're getting along just fine. We had a good night last night, and a good day today. I'm thinking that tonight might be even better, if you know what I mean."

I was pretty sure I did, it being her cheat week and all. But I'd heard enough. I changed the subject.

Chapter Forty-Six

"Did you really meet the governor today?"

"Yeah, I met him. I wasn't sure if I wanted to, though. Most politicians just want to use me to promote their own interests. They'll have me stand beside them in front of a bunch of photographers making it look like I support their cause.

"Usually without telling me beforehand what cause I'm supposed to be supporting.

"But this time, it was different. We met in private with no photographers around. He wanted to hear my thoughts on preventing school violence. Then actually listened to what I had to say. After we spoke, he thanked me for my time and we parted company.

"He was in Vero to speak in front of a large audience and could have tried to get me to go up on stage with him. But he didn't. He respected my privacy and promised he wouldn't use my name without my permission.

"I guess that's one of the reasons so many people in Florida like the guy. He does the right thing, even when no one else will ever know about it."

She was right about the Governor.

A lot of people in the state did like him. He kept his campaign promises, balanced the budget, was tough on crime, promoted education and environmental issues, and refused to be bullied by the federal government. That last thing was probably what people liked the most. That he stood up to the pols in DC.

Biscuit, Norah's aging beagle, didn't care much for us talking politics. He showed his displeasure by starting to whine a bit.

Norah picked up his leash. "Time for his walk. You want to come with us?"

I did, but wondered if we needed to get permission from Harris or O'Connor. They had told us to stay close, supposedly for our own protection.

As it turned out, we didn't need to ask for permission.

Agent Harris came over to check on us. Apparently, his meeting with Maddie had ended.

Seeing Biscuit tugging at his leash, he smiled at Norah. "Let's take him for a walk."

When the dog heard the magic w-a-l-k word, he took off, pulling Norah along with him. Agent Harris followed. Leaving me behind, wondering if I should join them or not. I quickly decided it might be better if I didn't.

I washed my hands at the outdoor faucet by the power pedestal and headed back to my RV. Along the way, I saw Maddie sitting at the picnic table, watching the boats on the waterway.

I decided to join her.

When I walked up, she said, "You didn't go off with them?"

"No. I got the feeling I wasn't invited."

She nodded. But added nothing.

Sensing that something might be bothering her, I asked, "So how are you doing?"

She looked at me, shook her head, and then turned to watch a sailboat pass just in front of us. A man and a woman were seated below the unfurled sail, with the man's hand on the wheel. The low rumble of a small diesel suggested they were under power, probably a wise choice while cruising the relatively narrow waterway.

The boat was moving slowly, the man and woman seemed relaxed. And happy.

Maddie nodded in their direction. "I should be doing something like that. Living on a sailboat, not worrying about what's happening in the rest of the world.

"I could get a dog and take him with me. Maybe a lab. They like the water. We could sail down to the Keys, and hang out for a month or two. Then maybe cruise to the Bahamas, find a sandy beach, and just chill."

I smiled. "Sounds good to me. You have any sailing experience?"

"A little. When I was a kid, we'd go to the lake and rent a Sunfish. A tiny boat with only one sail. We'd take turns sailing it across the bay. And paddling back when the wind died down.

"So yeah, I know how to sail. Probably just enough to get me in trouble on a bigger boat. But I could get someone to teach me. Maybe get a cabin boy to run the boat while I catch rays on the deck."

I smiled again. Having someone else run the boat would be nice. Especially if that person took care of all the chores and prepared the meals. But instead of a cabin boy, I'd prefer the company of a woman.

We sat at the picnic table watching boats go by. As each one passed, Maddie would say things like, 'That one's too big for me,' or 'too small', or 'too loud.' There was one boat she really liked. A twin-hull catamaran. With a wide deck and a navy blue sunshade over the open cabin.

She said it was the one for her.

After it passed us by, the next boat had several young men aboard, most with drinks in hand. Seeing Maddie, many of them waved. One yelled, "Babe, come join us!"

She waved back, but didn't say anything or get up. Apparently, she wasn't going to join them.

We were still sitting there, watching boats go by, when Agent Harris and Norah returned. Biscuit was with them, still on the leash, happy the way dogs are after they do their business.

When they came to the table, Norah took a seat beside me, Biscuit settled in on the ground at her feet.

Agent Harris didn't sit. Instead, he put his hand on my shoulder, and said, "Let's go for a walk. We need to talk."

It wasn't a suggestion.

Since he was packing a gun, and I wasn't, I got up and walked away with him, leaving the two women at the table to talk about their day.

Chapter Forty-Seven

Agent Harris walked beside me in silence until we reached the Ortona fishing pier. He stepped up on the deck and headed out toward the end. There was no one else on the pier. Agent Harris probably thought it would be a good place to talk.

The pier was made of weathered wood, and unlike most others, it didn't extend far out over the water. Instead, it went out a few feet, turned right and ran parallel to the shoreline. The design made sense. Had it extended further out, it would have been a hazard for the many boats using the waterway.

The layout made for a decent fishing platform, and a way to get a closer look at the boats as they went through the nearby lock. We didn't have fishing gear with us, I had a feeling we weren't there to just watch the boats go by.

I wasn't wrong.

When we reached the end of the pier, Harris turned to me. "You need to lighten up on Agent O'Connor. She's had a rough year and doesn't need anyone giving her more grief."

I nodded, wondering if she had told him about the clothing prank I had played on her earlier in the day. I didn't think she would have, but it was possible.

Harris continued, speaking low, at almost a whisper. "Her husband left her last summer. Her mother died in March. She lost her home in June to a fire and has been living in an apartment ever since. She's under a lot of pressure from DC to break the theft ring. If she doesn't get it done soon, they'll get someone else to take over.

"What you and Norah did yesterday created a major problem for her. If she doesn't figure out a way to sort things out quickly, it'll be the ruin of her career."

He paused, then continued. "What I'm saying is, go easy on her. Understand?"

I nodded. "Yeah. I won't cause any more problems."

We both turned to watch as another boat motored by. My thoughts immediately went to Maddie. I wondered if the boat was the kind she'd want to sail away on. Especially if the case she was working on, fell apart.

If she were replaced by another agent, would she actually do it? Get a boat, a dog, and sail off into the sunset?

Agent Harris tapped me on the shoulder. "Time to head back."

He turned and walked toward the steps leading up to the road. I followed.

When we got back to our campsite, Norah and Maddie were still sitting at the picnic table. At some point, Norah must have gone into her RV, because she had a glass of wine in her hand and a box of chardonnay on the table in front of her.

Maddie was sipping from a bottle of water. No wine for her. She was still on duty.

Seeing us walk up, Norah smiled. "What are you boys going to fix us for dinner?"

It was a good question.

If we would have had fishing gear, we could have tried to catch food. But we didn't have the option. Even if we had gear and had caught something, I wasn't sure any of us would volunteer to clean the catch.

It didn't matter though. We didn't have fish to clean. Or burgers or anything else to cook. As far as I knew, the only thing we had, were the frozen TV dinners in my fridge.

I had enough to share, and would if I needed to.

Fortunately, Norah had a better idea. "How about pizza? I picked up three supremes when we stopped at Walmart. I can pop one in the oven and we can be eating in fifteen minutes."

There was no need to vote. We all wanted pizza.

Fifteen minutes later, with the four of us sitting around the picnic table, we started in on the first of the three pizzas Norah was cooking for us.

Instead of being frozen and from a box, she had bought the fresh ones made daily at Walmart. And they were not bad.

By the time we finished the third one, we were all pretty happy. We'd had a long day, no one got killed, and we'd just been fed and there were no dishes to wash.

After dinner, Agent Harris and Maddie excused themselves and took a short walk. Not far enough that we couldn't see them, but too far for us to hear what they were saying.

Ten minutes later, they returned.

Agent Harris spoke first. "According to Agent O'Connor, the owners of the laptop are going to be here tomorrow. Just in case they show up early, two agents from O'Connor's team will be stationed outside the park gate tonight, posing as fishermen.

"When the suspects arrive, the agents will remain in place, until we have the detainees in custody. Or we need their help.

"Because there is a chance they might get here early, Agent O'Connor will be staying with Walker again tonight, and I will be with Norah.

"If all goes well and the suspects show up tomorrow, Agent O'Connor will, with Norah's permission, drive Buttercup to the gate and bring them back here. We'll take them into Walker's RV, and after they acknowledge that the laptop and phone belong to them, we will arrest them."

He paused, then looking at Norah, said, "No matter what happens, when the suspects arrive, you and Walker are not to get involved. You will remain in your RVs, staying in your bedrooms with the doors closed.

"I can not stress enough how important it is for both of you to stay safe and out of the way. We do not, and can not, have any civilian injuries or casualties. Understand?"

I nodded, as did Norah.

"Good. Our agents outside the gate will let us know if our targets arrive earlier than expected. That's probably not going to happen, but if it does, we'll be ready.

"In the meantime, stay close to your RVs. Don't go for walks unless one of us goes with you."

He closed by saying, "Tomorrow should be interesting, and hopefully, it will be the last day that either of you will be involved."

As it turned out, he was wrong about that.

Chapter Forty-Eight

After listening to Harris tell us what to expect, we retreated to our RVs. Norah and Harris to hers. Maddie and me to mine.

Inside, Maddie went to the bathroom to take care of her end-of-the-day business, while I waited on the sofa with Bob. He had been fairly patient with all the changes that had been going on. The new person staying with us, the dog, the long drive, and the commotion when Maddie scissored up my underwear.

Still, he needed some reassurance that things would be okay. He hopped up onto my lap, wanting some petting. I obliged, letting him know he was still loved and the changes in the RV were only temporary.

I rubbed his big head, stroked his back, and pulled his ears the way he likes them pulled. He settled deeper into my lap, started making biscuits with his big front feet, and began purring. The soft rumbling coming from deep within his body helped wash the stress away – for both of us.

When Maddie came back up front from the bathroom, she pointed to my bedroom. "If there's anything you need in there, now is the time to get it."

Apparently, she was going to make good on her threat to sleep in my bed and make me sleep on the sofa. I could have complained, even tried to change her mind, but decided not to. Harris had asked me to take it easy on her, and I figured me sleeping on the sofa while she got the real bed was a good place to start.

"Yeah, I just need to get a few things. It'll only take me a minute."

She stepped aside, giving me room to pass as I walked into the bedroom.

Inside, I grabbed a clean shirt, semi-clean cargo shorts, and the last clean pair of boxer shorts I had. She had destroyed the others, it was only sheer luck she hadn't found and cut up the clean pair hidden under a towel in the closet.

As I left the bedroom, she asked, "Is there anything in there I should know about? Anything that's going to poke me, jab me, or make me sick?"

I shook my head. "No, there's nothing in there like that."

It was the truth. Unless you counted the loaded pistol I kept under the bed in the fireproof safe. Or the thirty thousand dollars in cash and two rolls of gold coins in the same place.

I figured there was no reason she needed to know about those things. There was nothing illegal about them, but if she knew they were there, she would probably start asking the kind of questions I wouldn't want to answer.

Before going into my bedroom for the night, she said, "I'm going to leave the door open just slightly in case Bob wants to join me during the night. But only Bob. Not you.

"Keep in mind that I sleep with a loaded gun. If you come in unexpectedly, I might shoot you. Understand?"

I nodded. "Yeah, I get it. You're staying in there. I'm staying out here. Bob can stay where ever he wants."

She smiled. "One more thing. If anyone comes to the outside door, don't let them in. Turn on the lights and come get me."

With that, she went into the bedroom and closed the door

behind her, leaving it open just enough for Bob to go in and visit if he wanted to.

Since the bedroom was where he usually spent the night, I had no doubt he'd be joining her later on. But for the moment, he stayed up front with me. Maybe because it was around the time we usually played 'toss the treat'.

The way it worked was, I'd go to the kitchen and get out the bag of chicken-flavored treats he preferred. I'd shake the bag to get his attention, then say, 'Take a seat'.

I would hold a treat in my hand so he could see it, but wouldn't give it to him until he sat. It was the only trick I had been able to teach him. But it didn't always work.

Sometimes he'd be stubborn and try to wait me out instead of sitting. But usually, when he saw me holding the bag of treats, he'd immediately sit, without waiting for me to tell him to do so.

As soon as he sat, I'd toss a treat in the air and he'd try to catch it before it hit the floor. In most cases, he would.

Or he'd bat it with his paw and send it flying down the hall. Then chase it down and gobble it up.

'Chase the treat' was one of his favorite games.

He didn't get to play it the night before, because Maddie was with us. But with her out of the way in the back bedroom, Bob wasn't going to miss out a second night in a row.

I got the treats out, had him sit, and we played the game.

He caught the first two in the air like a champ. I tossed the third one like a fly ball, well over his head. As it came down, he hit it with a paw, knocking it toward the bedroom door.

He chased after it, hitting the brakes when he got close, then slid on the floor until he caught up with the little morsel. In a flash, he had it in his mouth, chewing his prize.

He took his time with it, since he knew the game was always over after the third treat. I was tempted to give him two more since he'd missed out the previous night, but didn't. I knew that if I did, he'd always want two more every time we played.

With the game over, Bob came over and sat by me on the couch. He put his paw to his mouth and licked the taste of the treats off. It was part of his nightly ritual. To clean himself before he went to bed.

It was still relatively early. I wasn't sleepy. I could have turned on the TV and checked to see if there were any local channels, but was afraid the sound would keep Maddie from getting a good night's sleep.

So, instead, I went to the microwave and got the laptop out. I wanted to check the thief's travel progress to see if they'd gotten any closer to us.

I powered it up, connected to my VPN, and checked their Google travel timeline.

To my surprise, it showed that their location was unchanged. They were still in Savannah. They hadn't started moving our way yet.

I refreshed the page to make sure I wasn't seeing a cached version showing the old results. But the newly refreshed page showed the same thing. They hadn't moved since the last time we checked.

I quickly disconnected from Wi-Fi and wondered if I should let Maddie know.

Chapter Forty-Nine

I decided not to tell her. If the thieves weren't on the road yet, there was nothing we could do about it. We definitely couldn't call and ask why they hadn't left. If we did, they'd know we were tracking them. They probably wouldn't like it.

The reality was, there was nothing we could do. Other than wait and see if they showed up like they said they would.

I disconnected the laptop from Wi-Fi and decided that since I already had it out, I might as well look and see if there was anything else interesting on it.

I started by checking the standard Windows folders. Downloads, documents, pictures, music, and videos. I checked each one, along with the subfolders they contained, and found nothing of interest.

Then, using File Explorer, I checked the system drive and found a few things that warranted a closer look. Including a folder named 'SIM CLONES'.

Clicking on it, brought up a window filled with subfolders – each one having a numeric file name. Opening one at random, I saw that it held a copy of a sim card taken out of a phone. One that was most likely stolen by the thieves.

The copied SIM could be used to create a ghost phone – one that could send messages and make calls that appear to be from the real phone, but weren't. The ghost phone could also be used for surveillance and identity theft. The SIM could also be sold on the dark web for a pretty good price.

Continuing my search, I found another interesting folder. This one was named 'CC Clones'.

When we found the laptop in the ambulance, it was connected to a credit card reader. The kind you slide a card through. With the right software, the card reader could be used to copy the info on the data strip on the back of the card.

With that, you could clone the card and use it to make purchases and cash withdrawals. You could continue doing this until the card owner noticed the transactions and had the card canceled. In the meantime, thousands of dollars of unauthorized charges and withdrawals could be made.

With just one cloned card number.

But the thieves had more than one. They had hundreds stored in the CC Clones folder on the laptop. The income potential from the contents of the SIM and CC Clones folder could easily be over a hundred thousand dollars. Maybe a lot more.

A quick scan of other folders revealed files that would be of great interest to the FBI. Including stored text messages, emails, money transfers, and contacts.

Whether the feds could legally gain access to and use the files in the laptop was questionable, due to the way Norah and I had obtained them.

In any case, I figured it might be smart to make a copy of the laptop's hard drive. It could come in handy should the device fall into the wrong hands or if the drive was somehow remotely wiped.

Making a backup would be easy. All I needed was an external drive and a USB cable. I had both in the RV with me. Along with other computer bits and pieces from back when I worked in the corporate world as a paid hacker.

The problem was, my external drive was stored on a shelf in

the bedroom closet. I couldn't get to it without going into the room where Maddie was sleeping.

She had warned me not to come in during the night. She'd said she slept with a gun and might use it if I came in unannounced. There was no way I was going to try to sneak in without her knowing it. Way too risky.

But maybe she wasn't asleep yet. And maybe she wouldn't shoot me if I tapped on her door and asked if I could come in and get what I needed.

I gave it a try.

I went to the bedroom door, tapped on it lightly, and asked, "Maddie, are you awake?"

From inside, "Yeah, I'm awake. What do you want?"

"I need to get something out of the closet."

"I'm in bed. Can't it wait till tomorrow?"

"No, I need to get it now. It won't take me long. I'll be in and out before you know it."

There was a pause. Then, "Give me a minute."

I heard her get up and move things around. Then, "Okay, you can come in now. But only to get whatever you need. Then you have to leave."

I didn't wait for her to change her mind. I opened the door and went in. She was sitting in the bed, with the sheet pulled up to her shoulders. My Kindle reader was next to her. It should have been in the top drawer of the bedside table where I'd left it the night before. She had gotten it out and was likely checking to see what kind of books I'd been reading.

I didn't mind. She'd find laid-back and sometimes funny novels by authors like Rodney Riesel, Mike Faricy, Don Bruns and a few others.

While she sat in bed watching, I went to the closet and dug around until I found the external drive and the USB cable I needed to make the backup.

As I turned to leave, she asked, "What'd you get?"

I held the drive so she could see it. "A backup drive. I'm going to make a backup of the laptop's main drive."

She sat up straight, causing the sheet that was covering her body to drop a bit, revealing her bare shoulders. I smiled, wondering if she slept in the nude. Most likely, she didn't. At least not in a stranger's bed.

"You're doing what?"

"I'm backing up the files on the laptop."

She leaned forward, not noticing the sheet was showing even more skin.

"You're backing up the laptop? Does that mean you turned it on?"

"Yeah, I turned it on. But I didn't connect to the Internet. It's not being tracked."

"You know that for sure?"

"Yeah, I'm sure. Without the Internet, there's no way it can be tracked."

She shook her head, and noticed the sheet had sagged and was showing the curve of her breasts. She quickly pulled it up to her shoulders. "Walker, listen to me carefully. Don't do anything with the laptop until I come out there and join you. Now get out of here so I can get dressed."

Reluctantly, I left the room, wondering what she was wearing, if anything, under the sheet.

Chapter Fifty

Four minutes later, Maddie joined me up front. She was wearing one of my tee shirts and a pair of bike shorts from Walmart. They fit her well.

She went to the fridge, grabbed a bottle of water, then joined me at the dinette. She pointed at the laptop. "Why do you need to back it up?"

I smiled. "Because it's full of files you might find interesting. Emails, text messages, spreadsheets, and folders with cloned credit cards and phone SIMs.

"And that's not all. There's more. Including names and addresses. And banking data. The kind of stuff that could expose their entire operation. It's no wonder the thieves want to get the laptop back. Or somehow remotely destroy the drive.

"So I figured it would be a good idea to make a copy of everything. Just in case.

"If you don't want me to copy it though, I won't. But I really think you should let me."

She thought for a moment, then said, "Do it. But don't tell anybody. It'll be our secret."

She watched as I connected the backup drive, and then typed in a string of letters and symbols into the Windows command line. After hitting the enter key, I sat back, crossed my arms, and said, "Now we wait."

Looking up from the screen, I saw that she was staring at me, a grin on her face.

"What are you looking at?"

The grin turned into a full-fledged smile. "I'm looking at the rough and tumble guy who has been secretly reading Romcoms on his Kindle."

"What do you mean?"

"You know exactly what I mean. Romantic Comedies. Like the A.R. Winters Cruise Ship Mysteries. You've got the whole series. And 'Pineapple Cruise' from Amy Vansant. and 'Cruise to Nowhere' by Lizzie Josephson.

"You have all these and more. Your Kindle shows they've been read. I'm assuming by you."

I couldn't argue. She had me dead to rights.

I'd gotten tired of reading books where the villains were serial killers, kidnappers, and mass murderers intent on inflicting pain and death in gory details. I didn't need any more of that in my life.

So I started looking for quick fun reads. The kind that leave you with a good feeling when you finish them. And I wasn't ashamed to admit it.

"Maddie, you got me. It's true. I've been reading those kinds of books lately. But I read other things as well. Scan through my Kindle library, you'll see."

Still smiling, she said, "Yeah, I saw what you've been reading. Romantic comedies, a few short stories, and several light-hearted mysteries. No war stories, no westerns, no shoot 'em ups. That tells me a lot about you."

"Really? You can figure me out by looking at the books I read?"

Before I finished asking the question, I knew the answer. The FBI and other federal agencies, along with Amazon and every company they sell their data to, can learn a lot about a person based solely on what he or she reads. They'll learn their interests, their dreams, their likes and dislikes, and if their choice of books runs toward the really weird or violent, they'll know who to watch a little closer.

"Walker, don't worry. I won't tell anyone. But I do think it's kind of funny."

I didn't see anything funny about it. But I wondered.

"What about you Maddie? What do you read?"

She shook her head. "You'll never know."

She pointed at the laptop. "When the backup finishes, check to see if the thieves have left Savannah yet. Then turn it off and put it back in the microwave."

After taking a last sip of water, she headed back to the bedroom, leaving the door slightly ajar.

Presumably for Bob, not me.

Chapter Fifty-One

An hour later, the laptop chimed, letting me know the copy process had ended. I unhooked the drive and put it in the cabinet over the sofa to keep it safe. I'd give it to Maddie in the morning.

Per her request, I connected to Wi-Fi to check if the phone we were tracking had left Savannah yet.

It hadn't. It was still in the same place it had been earlier in the day. There was no movement so far.

The thieves either hadn't left yet, or we were tracking the wrong phone.

My bet was, it was the wrong phone.

Whatever the reason, it wasn't worth waking Maddie to tell her that nothing had changed.

I powered down the laptop and put it back in the microwave with the phone. We'd get them both out in the morning and recheck.

With just about everything taken care of, I folded the jackknife sofa out into a bed, got the sheets and pillow down from the overhead, and got ready for a night's sleep.

But sleep didn't come.

The sofa, when folded out into bed mode, is extremely uncomfortable. At least for someone my size. The thin layer of foam covering the springs was designed for sitting, not for sleeping. To make matters worse, when folded out into a bed, there is a two-inch deep gully where the top and bottom cushions are hinged. It's in the center of the sleeping area, and there is no way to sleep on it without your spine dropping into the divide.

It would be difficult to design a better torture device for someone needing sleep.

Maddie had probably experienced this the night before. It could be why she'd claimed my bed and sentenced me to the sofa. She was back there sleeping comfortably while I continually tossed and turned, trying to find the elusive sweet spot on the sofa not-a-bed.

Other guests had stayed with me in the past. Some had slept on the sofa. Or at least, had tried to. None had complained though, most likely because they had no other place to sleep. Or were too tired to notice.

But I noticed.

I decided that after this little adventure with Maddie and Norah was over, I would rip the sofa out and replace it with something a lot more comfortable. Something that I and others could actually sleep on.

In the meantime, my temporary solution was to get two towels from the bathroom, roll them up lengthwise and stuff them into the sofa's gully in an attempt to create a more level sleeping surface.

It still wasn't comfortable, but the towels made it better. Eventually, I was able to drift off to sleep.

Not for long, though.

The next morning, Maddie was up early and full of energy. After spending a couple of minutes in the bathroom, she went back into the bedroom and did some kind of exercise. It had the RV bouncing up and down like a ship in heavy seas.

When she was finally done, she came up front with Bob cradled in her arms. He was purring as she spoke to him.

"Bob, you're a good kitty. It's a shame that Walker hasn't

cleaned your litter box lately. I'll make sure he takes care of it as soon as he gets up.

"You want down? Okay, I'll put you down."

She walked over to the sofa and put Bob down next to me. Then turning to the kitchen, just a few feet from where I was trying to sleep, she started opening cabinet doors, like she was looking for something. Not finding whatever it was, she closed each with a slam, then went on to the next one.

She did the same with the silverware drawers, opening and closing each with a slam.

When she slammed the pantry door, I'd had enough. I sat up. "What are you looking for?"

She turned to me. "Oh, you're up. I hope I didn't wake you."

We both knew that was exactly what she was trying to do. To wake me. But I didn't call her on it. Instead, I asked again. "What are you looking for?"

She pointed to the jar of instant coffee she'd picked up at Walmart. "A pot. To heat the water. You do have one, don't you?"

"Yeah, under the sink. But don't use it. Use the microwave. It boils water in two minutes."

She smiled while holding a cup already filled with water. "Oh, silly me. I should have thought of that before making all that noise while you were trying to sleep. Really, I didn't mean to wake you."

We both knew the truth.

As she headed to the microwave, she asked, "So, how did you sleep?"

"Not good. How about you?"

"It was great. I read a few chapters on your Kindle until I

couldn't stay awake, then went right to sleep. Woke up with Bob beside me. Well rested and ready to go."

I mumbled, "Yeah, I'm glad one of us had a good night."

"Did you say something?"

"No, just thinking out loud."

I got up and headed back to the bathroom to get ready for the day knowing that no matter what she said, I was sleeping in my own bed from now on. She could either sleep on the sofa or sleep with me.

It would be her choice.

Chapter Fifty-Two

Maddie was sitting at the dinette table drinking coffee. She'd toasted one of my pop-tarts and seemed to be enjoying eating and drinking while waiting for me to get ready.

Had I gotten up first, I would have cooked us a real breakfast – eggs, bacon, and toast. But that takes time and leaves a mess that has to be cleaned up. And it makes the inside of the RV smell like bacon for the rest of the day.

Wanting to avoid that, I passed on the bacon and eggs and had what Maddie was having – a pop tart.

She was just finishing her coffee when the toaster pastry popped up. I quickly slathered it with butter, grabbed a napkin and a glass of orange juice, and sat at the table across from her.

She had a smile on her face, something I'd rarely seen since our little adventure had begun. Maybe it was the coffee she was drinking, or the good night's sleep she'd had. Whatever it was, it was nice that she wasn't in the same cranky mood she had been in the day before.

I was about halfway through my pop-tart when she stood and said, "I'm going to go see if Agent Harris is up. Come join us when you finish eating."

She took two steps toward the door, then stopped and turned back toward me. "Don't forget to clean Bob's litter box. I promised him you'd take care of it today."

I smiled. "So you and Bob are besties now? Is that it?"

She nodded. "Yep, me and Bob. We're tight. He likes me, and I like him. And he'll like you too, if you clean his box."

She headed outside.

I stayed in and finished my pastry. After washing it down with orange juice, I went to the back of the RV to look for him. I figured he'd be on the bed, having probably spent most of the night there. Like most cats, he loves to sleep. Usually around eighteen hours a day.

Checking the bedroom, I saw that the bed had been made, the pillows had been fluffed and lined up against the wall that served as my headboard. Bob was stretched out on the bed, on his back, feet in the air. His eyes were closed, and he could have been sleeping.

But I knew better.

He would have heard me coming and would have been wide awake by the time I got to him. When I called his name, one of his ears twitched.

Yeah, he was awake.

"Bob, did you sleep with her all night? You didn't even come to see how I was doing. What if I was sick or something? Who would feed you if something happened to me?"

He didn't answer. Instead, he opened his eyes, blinked twice, and covered his face with one of his paws. He was telling me he didn't want to be bothered.

I got the message. I headed to the bathroom where I kept his litter box. Using the plastic litter shovel, I scooped out the clumps he'd deposited overnight and put them in a trash bag. I would drop in an outside bin later on.

After checking myself in the mirror, I went out to see what Agent Harris and Norah were up to.

As it turned out, it was apparently nothing, or at least nothing that they wanted me or Maddie to know about. They were still in Norah's RV.

They hadn't come out yet.

Maddie was sitting at the picnic table alone. I walked over and sat down across from her. "Where are they?"

She shrugged. "Inside I guess. I knocked on the door, but there was no answer. Maybe they're sleeping in."

I smiled, remembering that it was Norah's cheat week. Maybe she and Agent Harris were doing more than sleeping.

Before I could say something about that, Maddie stood and waved to someone behind me. I turned to see Agent Harris and Norah walking toward us, coming from the direction of the fishing pier.

Harris spoke first. "We were up early. Just as the sun was coming up. We had breakfast, then came out here and waited for you two to join us.

"When you didn't show, we decided to go for a walk. We went to the front gate, then to the pier. We sat there for a while, watching the boats go by.

"When we got tired of doing that, we decided it was time to come back and wake you if you weren't up yet.

"Glad we didn't have to."

He paused, then asked, "O'Connor, what's the plan for today?"

She smiled. "It all depends on whether the goons show up or not. If they do, we'll detain them and my agents will take them away for questioning. Hopefully, we'll learn enough to get a warrant and take down whoever's in charge.

She looked at me, then back at Agent Harris. "Assuming they do show, they'll expect to see me and Walker together. They saw us on video and think we're married. If they see anyone else with me, they might be suspicious and run.

"So even though I don't like it, it'll be Walker and me who

meet with them when they get here. We'll show them the laptop and phone, and if they can prove they are the owners, we'll get them to pay us. Once we get the money, we'll have all we need to detain them."

Harris wasn't too happy with the plan. "I'm not sure I like the idea of Walker being in this with you. He's a civilian. It'll look bad if he gets hurt. It'd be better if it were me with you instead of him."

Maddie nodded. "I agree. It would be a lot better if we didn't have civilians involved. But the people coming for the laptop expect to see me and Walker. Not you."

"Walker looks like a civilian. You don't. You look like a fed. Even dressed like a tourist, you still look like a fed. They see you, they'll know something's up.

"It has to be Walker."

Harris frowned. "I still don't like it. If this goes sideways and he gets hurt, it's going to be on you."

Maddie nodded. "I know. But it has to be that way."

Norah, who had kept quiet, spoke up. "I think Walker can take care of himself. And anyway, he and Maddie make a cute couple. It's totally believable that they might be married, or at least living together.

"The way she's dressed in those tight shorts and sports bra, no one would think she's a fed."

I smiled, because it was true. With the bike shorts and the sports bra she was wearing, she definitely didn't look like a fed. She looked more like a hot Pilates instructor on her day off.

Of course, I didn't tell her that. But I sure thought it.

She pointed toward my RV.

"Walker and I are going to go set things up so if they call, we'll be ready."

Chapter Fifty-Three

Back in my RV, I got the thieves' phone and laptop out of the microwave. After powering both up, we checked to see if we'd missed anything.

The recent call log showed there had been no incoming calls since we'd spoken to them the day before. They hadn't tried to call and tell us they were on their way.

At least not yet.

The travel timeline showed their location hadn't changed. It still showed Savannah. I refreshed the page and got the same result. The phone we were tracking hadn't moved.

Since we were still connected to the Internet, I turned the laptop's Wi-Fi off so they couldn't listen in. I didn't want them to hear what I was about to say.

"Maddie, they're still in Savannah."

"What? Are you sure?"

"Yeah, I'm sure. The track hasn't moved since yesterday. The dot on the screen still shows Savannah."

She shook her head. "They said they were eight hours away and would be here sometime this morning. If they haven't left yet, they won't get here until late this afternoon. If they get here at all.

"If they don't show, I'm screwed. My bosses told me I needed to wrap this up quickly. It doesn't look like that's going to happen. At least not with me in charge.

"This was supposed to be my big chance to redeem myself. To show I could run an operation like this. But if it falls apart, they'll pull me from the field and put me on desk duty. They'll have me shuffling paper as they ease me out the door."

She sat on the couch, holding her head in her hands. Bob, sensing that something was wrong, came up front. Seeing Maddie in distress, he trotted over and rubbed up against her ankles. Then hopped up on the couch and sat next to her. Putting a paw onto her lap, he meowed softly. Almost like he was saying, 'It'll be alright.'

Without even realizing it, Maddie began stroking his back, with long slow strokes, the kind he enjoyed. He rewarded her by settling into her lap and purring loudly.

She continued to stroke his back and he continued to purr.

Eventually, she started to rub his ears, something he really likes. He responded by kneading her bare legs with his paws. Making biscuits.

The more she rubbed, the more biscuits he made. They both seemed to enjoy it. At least, until his claws came out. That's when Maddie said, "Ouch! Don't do that. It hurts."

Bob jumped down, twined between her legs to show his appreciation for the pets, then headed back to the bed.

Maddie looked up at me. "So, they're still in Savannah, right? Does that mean they're not coming?"

"No, it doesn't mean that at all. We don't know who the phone we're tracking belongs to. It was just a guess that it was one of the crew's. But maybe it isn't. Maybe it belongs to someone else. Even if it does belong to one of the crew, we don't know if they're carrying the phone with them on the way here.

"All we know for sure, is they want to get the laptop back before it falls into the wrong hands. You've seen what's on it. They know it could hurt them. They have to get it back.

"So they're still coming. They may not make it this morning, but they're coming. They want the laptop."

She nodded.

"You're right. The laptop is the key. They have to get it back. Sooner or later, they'll come. That means we have to be ready for them.

"I'm going to go let the others know it may be this afternoon before they get here. You do whatever you need to do in here, then come out and join us."

She went outside, carrying the phone the thieves had called her on earlier. If they called back, she wanted to have it with her.

While she was outside talking to Agent Harris, I stayed inside. I wanted to make sure the laptop was secure, and if the thieves came into the RV, nothing inside would make them think it was part of an FBI sting operation.

As far as I could tell, everything looked good. Nothing seemed to say that the feds were hiding nearby.

Satisfied with the way everything looked, I went back outside, expecting to find Harris and Norah at the same picnic table we'd left them at a few minutes earlier.

But they weren't there. They were gone.

And so was Maddie.

I figured they had either moved over to the other picnic table, the one by Norah's RV, or had gone inside her rig to talk.

Her table was on the far side of her RV and wasn't visible from my site. It would be a good place for us to meet until the thieves got close. When they arrived, Maddie and I could go back to my place and wait for them there.

I walked around Norah's RV, and just as I figured, the three of them had moved to the table on her side. I took a seat next to Maddie. She and Harris were talking about what charges could be used to detain the crew when they showed up.

They quickly came up with a long list, including various computer crimes, interstate commerce, and identity theft. The kind of charges that could put the crew behind bars for years. Or used as leverage to get them to talk about the people at the top of the operation.

To speed things along, Maddie called her office and had warrants prepared. The name or names of the individuals being charged would be filled in later.

With a plan in place and warrants being drawn, the only thing left was to wait for the thieves to show.

We figured it'd be a long wait.

As it turned out, it wasn't.

Chapter Fifty-Four

Norah was about halfway through a funny story about an emergency room visit by three frat boys. Something about a Barbie doll that one of the boys supposedly sat on while naked.

Just as she was getting to what we assumed was the good part, the phone that Maddie had been holding, rang. She answered it quickly, putting it on speaker so we could hear what was being said.

"Hello."

A woman's voice said, "Uh, yeah. I'm here at the front gate. I'm supposed to pick up a laptop. The guard won't let me through."

Maddie smiled. "Glad you made it. I'll call and tell him to let you through. We're in site twenty-two. I'll be outside in front of our RV waiting for you."

"Cool, I'll head that way as soon as he opens the gate."

The call ended.

When we first got to the campground, the gate guard had given us a handout with the rules and a map to our site. It had his phone number on it and he said to call should we need anything.

Maddie made the call, telling him to let the visitor to site twenty-two, through the gate. He said he would.

As soon as she ended the call, I took the phone from her and powered it down. Now that someone was coming to get it, there was no reason to leave it powered up. And plenty of reasons not to.

Maddie nodded at me, understanding what I was doing and why. Then she said, "This is it. It's time we reel them in."

She looked at Agent Harris. "I'm going to put you on a video call so you can watch everything as it happens."

Hearing his phone ring, he answered and saw that the video feed was working. He gave her a thumbs up. Then he said, "Whatever you do, don't let them leave with the laptop. If things go sideways, just say the word 'casino', and I'll come running."

"Casino?"

"Yeah, 'casino'. Say it and I'll come over with guns blazing."

Maddie shook her head. "No, no shooting. We need them alive."

She turned to me. "We need to get to your RV before they get here."

Leaving Agent Harris and Norah sitting at the picnic table at their site, we went to our place and took a seat at the picnic table. We sat across from each other, doing our best to look like a bored married couple on a camping trip.

Maddie looked a little too perfect to pull it off. I reached over and tousled her hair. She was about to swat me away when we heard a car pull up.

An older Kia or Hyundai, hard to tell them apart. Gray in color, two door, with a woman about thirty, at the wheel. No one else with her. Unless they were hiding in the back seat.

She rolled her window down. "I'm here to pick up a laptop. Is this the right place?"

Maddie stood. "Yeah, we've got it inside."

She turned and headed toward the RV. The woman driving the car got out and followed her, but slowed when she saw me. "Who are you?"

"I'm her husband. Do you have the money for the laptop?"

"Yeah, I got it. But I'm not supposed to pay until I have it in my hands. There's supposed to be a phone too, right?"

"Yeah. It's inside the RV."

Up close, the woman looked young. Maybe not even twenty. Five six, and skinny. Tattoos on both arms. Stringy black hair, dark circles under her eyes. Wearing cut-off jeans and a faded Death Leopard tee-shirt.

It could have been a look she was going for, or the reality of her life. Her appearance gave off the impression she wasn't a stranger to meth. Or something stronger.

Maddie was waiting for us at the door of the RV. "Come on, the laptop's inside."

The woman followed her in. I brought up the rear.

Inside, Maddie introduced herself. "I'm Maddie. The guy behind you is Walker. And you are?"

Before answering, the girl looked around, and pulled out a vape pen. "Okay if I smoke?"

Maddie shook her head. "No. Not in here. But we won't be long."

She pointed to the laptop. "It's ready to go. You got the money?"

The woman, who still hadn't told us her name, reached into her pants pocket and pulled out three crumpled one-hundred-dollar bills.

Taking the cash, Maddie asked, "So you drove all the way here from Savannah?"

The woman looked confused. "Savannah? No. I've never been there. I live in Okeechobee."

"Really? You've never been there? I thought that's where the owners of the laptop were calling from."

The woman shrugged. "I don't know nothing about that. All I know is I got a call yesterday asking if I could pick up a laptop and take it to Miami."

"You got a call?"

"Yeah, I run a local delivery service in Okeechobee. Picking things up and dropping them off for people. Usually just around town, though. I normally don't go as far as Miami. But if the money is right, I will.

"When the guy called, I told him I'd do it for eight hundred. Paid upfront. In cash. I didn't expect he'd go for it. But he did.

"This morning, FedEx brought the money, a phone, and an extra three hundred dollars. And a page of instructions telling me what to do.

"It said to come here, pay you the three hundred, and pick up the phone and laptop. I've done that. So, I guess I'll be on my way."

Maddie shook her head. "Sorry honey, it doesn't work that way. You're not going to Miami today. You'll be staying here."

The woman started to protest, but Maddie held up her hand. "Don't worry, we'll still pay you the eight hundred, and even give you a bonus. But you won't be doing the delivery. I will."

The woman shook her head. "No, he paid me to do it. He said I'll get a big tip when I deliver. So why should I let you go instead of me?"

Maddie looked at the woman for a moment, then asked, "What's your name?"

"Luna. Luna Day."

Maddie nodded.

"Luna, have you ever been arrested?"

She didn't answer.

"How about it, Luna? Any warrants?"

Again, no answer.

Maddie took a deep breath.

"Luna, the laptop is stolen. You just paid me to give it to you. That means I can have you arrested for dealing in stolen property.

"When the cops get here, they'll fingerprint you and learn your real name. If you have warrants or are out on bail, they'll cuff you and put you in jail.

"You probably don't want that. I don't want that either. So let's make a deal.

"You let me do the delivery. You keep all the money they paid you. And on top of that, I'll give you the three hundred you gave me for the laptop. That'll be a total of eleven hundred dollars you get, and you won't have to go to Miami.

"And, just to make sure things work out for you, I have a friend who'll be staying with you the rest of the day. He'll buy you lunch and take you shopping and buy whatever you want.

"How does that sound?"

Luna answered in a whisper. "Better than jail."

Chapter Fifty-Five

We went outside to Luna's car to get the FedEx package that had been sent to her by the people wanting to get the laptop back. When we stepped outside, Luna fired up her vape. Judging by the smell, I assumed she had a medical marijuana card. Otherwise, what she was smoking was currently illegal in the state of Florida.

Her car door was unlocked. The FedEx package was in the passenger seat. The back seat was piled high with dirty clothes and littered with empty fast food bags. She could have been living in the car. It wouldn't surprise me if she were.

Maddie grabbed the FedEx package and walked Luna to the nearby picnic table. I stayed back, not wanting to get in her way.

Agent Harris, who had been watching everything on his phone, came over to where Maddie and Luna were sitting. Norah came with him, but instead of going to the table, she approached me.

Nodding toward Luna, she whispered. "She's not what they were expecting, is she?"

"No, she's not. But maybe this will be better. Maddie can deliver the laptop herself. Maybe even meet the people in charge."

Norah nodded. "Yeah, it'd be nice if it worked out for her."

She paused, then said, "I don't want to sound like this hasn't been fun, but I don't have many days left in my cheat week. I'd like to be able to enjoy them before I have to go back to work. Know what I mean?"

I nodded like I understood, but didn't say anything. I hoped the remainder of her cheat week plans didn't include me. The oyster evening we shared had soured me on the idea.

Maddie, Harris, and Luna were at the picnic table talking. We inched a little closer so we could hear what was being said.

From what we could tell, Maddie had called the two FBI agents who had been posing as fishermen near the front gate and told them to come join us. She had a job for them.

While they were on their way, Harris asked Luna why they had chosen her to pick up and deliver the laptop.

Still puffing on her vape, she said, "I sometimes drive for Uber. They probably found me that way. Or maybe they saw my website. It says I pick up and deliver in Okeechobee and surrounding areas, including Ortona Campground. Maybe they searched Google for Ortona and my page came up.

"Yeah, that's probably how they found my phone number. On my web page."

She took another puff on her vape.

"I don't get many calls about doing a long-distance delivery, but when I do, I always take the job. No matter what it is. Cause I need the money."

She should have stopped talking then, when she'd answered the question. But she couldn't help herself. She was on a roll and kept going.

"Usually, I don't know what's in the packages I pick up and deliver. As long as it'll fit in my car and it pays, I'll take the job.

"Of course, I wouldn't deliver anything illegal. At least if I knew for sure it was illegal. But like I said, I never know what's in the packages they give me. I don't ask, and they usually don't tell me."

She pointed to her car. "If you're done with me, I'd like to get going. I've got other things I want to do today."

She started to stand, but Harris stopped her by grabbing her arm. "Sit. You're not going anywhere. Not until you answer a few more questions."

She rubbed her wrist where Harris had grabbed her and quickly sat.

"Luna. Are there any weapons in your car?"

"No. Just a knife. Under the driver's seat."

"Any illegal drugs?"

She didn't answer.

He repeated the question. "Any illegal drugs?"

She hesitated, then said, "None that are mine. It's possible someone left something in there that I didn't know about. But if they did, it's not mine."

We all knew what that meant. Harris didn't press her on it. He had more questions.

"So, this delivery. How was it supposed to work?"

She pointed to the FedEx package.

"The directions they sent me are in there."

"What do they say?"

She shrugged. "I can't remember everything. You probably ought to read them yourself."

Harris picked up the package and pulled out the contents. A page of printed instructions and a burner phone.

He read the instructions out loud.

"Step One. Go to Ortona South Campground and use the enclosed phone to call the number below. Tell them you are there to pick up the laptop.

"Step Two. Pay the people three hundred dollars for the laptop and phone. Be sure to get both.

"Step Three. Use the enclosed phone to take a picture of the laptop and the phone on the hood of your car. Text the photo to the number below.

"Step Four. After you send the text, you will receive a return text with an address in Miami. Go to that address and ask for Rick. He'll tell you what to do next.

"You must arrive at the address in Miami no later than five today, with the laptop and phone, if you want a hundred-dollar bonus."

He looked at Luna and tapped the page. "These are pretty detailed. Did they tell you you'd be doing all this before you took the job?"

"No, I thought it was a simple pick-up and delivery."

He nodded. "One final question. Where's your personal phone?"

She pointed to her car. "In the console."

Harris turned to O'Connor. "Your turn."

Maddie looked at Luna. Then smiled, and said. "Here's what's going to happen now. We are going to search your car. If we find anything illegal, we will hold it until the end of the day. If you do what we tell you, and don't cause any trouble, you'll get everything back, no questions asked. No charges.

"But if you cause problems or try to get away, you'll be taken to jail where you'll be held for at least the next thirty days.

"Understand?"

Luna nodded.

An older minivan decked out with fishing gear, pulled up behind Luna's car. Two men stepped out and walked over to O'Connor.

"Agent Wallace, Agent Burke, how's the fishing?"

Neither man answered. They knew she didn't expect a reply.

She motioned toward Luna. "This young lady will be spending the day with one of you. You are to take her to lunch, then shopping. You are not to let her out of your sight, nor let her use the phone or a computer. Other than that, she can do whatever she wants. But no contact with anyone.

"Who's going to volunteer?"

The youngest of the two agents, the one O'Connor had said was Wallace, raised his hand. "I'll do it."

Luna looked at him and smiled. He didn't smile back.

O'Connor continued. "She'll ride with you in the minivan. Don't let her out of your sight."

She turned to the other agent, whose name was Burke. "Since you didn't volunteer to spend your day with her, you get to search her car. If you find anything illegal, tag it and put it in her trunk. Then drive her car to Okeechobee and meet up with Wallace. Stay with the two of them until I call and tell you it's time to let her go.

"Any questions?"

Neither agent had one.

She turned to Luna. "Today is your lucky day. Don't blow it by doing anything stupid."

She told Wallace to take her away.

Chapter Fifty-Six

After Agent Wallace left with Luna, Agent Burke went to her car and began his search. Almost immediately, he found the knife that Luna had said was under the driver's seat.

Instead of being a pocket knife, it was a machete with a black plastic handle and an eighteen-inch blade. The kind of 'knife' you take with you when you need to hack a path through a jungle or fight off zombies.

The agent held it up so we could see. He put it on the roof of the car with the other items he had pulled out of the front seats. A moment later, he held up a baggie with white pills. And then another filled with a green leafy substance.

Luna had claimed there were no drugs in the car. At least, none that she knew of. She also said that if any were found, they didn't belong to her. With that statement, she had given the agent no reason to return the drugs. They would be destroyed.

While the search of the car continued, Maddie turned her attention back to the FedEx package and the delivery notes Luna was supposed to follow.

"These guys called and spoke to her. They know she's a woman. They'll expect a woman to deliver the package. So it has to be me.

"The instructions say to take a picture of the laptop and phone on the hood of the car making the delivery. We could take Luna's, but it looks like it's on its last legs. It'd be bad if it broke down and I couldn't get there by their deadline. No telling what kind of diseases I might catch driving it. So that's out."

She turned to Norah. "You're the only one here with a car. So, with your permission, I'd like to borrow it and take it to Miami. But only if it's okay with you."

Norah frowned. "Buttercup? You want to take my Buttercup to Miami? What if something happens to her?"

Then, with a smile, she added, "Just kidding. Yeah, you can take her. Just be careful."

Maddie thanked her, then picked up the burner phone that had been in the FedEx package. "They want to see a photo of the laptop and phone on the hood of the car I'm going to show up in. Let's take care of that now."

I went to the RV to get the laptop and phone. When I came back out, Norah was waiting at Buttercup. Like a protective mother, she said, "Be careful with the paint. Please don't scratch it."

She watched as I gently placed the phone and laptop on the car's hood, being careful not to cause any damage. When Maddie was satisfied with the placement, she gave me the burner phone and told me to shoot a photo with her arm pointing at the two items.

I started the camera app, carefully framed a shot of Maddie's hand pointing at the laptop on Buttercup's bright yellow hood, and shot the photo. When I showed it to Maddie, she approved. "That'll work. Send it to the number listed in step three of the instructions."

Back at the picnic table, Norah had a question for Maddie.

"Can you drive a stick?"

"A stick? What do you mean?"

Norah pointed to Buttercup. "It has a manual transmission. Five-speed stick. You have to shift gears using the clutch. Do you know how to do that?"

Maddie shook her head. "Uh, I've never driven a stick. But I can learn, right?"

Norah was about to say something, but Harris spoke first. "There's no reason for her to drive the car to Miami. We can tow it behind the RV. When we get close to the drop-off point, we can park and unhook the car. She'll only have to drive it a few blocks. Shouldn't be a problem."

The burner phone from the FedEx package buzzed with an incoming text. Maddie read the message aloud. "Take the package to Bus and Boat Salvage on Forty-Seventh Street in Miami. Get there before five."

I pulled out my phone and checked to see how long a drive it'd be. According to Google Maps, the place was a hundred and fifteen miles from where we were. Almost a straight shot down Highway twenty-seven. A two-hour drive, depending on traffic.

The street view of the place showed a row of decommissioned ambulances in the front parking lot. All had 'for sale' painted on the windshields.

I turned to Maddie. "Look at this."

Seeing the picture, she nodded. "Looks like we're going to the right place."

Going back to the map view, I clicked on 'satellite', and saw that there was an empty parking lot on the same block as Bus and Boat Salvage. With plenty of room to park two RVs.

"It looks like it's about a two-hour drive from here. If we leave soon, we can be there before three. There's an empty parking lot where we can park the RVs and unhook Buttercup. Agent O'Connor can take it from there."

Maddie nodded. "Yeah, let's do that."

Harris shook his head. "No. We don't need to take both RVs.

Just Norah's. With her car towed behind. Walker doesn't need to go with us. He can stay here, or go wherever he wants. But he's not going with us to Miami."

I was surprised to hear him say that, but also, kind of relieved. It meant I was no longer part of the FBI's case. I could get on with my life without having to seek permission from either of the two agents.

But Maddie wasn't going for it.

"No, he doesn't get off that easy. He's going to Miami with us. If this case falls apart, he's going to shoulder some of the blame. We need him to stay close. We don't want to have to chase him down if we need to bring him in. He's going with us."

Agent Harris didn't argue. Instead, he asked, "You riding with him?"

She shook her head. "No, I'm going with you and Norah. Walker can go alone, leading the way. We'll follow a few miles behind. If he runs into traffic or anything else that can slow us down, he can call and let us know.

"If all goes well, we'll meet back up in Miami. At the parking lot close to the Bus and Boat place."

She looked at me. "Any questions?"

I didn't have any. Neither did Agent Harris or Norah.

Back at my RV, I got everything ready to hit the road. I unhooked from shore power and water and closed and locked the outside compartment doors. Inside, I put loose items away, latched the cabinet doors, and made sure Bob was safe in bed.

When I entered the address of the empty parking lot into my GPS, it gave me two route options. One had me staying on county road twenty-seven all the way into town. The other put me on I-75 with an exit into downtown Miami. Knowing how much of a mess I-75 could be, I chose the county road.

I was about to start the engine when I saw Norah outside her RV with Biscuit. She waved for me to come over and join her. I figured she might need help getting Buttercup hooked up to her RV.

I went over to help.

Chapter Fifty-Seven

When Biscuit saw me heading his way, he ran over, sniffed my shoe, and flopped down onto the ground, ready for a belly rub.

I gave him a quick rub, just to show I cared, then stood and told him that was all he was going to get. Seeing me stand, he got back on his feet and tugged hard on the leash Norah was holding, letting her know he needed to take care of business.

She was carrying a small plastic bag. We both knew what it was for.

I smiled. "You want me to walk with you?"

"Yes, that would be nice."

We headed toward a grassy spot across the road. Seeing the greenery in the distance, Biscuit pulled hard on his leash. Apparently, he was in a hurry.

When we got to the grass, he sniffed around until he found the perfect spot, and then got into position.

Norah and I turned away, not wanting to watch as he dropped his load.

When we heard him digging with his back feet trying to cover it up, we turned to check his work. He'd made a small deposit and was standing in front of it, proud that he'd accomplished his mission.

Norah congratulated him. "Good job, Biscuit. Let me clean that for you."

She went over and scooped up the warm doggy poo into

the plastic bag she was carrying. Coming back to me, she said, "You want to hold this?"

I shook my head. "No, I think I'll pass."

"That's what I figured."

On the way back to the RVs, Norah dropped the bag into the nearest trash can, then stopped to talk.

"Walker, does anything about this bother you? Going to Miami? With federal agents? To break up an international crime ring? Don't you think it might be a little dangerous?"

I'd already been thinking along the same lines.

Heading into Miami is always dangerous. Go into the wrong part of town at the wrong time of day, and you might not make it out alive. Traveling with two federal agents intent on breaking a major case by confronting suspects on their own turf, could make it even more dangerous.

But I wasn't going to say that. Norah probably already knew.

Instead, I said, "Look, back when we were in Titusville, you said you wanted to go to Key West. Going to Miami will get you halfway there. When this thing is over, it'll be a short drive to the Conch Republic."

She smiled. "I guess you're right."

We headed back to our RVs and got ready to hit the road.

Had we known what was going to happen when we got to Miami, both of us would have headed in the opposite direction, getting as far away from there as we could.

Chapter Fifty-Eight

With Bob in the passenger seat, I headed for Highway Twenty-seven. According to the GPS, it would take me into the middle of Miami. If traffic wasn't bad and I didn't make any unplanned stops along the way, I'd arrive at my destination at one-fifteen.

Being in a motorhome, you never know what to expect when it comes to traffic. Especially when heading into a big city like Miami. Motorhomes aren't easy to turn around. If you go down the wrong road, you might not be able to get back out. Narrow streets, dead ends, and low shoulders can cause major problems. Something as simple as a car double parked in the wrong place could keep you from going any further. You might have to wait hours for the driver to return and move the car out of your way.

I wanted to avoid these kinds of problems, so before leaving, I used the satellite view of Google Maps to check my route again. It showed Highway twenty-seven was a divided road that missed most of the heavy traffic and congestion around Miami. It skirted the western edge of the city until it turned toward the airport. Traffic would be heavy from that point on, but I'd only be going a few blocks in it until I reached our destination.

Twenty minutes after leaving the campground, my phone chimed with an incoming call. The hands-free Bluetooth on my in-dash radio answered it.

It was Maddie.

"Walker, we just got on twenty-seven. Everything's fine on our end. How are things going for you?"

"No problems so far. Not much traffic. The road's in good shape. I'll call if anything changes."

For the next hour and a half, the drive went smoothly. No wrecks, no traffic jams, no typical Florida weirdness. Just an open road under blue skies with almost no wind to push the RV around.

As I got closer to Miami though, things changed.

Traffic picked up. There was a stoplight about every four blocks. Impatient drivers honked and sped around me, often cutting me off when they pulled back into my lane.

Some would flip me off, letting me know they didn't like being stuck behind a tall motorhome in traffic. Nothing unusual about that. That's the way it is, when driving an RV. No matter how fast you go, there's always someone wanting to go faster.

I learned long ago not to take it personally when other drivers get upset. Just let them do their thing, and don't do anything to antagonize them further. Especially in a place like Miami, where a lot of people carry guns in their cars and aren't afraid to use them.

After stopping at the fourth light in a row, Bob had had enough. He jumped down from the passenger seat and headed back to the safety of the bedroom.

I didn't blame him. If I didn't have to drive, I'd be doing the same thing.

The GPS eventually led me into the industrial section of town, near the airport. Most of the shops in the area seemed to be in the business of dismantling cars and selling off parts. Nearby crushers would take the remaining carcasses, pound them flat, and sell them as scrap metal.

The boatyards in the area looked to be doing the same thing. Taking in vessels that were on their last legs, decommissioning them, and selling what was left for parts and scrap.

The one thing that all these businesses had in common was their lots were walled off with chain link fences topped with razor wire, It suggested the neighborhood might have a crime problem. I'd have to keep that in mind if we left our RVs parked in the area overnight.

Ten minutes after the GPS put me in the industrial section, it let me know my destination was coming up on my left. I slowed until I reached an empty parking lot in front of what had once been a radiator repair shop.

The asphalt surface was cracked. Grass was growing through the seams. There were scattered patches of broken glass. But other than that, the lot looked okay. The driveway was wide and there was plenty of room to park two RVs side by side.

Thinking that I might have to make a quick exit, I pulled into the lot and backed into a parking spot, with the front of the RV facing the road. I'd tell Norah to do the same. That way, when we needed to leave, we could get out quickly without having to do any backing.

The business next door had a sign saying they were a paint and body shop, but the high fence surrounding it kept me from seeing what they might really be doing over there. The fence kept them from seeing what we might be doing as well. A good thing.

On the other side of the lot, a diesel repair shop. It too had a high fence topped with razor wire, again suggesting the neighborhood might not be the best place to spend the night.

Hopefully, we wouldn't have to.

But, when it came to parking, the lot we'd picked out was our only choice. It was the closest place to the drop-off point that was vacant and big enough for both our RVs.

Thinking that Norah was probably twenty minutes behind me, I gave her a call.

Agent Harris answered.

"Walker, any problems?"

"No, except for a few crazy drivers."

"Yeah, same here. How's the parking lot?"

"Not bad. Surrounded on three sides by tall fences with razor wire. Probably not the best neighborhood. Wouldn't want to be here after dark.

"But there's enough room for both RVs. You'll want to stop and unhook Buttercup before you get here though. Not enough room to do that here."

"Good to know. We'll stop and do that in the next parking lot we see. Call if anything changes on your end."

He ended the call.

I knew that when they arrived, they wouldn't want to waste time. They'd want to do the drop and see how things went from there. With that in mind, I figured it'd be a good idea to lock down the RV just in case they wanted me to go with them. I closed all the shades, pulled the windshield curtain so no one could see in, and double-checked that all the doors and windows were locked.

It was cool enough outside that I wouldn't have to worry about it getting too hot inside for Bob. But just in case, I turned on the overhead fans to keep the inside air moving.

One thing I noticed about the lot was the constant noise. Not only were we parked in the industrial section surrounded by auto and boat dismantlers, but we were also directly under Miami International Airport's flight path.

Every few minutes a heavy passenger jet would roar overhead as it tried to gain altitude leaving the airport behind.

The noise would be bothersome if we were trying to sleep.

As I found out later on, the noise could also work in our favor.

Chapter Fifty-Nine

Norah's RV pulled into the lot thirty-seven minutes later. Agent Harris was driving. Maddie was in the passenger seat.

He waved, then parked the same way I had, with the front of the RV facing the street. A minute later, Norah pulled into the lot driving Buttercup. She parked in front of her RV, got out, and went inside. I went over to join them.

Inside, Maddie, still wearing bike shorts and a sports bra, was filling us in on her plan.

She would drive Buttercup over to the Bus and Boat Salvage yard. There, per the delivery instructions from the FedEx package, she would go inside and ask for Rick. She would not take the laptop in with her. She'd leave it in the car.

Same with her gun. She wouldn't be able to conceal it in the skimpy outfit she was wearing. She'd leave it under Buttercup's driver's seat, within easy reach should she need it.

She'd have her phone with her and it would be sending video and audio to Agent Harris.

If things went south, he would go to her aid.

Norah and I were to stay put in her RV. We were not to go anywhere. Maddie told us twice. "Stay in the RV, out of the way. No matter what happens, do not get involved."

She had already called the FBI office in Miami and let them know what she was working on. She asked that they have a team ready to assist her if needed. They said they would.

After telling us this, she said, "It's time. I'm going over to see Rick."

Norah gave her the keys to Buttercup and went outside to show her how to use the clutch and put the car in gear. Maddie had never driven a car with a stick, and it quickly showed.

After three attempts to move the car out of the lot, she only managed to go four feet. She stalled the motor every time she let the clutch out.

She was trying her best, and in time, could have learned to do it right. But she didn't have time. She needed to get to Bus and Boat and see Rick.

Finally, frustrated that she couldn't do it on her own, she turned to Norah. "You drive."

Agent Harris wasn't having it. He stepped between Norah and Buttercup. "No, she can't get involved. I'll do it."

Maddie shook her head. "That won't work. You look too much like a fed. It has to be Norah."

Harris frowned. "Then what about Walker? He doesn't look like a fed. Let him drive."

"No, that won't work either. They're expecting a woman. If I show up with a man, they'll be suspicious. It has to be Norah. Get out of the way and let her drive."

Harris wasn't happy about it, but he let Maddie have her way. He stepped back, letting Norah open the driver's door.

Maddie got out and went over to the passenger seat while Norah took her place behind the wheel. She put the car in gear, and smoothly pulled out of the lot, heading one block east toward Bus and Boat Salvage.

Agent Harris quickly turned and headed into Norah's RV. I went with him.

Inside, he monitored the audio and video coming from

Maddie's phone. At first, there was nothing but the sound of Norah shifting through the gears. Then Maddie said, "There it is, pull in and park."

A moment later, she said, "Stay out here in the car. Leave the motor running. Lock the doors."

The next sound was Maddie leaving the car. We could hear the passenger door open, then close.

A moment later, Maddie said, "I'm here to see Rick."

She was inside Bus and Boat Salvage.

A man's voice spoke. "Rick? You're here to see Rick?"

"Yes, I've got a delivery and was told to come here and ask for Rick."

The man spoke again. "Are you sure you're at the right place? We don't have anyone here named Rick. Or Ricardo or Richard. There's just the four of us. No one goes by Rick."

A pause, then Maddie said, "Check again. I've got a package I'm supposed to deliver. I was told to come here and ask for Rick."

The man spoke again. This time his voice sounded like it was on loudspeaker. "If there is anyone here who goes by Rick, come to the front desk. Right away."

We heard nothing but the buzz of machinery.

After a minute, the man said, "See, there's no Rick here. You're at the wrong place."

Maddie spoke. "I was told to deliver a package here. No one told you to expect me?"

"Lady, the only package we're expecting is a front bumper for a Ford F-450. If you've got that, bring it in. Otherwise, I can't help you."

A moment later, Maddie said, "I'm back outside. Going to

the car to check the instructions to make sure this is the right place."

Then, "Norah's gone! The car is still here, but Norah's gone. The laptop and phone are gone too!"

"I'm going back inside. Someone in there must know something."

Agent Harris looked at me. "Time to go. Lock the doors. Follow me."

He tossed me the keys to the RV and headed outside. I followed, locking the door as I left.

There are no sidewalks in this part of Miami. No reason for them. Only a fool would be out for a walk in this area. We were on foot and had to take to the streets.

Agent Harris didn't hesitate. He ran out onto the pavement, dodging oncoming traffic. I followed, doing the same. It was a short run, just a couple of blocks.

We reached Bus and Boat in less than a minute. Buttercup was still in the parking lot. Norah wasn't in it.

Agent Harris stopped at the car and turned to me. "You stay here. With the car. I'm going inside to help Agent O'Connor."

He ran to Bus & Boats' front door. I stayed out with the car.

The passenger door was unlocked. The keys were still in the ignition, but the motor was off. The driver's side window was down. Norah's purse was on the floor, between the seats, just under the dash. But still, no Norah.

I opened the passenger door and climbed in, thinking I might find something to tell me what had happened to her.

Remembering that she kept a gun in her purse, I checked to see if it was still there. It was. A Glock 43X. With nine rounds in the mag. Next to it, her phone. She hadn't taken it with her.

Maddie had said she was going to keep her gun under the driver's seat. I checked to see if it was there. From where I was sitting in the passenger seat, I had to lean over to my left and duck down under the steering wheel to look.

If I were a gymnast, it would have been easy to do. But I wasn't a gymnast. I was a full-grown six-foot tall man, and it took a lot of bending to get around the stick shift, and under the steering wheel just to feel around for the gun.

I had just squeezed my arm under the seat when I felt the car move. I figured Agent Harris had come back.

But it wasn't him.

I knew that for sure when the front end of the car rose up off the ground. At least three feet above the pavement. The angle, along with the pull of gravity, kept me pinned under the steering wheel. I tried, but I couldn't get upright.

With my head down close to the floor, I couldn't figure out was what going on. All I knew for sure was the front of the car had been lifted off the ground, and soon, we were going down the road at a pretty good pace.

It was a strange feeling to be moving so fast in a car without the motor running.

I'd soon find out how that was possible.

Chapter Sixty

With my head stuck under the dash, I couldn't see out the front window to know what was going on. But I suspected Buttercup had been picked up by a tow truck using a wheel lift and we were being towed away.

An experienced tow driver using a wheel lift can grab a car and be gone in less than thirty seconds. Sometimes even quicker.

Being stuck down under the dash, the tow driver wouldn't have seen me when he hooked Buttercup. He wouldn't know I was in the car. He probably never even looked. In Miami, as in most major cities, tow drivers don't like to leave the safety of their trucks. They know a lot of people carry guns, and some will pull them when they see their car being towed away.

The drivers prefer to grab a car quickly without getting out and be gone before anyone can say anything.

He had done that with Buttercup, not knowing I was inside. The big question was, why was he taking Buttercup and where was he taking it?

It wasn't likely that he was trying to steal the car. Being an older Ford Focus, it didn't have much resale value. It wouldn't be worth the trouble to part out.

That meant it was being towed for some other reason. Probably having something to do with the laptop and Norah's disappearance.

If I was right, and lucky, the driver would tow the car to where Norah was. That might give me a chance to help her escape – assuming she was being held against her will.

Since the driver didn't know I was along for the ride, I figured it'd be a good idea to keep it that way. I kept my head down and hoped he would drop the car the same way he'd picked it up. Quickly, without bothering to get out of his truck and look inside.

As I was laying there, under the dash, Norah's phone chimed with an incoming call. The phone was close, still in her purse, in front of the shifter.

I wasn't sure I could reach it, but I knew I had to, for two reasons.

The first being, I didn't want the ringing phone to alert the tow truck driver to my presence. While there was no way he could hear it up in his truck, he might hear it once we stopped. Then come back and find me.

That wouldn't be good.

A better reason to answer was to let Agent Harris and Maddie know what was going on. I assumed it had to be one of them calling.

Reaching back behind me, I stretched my arm out and tried to find Norah's purse. It had fallen off her seat when the car was lifted and had landed in the space under the dash. Fortunately, I was able to reach it.

I pulled it close. On the fifth ring, I answered the call.

"Hello?"

"Norah?"

"No. It's me. Walker."

"Why'd you take the car? Bring it back. We need it."

It was Agent Harris speaking.

"Sorry, no can do. I didn't take it. It was towed away. With me inside."

"Towed? What do you mean towed?"

"What I mean was I was looking under the dash, trying to see if Norah had taken Agent O'Connor's gun when a tow truck showed up and hauled the car off.

"I'm inside. The tow truck is going down the road. I have no idea where we're going."

Harris paused, then asked, "Is O'Connor's gun still under the seat?"

"Yes, it is. Along with the gun in Norah's purse."

"Okay, here's what I want you to do.

"Stay in the car until the driver drops it off. Then use the phone to find out where you are. Text me the address.

"And Walker, don't get out of the car or use the guns for any reason. Just stay hidden until we get there."

Harris ended the call before I could ask about Maddie.

It was good timing on his part. The tow truck slowed and made a sharp right turn. Then came to a full stop.

Still crouched under the steering wheel, I listened carefully for the sound of a car door opening. If I heard it, I'd know the tow driver was getting out. Probably to come back and check the car before dropping it off. If he found me in it, no telling what might happen.

Preparing for the worst, I grabbed Maddie's gun and chambered a round. I hoped I wouldn't need to use it, but if the driver pointed a gun at me, I wanted to be able to point one back.

Fortunately, it didn't come to that. Instead of hearing a car door open, I heard the distinctive sound of a garage door rolling up. When it stopped, the tow truck pulled forward several feet.

Then made a sharp right turn and backed up several feet before stopping again.

Almost immediately, I could hear a mechanical whining sound as the front end of the car dropped to the ground. After a few pops and the sound of the lift arm being retracted, the tow truck drove away.

Leaving me behind, wondering where I was.

Chapter Sixty-One

I waited a full minute before crawling out from under the dash. Then waited another minute, just listening to my surroundings. I wanted to be sure that when I popped up, there wouldn't be anyone around to see me.

Not hearing anything, I slowly lifted my head and peeked out over the dash. There was nothing to see. It was pitch black. Or at least, it appeared to be. If the place had lights, they weren't turned on.

As I looked around trying to see anything I could recognize, my eyes slowly adjusted to the darkness. As they did, I saw that the building I was in was a large warehouse, full of cars. Two rows of them. Backed up against the walls on both sides of the building. There was enough space between the rows to drive a car or a tow truck to the other end of the warehouse.

Light leaked in from the bottoms of closed roll-up doors at each end. Another light, much fainter, spilled out from under a doorway near the middle of the building.

As my eyes adjusted, I could see that most of the cars were high-end collectibles. Ferraris, Rolls, Lambos, and a few Porsches. Most looked fairly new and fully intact.

My first thought was the place was a chop shop. Where stolen cars were taken to be stripped for parts. But looking around, I didn't see any of the tools you'd expect in a chop shop. No car lifts, no plasma cutters, no tools of any kind. No mechanics to strip the cars.

Along with the exotics, there were at least three

ambulances, all looking a lot like the one Norah and I had broken into two days earlier in the Buc-ees lot. It was either a very weird coincidence they were in the same warehouse where Buttercup had been taken to, or I had stumbled into one of the operation centers belonging to the people Maddie was looking for.

Agent Harris had told me to text my location when the car was dropped off. Using Norah's phone, I brought up Google Maps to see if it would show where I was.

It didn't.

Instead, it said no signal, which made sense as I was inside a warehouse, presumably with a metal roof, which prevented the phone's GPS from getting an exact fix on my location.

Fortunately, Google did have the address of the last place the GPS had a signal. Near the 3600th block of North River Road in Miami. The accompanying satellite view showed a large warehouse spreading over two city blocks, surrounded on both sides by what looked like automobile junkyards.

The street side of the warehouse was on River Road. The back faced the Miami River and had what looked like an older flat-top barge docked at the seawall. A fairly large motor yacht was docked behind it.

The satellite photos were not real-time, which meant the barge and motor yacht could be long gone.

I texted the address to Harris. He texted back and said they were on their way and for me to stay put.

It was a little stuffy in the car, so I rolled the window down to get some fresh air. But the air wasn't fresh. It smelled of old cars, gasoline, and salt water. Seeing no one around, I wanted to get out of the car to get a better idea of the layout of the place and see if I could find where they were holding Norah.

Harris had said to stay put. He didn't want me going

anywhere. I should have listened to him.

But didn't.

I had two guns with me. Agent O'Connor's Sig, and Norah's Glock. I knew how to use both. And I wasn't much for waiting around when someone I knew might be in danger. So, instead of waiting for the cavalry to show up, I put the pistols in my pants pockets. One on the left, one on the right.

With the confidence the firearms gave me, I got out of the car, still keeping my head down, and looked around.

Just as I first figured, I was in a giant warehouse, long and wide, with high ceilings. Any sound inside would echo in the open space above. The row of expensive cars lining the walls went further than I first thought. Instead of being just under twenty cars, there had to be at least a hundred, with fifty against each wall. Plus, three ambulances. If the lights were on, the place would have looked like a huge exotic car showroom, minus the salespeople.

Staying low, I moved away from Buttercup to the next nearest car. A late model Bentley. It was big enough to give me cover as I tried to figure out what to do next.

My goal was to find Norah. To do that, I needed to check out the room where I had seen light coming out from under a door. Maybe it was an office and they were keeping her there.

Moving away from the Bentley, I headed toward the light. As I moved, I kept my back to the wall and squeezed between it and the rear bumper of each car I passed. This would make it more difficult for anyone to detect my movement and would also provide instant cover if I needed it.

Moving slowly, it took me two minutes to get to the car nearest what I assumed was an office door. From there, I could hear two men speaking inside.

"What does he want us to do with the car she was in?"

"He said to shred it and put it on the barge with the others."

"What about the girl? What do we do with her?"

"Take her to the boat. Then forget about her. As far as you're concerned, she was never here. Understand?"

An answer was mumbled, which I assumed meant the man understood.

I understood as well.

It was time for me to do something other than just listen to the men talk about doing away with Norah.

Chapter Sixty-Two

Agent Harris and O'Connor still hadn't shown up. Or if they had, they were waiting outside for other agents to join them. I wasn't going to wait, though. I was going to find and hopefully rescue Norah. Or get shot trying.

When the men in the office were talking about what to do with her, one had said they needed to take her to the boat. If he meant the one that Google Earth showed docked behind the warehouse, it might mean she was close. Maybe in the same room they were in, or one close by.

I needed to find out but didn't want to go in with guns blazing and face off the two men, or however many others were in the office with them. I didn't know if they were armed but was pretty sure they wouldn't be happy to see me if I barged in and tried to take Norah.

It would be better if I could figure out a way to get them out of the office so I could go in and look around without them knowing about it. That way, if I found Norah, we could try to escape unnoticed.

The question was, how was I going to get everyone out of the office without them finding me?

I thought for a moment and came up with an idea. One that usually worked in the movies.

I'd create a huge distraction. One the people in the office couldn't ignore. One that would give them a good reason to come out and see what was going on.

I figured the best way to do that, was to start setting off the security alarms in the cars parked in the warehouse. Most of them were expensive and were sure to have alarm systems. If I could trigger a few, the annoyingly loud horn blasts and accompanying sirens couldn't be ignored.

The guys in the office would have to come out and check. While they were trying to disable the alarms, I'd sneak in and look for Norah.

To keep from being found, I went back to Buttercup and jiggled the driver's door handle on the Bentley next to it. Nothing happened. No alarm. I tried again, same results. No alarm.

I tried the door, and surprisingly, it was unlocked. Looking in, I saw the car keys were on the seat, in plain sight.

I picked up the key fob and pressed the panic button. That set off the alarm. The horn blared and the lights flashed. I quickly got out and moved to the next closest car, a red Ferrari.

Like the Bentley, the doors were unlocked. The keys in plain sight, on the seat. I pressed the panic button, setting off the alarm.

The next car was a blue Maserati Ghibli. Like the Ferrari, the keys were in the seat. I opened the door and pressed the panic button. And just like with the first two, the alarm screamed. I got out quickly, but this time, I kept the keys with me. I figured the alarm couldn't be reset without them. I did the same with the next three cars. European exotics with piercing horns that couldn't be ignored.

Or so I thought.

Even with the blaring horns of six cars, no one came out of the office to see what was going on.

But I wasn't going to give up. I kept going, car to car, setting off alarms and flashers on each. I was surprised that most were unlocked with the keys in clear view. But maybe the thieves felt their warehouse was secure. Or maybe it was just easier to keep up with the keys to over a hundred cars by leaving them inside each one.

Whatever the reason, it made my job a lot easier.

By the time I finished with the tenth car, two men carrying guns came out of the office. They were yelling at each other, but I couldn't hear what they were saying over the blaring horns. They probably couldn't hear each other either. The larger of the two pointed to the first car I had set off, the Bentley. The other man nodded and both of them headed toward it.

I stayed hidden until they walked passed me, then made my way to their office. I quickly went in, locking the door behind me.

It was a small room. An older metal desk sat in the middle. A rolling chair behind it. Two well-worn plastic chairs off to the side. Three metal file cabinets behind the desk. A stack of license plates from various states on the floor to the right of the desk.

No Norah.

A door behind the desk was closed. It likely led to a bathroom. Or maybe a hallway leading to other rooms.

I needed to find out. But I knew I didn't have much time. The two guys outside would eventually figure out that someone in the building was setting off the alarms.

When they did, they'd come looking for me.

I wasn't going to wait for them.

Instead, I tried the door behind the desk. It was unlocked. I pushed it open and was surprised as well as relieved to find Norah. Sitting on the toilet. Feet and arms bound with duct tape, a bandanna around her mouth.

Seeing me, her eyes opened wide. She tried to say something, but her words were muffled. I tore the tape away from her arms and legs, then removed the bandanna.

She took a deep breath, rubbed her wrists, then said, "Walker, good to see you. You alone?"

"Yeah, it's just me. Harris and O'Connor are on their way."

She pointed to the door. "They have guns. We need to get out of here."

Before I could tell her I was armed, shots rang out from within the warehouse. Three quick ones, a pause, then four more.

We could hear yelling, then a voice shouting, "FBI!"

The gunfire stopped.

Norah stood. "We need to get out of here."

I shook my head. "No, we don't. Not while they're shooting. We don't want to get caught in the crossfire. Or shoot our way out and accidentally hit Harris or O'Connor.

"We'll stay in here."

I showed her the two guns I'd found in Buttercup. One was hers, the other O'Connor's. "If the bad guys come back, we can protect ourselves."

Norah nodded and held out her hand. She wanted her gun.

I gave it to her. "I don't want to shoot anyone. But if they come in here and start shooting, I will."

I felt the same way.

Norah's phone chimed with an incoming call. It was in my pocket. I pulled it out. The caller ID said O'Connor. I answered and put it on speaker so Norah could hear.

"This is Walker."

"Walker, where are you?"

"In the warehouse. Norah's with me. We're safe. In the office."

"Do you have my gun?"

"Yeah."

"Good. Harris has been shot. I'm pinned down behind Buttercup. I've got his Glock, but I'm down to three rounds.

"Backup hasn't made it yet. They say they're ten minutes away.

"If the bad guys start shooting again, I may not make it. When the other agents show up, tell them what happened."

She ended the call.

Chapter Sixty-Three

There were three more gunshots from outside. And still no sign of FBI backup.

I pointed to the door. "I'm going out to see if I can help her. You stay in here until it's safe. Lock the door as soon as I go out."

"Walker, wait. What's your plan?"

"I don't have one. I'm just going out there and start shooting at anyone who isn't FBI."

She reached over and grabbed my arm. "No, you can't do that. You might get shot, and if you do, who will rescue Harris and O'Connor?"

I thought for a moment. "There are three ambulances right outside the office door. The kind the thieves have been using. If we can get one started, I can try to get to Harris and O'Connor and get them out of the building.

"If the bad guys get in the way, I'll drive over them."

Norah frowned. "You know they aren't bullet-proof, right? The ambulances. They won't stop a bullet."

"Does that mean you're not coming with me?"

She racked the slide on her pistol. "I'm ready if you are."

I pointed to the door. "They're on our right. Let's see if we can sneak out and get one started."

I went to the door, unlocked it, and opened it just slightly. Peeking out, I couldn't see or hear the bad guys. The sirens and blasting horns I'd set off were still going strong, hopefully giving us some cover as we made our move.

I pushed the door open just far enough to slip out. Norah followed. We quickly made our way to the nearest ambulance. The back door was unlocked. I opened it for Norah and she went in. I stayed outside ready to put down cover fire if needed.

Norah must have found the keys because I heard the motor turn over. It didn't start, though. She tried again, but still, no start. I could smell diesel, which would explain the problem.

"Norah, don't turn the key until the glow plug light goes out, then try it again."

Five seconds later, the engine came to life with a roar. Norah moved to the passenger seat as I jumped in. I handed her the phone. "Call O'Connor. Tell her we're coming."

I put the ambulance in gear and eased out into the middle of the warehouse. The lane between the rows of parked cars led to a large overhead door that would take us outside. The door was closed.

I'd worry about that later.

Maddie had said she was pinned down behind Buttercup. I knew where it was parked. I headed that way.

But didn't get far.

A man stepped out from behind a Rolls Royce wit a gun pointed in our direction. He didn't look like FBI. I was ready to shoot, but before I could, Norah grabbed the handle of the ambulance's spotlight and pointed it directly at the man, temporarily blinding him.

He fired anyway. Hitting the ambulance just above the windshield. The bullet went through the fiberglass topper and continued on until it exited out the back.

If it had hit either one of us, we wouldn't have survived.

Norah kept pointing the spotlight at him. He kept

shooting, aiming at the light, which was about a foot from where she was sitting.

I steered toward the gunman and accelerated. He had to choose quickly. Jump back out of the way, or get run over.

He made the right choice.

As we passed, he fired three shots into the side of the ambulance, not hitting anything that mattered. At least to us.

When we got to Buttercup. I pulled up at an angle, using the bulk of the vehicle to block the bad guy's view and any bullets coming our way.

O'Connor popped up, pushing Harris toward our passenger door. Norah opened it and pulled him in. O'Connor followed.

I pressed the go pedal and headed for the closed garage door.

We hit it at twenty miles an hour. Not particularly fast unless you're hitting something head-on.

The roll-up door, like many in Florida, had extra braces, making it what insurance guys call 'hurricane proof'.

It might have been able to withstand hurricane winds, but it didn't have a chance against the speeding ambulance.

We broke through like it wasn't even there.

Outside, O'Connor's backup team was just pulling into the lot. I slammed on the brakes, skidding the ambulance to a stop, just barely missing the first black SUV through the gate. Three others followed, close behind.

Twelve guys, wearing body armor, poured out, carrying assault rifles, all pointed in our direction.

Chapter Sixty-Four

We were ordered to stay in our vehicle with our hands over our heads. Maddie was the only one who didn't comply.

Instead of putting her hands up, she pulled out her phone and punched in a number.

Outside, we watched as one of the agents reached into his vest and pull out his phone.

We couldn't hear what he was saying, but we could hear Maddie's side of the conversation.

"I'm Agent O'Connor. I'm in the ambulance with Agent Harris of Homeland. He's been shot. We need an ambulance. The two other people in here are kidnap victims. They are both safe.

She continued. "There are at least two armed men inside the warehouse. They opened fire on us. One of them shot Harris.

"We are going to step out of the ambulance. I will get out first, then Agent Harris, followed by the female civilian, and then the male, who is behind the wheel."

The agent standing in front of the lead SUV nodded in Maddie's direction, then had his agents lower their weapons.

O'Connor opened the passenger door and stepped out. Harris did not follow. Neither did Norah.

I turned to let them know it was time to go. They weren't listening.

Norah, the traveling nurse who had worked in emergency rooms, had found a first aid kit in the decommissioned ambulance. She was using it to tend to Harris's gunshot wound.

It was obvious he was in pain, but also obvious he liked the attention he was getting.

I called back to her. "How's he doing?"

She was quick with an answer. "The bullet missed his vitals. He'll be sore for a few days, but he'll live."

Norah stayed with him until a real ambulance with EMTs pulled into the lot. When they came to his aide, she explained how she had treated the wound. She stayed with him as they wheeled him away.

I was the only one left in the ambulance and was about to step out when I heard the unmistakable sound of a Ferrari revving its motor from inside the warehouse.

As far as I knew, the only people left inside were the two guys who had shot Agent Harris. If they were trying to escape, a Ferrari might be a good car to be in, if the coppers gave chase.

The warehouse had two roll-up doors, one at each end of the building. The crooks could go out either way. If they were smart, they'd take the Ferrari out the door I hadn't crashed into. But maybe they saw the gaping hole I'd made and didn't know the lot outside was swarming with FBI agents.

If they could get the Ferrari through the busted door without having to get out and open it, it'd save them time and make for a faster getaway. At least that's what they must have been thinking when I heard the sound of burning rubber and saw the sleek sports car heading my way.

If they timed it just right, they could get through the door, then weave through the parking lot and out onto the street. If they could get that far, they'd be long gone before the agents could give chase.

So without too much thought, I started the ambulance, put it in reverse, and backed toward the warehouse door.

My timing was perfect. Just as I reached the door, the Ferrari came through and slammed into the back of the ambulance. The front of the sports car crumpled as it slid under the rear end of the far heavier truck.

Smoke poured out of the front-engined Ferrari while the two occupants struggled to get out. The force of the wreck had warped the doors, trapping the men inside. The Ferrari was built before the invention of airbags and there was nothing to soften the blow of the crash.

Fortunately for the two men inside, the EMT crew that had come to help Agent Harris was still in the parking lot. They, along with six FBI agents, rushed to the car to provide aid.

I moved the now-wrecked ambulance out of the way, giving the agents and EMTs more room to work. Then I parked and went over to see Maddie.

When I got close, she said, "I told you not to get involved. And did you listen? No, you had to be the hero, didn't you?"

I smiled and moved closer so no one but her, could hear what I said. "Agent O'Connor, I apologize for saving your life. Can't promise I won't do it again though, if the need arises."

She shook her head and started to walk away, but stopped when I said, "Those guys in there, the ones who were shooting at you, are just low-level goons. The main guy, the one you really want, is in the boat behind the warehouse. If you hurry, you might be able to catch him before he gets away."

She stopped walking and turned to face me. "What? What main guy? What boat?"

I pointed toward the river that bordered the warehouse. "The boat over there. The guy you want is in the boat."

Instead of asking more questions, she called over four agents and they, along with her, headed toward the dock behind the warehouse.

About two hours later, having been interviewed by three different agents, Norah and I were allowed to leave. We didn't get to say goodbye to Harris or O'Connor, but we were able to convince the agent in charge, to let us leave in Buttercup.

We got in and drove away before he could change his mind.

Chapter Sixty-Five

Back at our RVs, the first words out of Norah's mouth were, "Let's get out of here before dark. I don't want to be around when the sun goes down."

I didn't need to ask why. The burned-out wrecks and the razor-wire fences told me all that I needed to know.

"Yeah, we should leave. Give me ten minutes to get cleaned up and I'll be ready to go."

She nodded, gave me a peck on the cheek, and went to her RV. I watched as she unlocked the door to make sure she got in safely. In the neighborhood we were in, it seemed like a good thing to do.

Back inside my place, Bob met me at the door. He meowed a welcome, then trotted back to the bathroom where his food and water bowls were kept.

I'd filled them before we'd left and knew they weren't empty, but went back to check anyway. Bob always appreciates it when I do.

As expected, both bowls were nearly full. He hadn't eaten much in the three hours I'd been away. Most likely, he'd spent most of that time sleeping on my bed.

With Bob reassured that he wasn't going to starve anytime soon, I washed up. The shirt I was wearing was splattered with blood, grease, and grime from the warehouse. I pulled it off and put on a clean one.

Then I went back up front, grabbed a bottle of water, and sat on the sofa waiting to hear from Norah.

She showed up at my door a few minutes later.

"Walker, like I said, I don't want to spend the night here. I want to go someplace quiet where there won't be many people around. A place I can relax without worrying about being kidnapped or shot. You know of anything like that nearby?"

I did.

"We could go to Midway. It's part of the Big Cypress Preserve on Alligator Alley. It'll be quiet there, and it's only an hour's drive from here.

"The sites are first come first serve. This time of year, you never know if they'll be any available. If there aren't, we can go to the nearby Miccosukee Casino. It won't be quiet, but they have a place where RVs can park overnight. And they have security guards to keep the peace."

"Sounds good to me. When do we leave?"

"Right now, if that works for you. All we need to do is hook up Buttercup."

Fifteen minutes later, we had the little car connected to her RV.

Before leaving the lot, I programmed Midway's address into Norah's GPS, so we would both be taking the same route to get there. We'd agreed that I'd go first and she'd follow. If she got lost, the GPS would get her back on track.

Traffic was what we expected. Mostly stop and go until we turned onto US 41. From there it was smooth sailing all the way to the entrance of Midway Campground. Norah stayed several miles behind, so we didn't create a rolling roadblock with the two large RVs.

I got to Midway first. A sign on the gate said, 'Park Is Full. No Sites Available.'

I called Norah. "Midway is full. We'll have to stay at the Casino. I'll meet you there."

Twenty-five minutes later, I pulled into the casino lot. Having been there before, I knew the best place to park an RV would be in the back, where the pavement ended and the grassy Everglades took over. Most people avoided that area, thinking it was too far a walk from the Casino doors. Since we weren't planning on going in, the back lot would work for us.

I found a spot I liked and pulled in. Norah pulled in beside me. There were no hookups. But it didn't matter. Just about everything in our RVs except air conditioning was powered by the coach batteries.

After parking, Norah stepped outside and I went over to talk.

"What do you think?"

She smiled. "I like it. Plenty of places for Biscuit to take care of business. No one parking near to bother us."

She pointed to the casino building. "They have food in there?"

"Yeah. Three or four cafes and an all-you-can-eat buffet. I'll treat you if you want to go in."

"Good. I'll need a nap first, though. Come get me around seven and we'll go eat."

Chapter Sixty-Six

As planned, we ate dinner at the Casino buffet. The food was decent and there were plenty of options.

They had three different kinds of seafood along with fresh oysters, but I wasn't going to take a chance. I was done with oysters. I'd learned my lesson.

I stuck with meat, potatoes, and chocolate cake for dessert.

Norah had the same.

After dinner, we went back to her RV and talked.

"So Walker, where are you going next? After we leave here?"

"I haven't thought about it. Except I'm pretty sure I won't be going back to Miami anytime soon."

"Me neither. In fact, I think I'll go in the opposite direction. To Orlando. Might even leave in the morning and head that way.

"My job there doesn't start for another three days, but I need to go somewhere and stay put for a while. To chill. The last few days have been crazy."

I understood completely. Downtime would be nice.

"Norah, I'll probably do the same. Find somewhere quiet and do nothing for a few days."

She laughed. "Isn't that what you do most of the time? Just lay around doing nothing?"

I grinned. "Yeah, that's me. Doing nothing. Except when I'm being seduced by traveling nurses who somehow get the

FBI and Homeland Security involved."

She smiled, then reached out to take my hand. "Walker, you poor baby. You have it so hard. Going wherever you want, whenever you want. And being chased by women at every stop.

"Maybe if you settled down, got a real job, and moved into a real house, things would be better for you."

I shook my head. "A real job? Me? Are you kidding? I tried that once. It didn't work out. I'll stick with living on the road."

We talked a bit more, drank wine, and had a pleasant evening. We promised that no matter where we went, we'd try to stay in touch and agreed if our schedules meshed in the future, we'd get together again."

Around eleven, Norah said it was bedtime. She kissed me on the cheek and went to her RV.

I stayed up until I saw her lights go out. Then I pulled my blinds, locked the doors, and crawled into bed. Ten minutes later, I was out.

Bob slept with me most of the night. When we woke, Norah's RV was gone. She'd left a note on my windshield saying, 'At least it wasn't boring.'

She was right about that.

I stayed in the casino lot for two more days. On the morning of the third, Agent Harris called.

"Walker, how you doing?"

"Pretty good. How about you? How's the arm?"

"Still hurts when I forget to wear the sling. But getting better every day. The doc says I'll be good to go in a month."

"Glad to hear. But I'm guessing your health is not the reason you called."

"You're right. I wanted to give you an update on what's been happening since the shooting.

"First, all those cars in the warehouse were stolen. Valued at almost thirty million dollars. Finding them was a big deal. It made a lot of wealthy people happy they were getting their cars back. The insurance companies were happy too. They didn't have to pay big buck settlements.

"Busting the theft ring made the FBI look good. Something that's been in short supply lately.

"Agent O'Connor is getting all the credit, as she should. She and her team were the ones who cracked the case. In case you missed it, when she went to the boat behind the warehouse, she captured an Iraqi national who was behind the whole thing.

"He was using the warehouse location on the river to ferry stolen cars out to larger ports where they would be loaded onto freighters and sold to overseas buyers.

"Breaking the case was a big deal for O'Connor. She should have gotten a commendation. But she didn't.

"Instead, they suspended her for ninety days. The agency will be using that time to determine if she broke agency rules regarding the use of civilian assets during the investigation.

"It's pure politics. She cracked one of the biggest cases of the year, She should be getting a promotion instead of a suspension. But someone decided otherwise. They don't want to see her move up the ranks.

"Anyway, thought you might want to know."

"Yeah, thanks for telling me. How's Maddie taking it?"

"I don't know. Why don't you give her a call?"

I had her number and said I would.

But I wasn't sure if I should.

She probably believed, and rightly so, that my getting involved in her case and not following her orders to stay out of the way, were the cause of her suspension.

Even so, I knew I should call her. And apologize.

I was debating the best time to call when my phone chimed with another incoming call.

From Norah.

I answered on the second ring.

"Hi, Norah. How's the job in Orlando going?"

"Not good. That's one of the reasons I'm calling.

"The nurse I was supposed to fill in for, chose not to use her vacation days. She decided to work instead, which meant they didn't need me.

"They went ahead and paid me half of what I was due and sent me on my way.

"That means I have three months free to do whatever I want. But not just me. As you probably know, Maddie also has free time on her hands. Not by choice, but it is what it is.

"I called her this morning and asked if she wanted to get together. Maybe go some place where no one knew us and we could just chill for a few days. Somewhere warm and near the water.

"She wasn't sure at first, saying that maybe she should just stay in her apartment and do nothing. But I wasn't going to give up. I told her among other things, it would be good for her health to get away.

"It took some doing, but I finally convinced her to go with me. She had one condition.

"She didn't want to stay in a motorhome. It has to be an upscale resort with real beds, room service, and a pool. If I couldn't find a place like that, she wasn't going to go.

"So right away, I started looking. Checking all the oceanfront resorts in Florida. It turned out to be a bust. With it being snowbird season, there are no rooms to be had.

"I thought I'd call and see if you could think of a place we could get into. It was actually Maddie's idea that I call you. She hinted it might be nice to have you go with us.

"So, what do you think, Walker? Know of a place? And would you want to join us?"

Chapter Sixty-Seven

"Are you sure Maddie wants me to come? I mean, she might not be too thrilled to have me around. It was my fault she's in trouble with the Agency."

"Walker, she doesn't blame you for what happened. Or me. She said her suspension was politics within the Agency. Some people don't want to see her rise in the ranks. They are trying to create a reason for her not to.

"So yes, she wants you to come. But only if you want to. If we can find a place where we'd each have a separate room and I can bring Biscuit and you can bring Bob, it would be great. Having room service would be a plus.

"Any suggestions?"

I thought about it. It would be hard to find that kind of thing, this time of year in Florida. Especially one that allowed pets.

Fortunately, I knew someone who might be able to help.

Two years earlier, while on the Treasure Coast, I met Francis Ford. I had trespassed onto her oceanfront property, looking for a lost dog. And she'd pulled a gun on me.

It could have gone badly, but didn't. In the end, I found the dog, and while on her property filling in a hole the dog had dug, I found her grandmother's wedding ring, which had been lost for years.

As a reward, she gave me her card and said if I ever needed a place to stay, give her a call. I found out later she was the majority stockholder in a company that owned hotels, condos, and vacation homes throughout Florida.

I decided to call and see if she knew of a place that might be available.

I punched in the number on her card and listened as the call went through. On the fifth ring, just when I thought it was going to voice mail, she answered.

"Hello?"

"Francis, this is Walker. I don't know if you remember me or not. We met in Vero. I was looking for Jake, the wonder dog."

There was a moment of silence, then, "Walker, of course, I remember you. And that cute girl you were with. You still seeing her?"

"You mean Anna Parker? Yeah, we're still in touch. She's selling real estate on the Gulf side of the state, and doing quite well.

"How about you? Are you staying healthy? Seeing anyone?"

"Walker, I'm doing about as well as can be expected at my age. I'm still with Walt. And Jake. Thanks to you."

"Glad to hear it. Walt is a good man. And Jake is the best dog in the world.

I hesitated, then said, "Francis, did you hear about the FBI and that stolen car ring they busted in Miami last week?"

"Yes, I heard about it. In fact, they recovered one of my cars. A white Rolls. Why do you ask?"

"Well, I was there. In the warehouse when the shooting started. Along with the lead FBI agent.

"Norah Shepard was there too. You might have heard of her. She's the woman who stopped a school shooter a few years back. She's one of the reasons I'm calling.

"The lead FBI agent who solved the car case, Maddie O'Connor, was suspended for ninety days. It was because Nurse Norah and I were with her when the shooting started in the car warehouse.

"Even though Agent O'Connor broke the theft ring, captured an international terrorist, and saved a lot of lives. the FBI suspended her.

"Nurse Norah and Agent O'Connor are both looking for a place to stay and chill out for a month. Something nice, maybe close to the ocean. Norah has a beagle rescue, so the place has to allow pets. I still have a cat and might be staying with them, so the place has to be pet friendly.

"I know it's a long shot, but Nurse Norah and O'Connor both deserve something nice. Do you by any chance know of something that might be available?"

Francis Ford answered quickly. "Walker, this time of year, there's no apartments or condos available anywhere close to the beach. Even if there were, none would allow a dog or cat on the premises."

When she paused to take a breath, I said, "That's what I figured. I guess we'll just keep looking. You stay well."

I expected her to say 'Sorry,' and end the call. But she didn't.

Instead, she said, "Hold on. I know a place. My villa in Key West. No one's using it this time of year, and for you, I'd allow pets.

"It has five bedrooms, plus a cottage by the pool for the house manager. It's in a quiet part of town, away from the crowds, but just a short bike ride to Duval Street and Mallory Square.

"It's fully stocked and the house manager takes care of everything, including preparing meals.

"If you and your two friends would like to stay there for a month, it's yours. Do you want me to call and set it up?"

I was stunned. I certainly didn't expect her to offer her personal villa.

"Francis, I appreciate the offer, but I don't want to put you out. If it's your personal home, or if you have someone else staying there, I don't want to create a problem. We can find something else."

"Walker, you don't understand. It's a villa I only use a few times a year, but mostly it just sits empty. It won't be a problem for you to use. In fact, I would be honored to have you and your FBI friend and Nurse Nora stay there. And of course, you can bring your pets.

"With one condition. I want to personally meet the FBI agent who solved the case and thank her for her service. I also want to meet Norah. Would that be possible?"

"Of course. I'm sure they would both love to meet you. And yes, it would be great if we could stay at your villa. Both Norah and Agent O'Connor are free for the next sixty days, so anytime within that time frame would work for us. I can send you payment right away."

I didn't care what it'd cost. The villa sounded perfect and I owed it to Maddie to find something nice where she could relax and recover from the problems I caused.

"Walker, you know I'm not going to charge you anything. Especially since you're helping out the FBI agent who recovered my car along with Nurse Norah who saved all those kids.

"I'll call the house manager today and let them know you and your guests are on the way. She'll have the place ready for you as soon as tomorrow.

"And Walker, if you need anything else, call me. I still owe you."

We said our goodbyes and I ended the call.

Chapter Sixty-Eight

A few minutes later, Francis texted me the address of her villa along with the phone number of her house manager.

Before calling Norah and sharing the good news, I entered the villa's address in Google to see if there was room to park my RV along with Norah's.

There wasn't.

Even though the property itself was massive, the narrow streets of Key West meant there was no room to park an RV anywhere close by.

It didn't really matter though. Not after I got a look at the villa.

It turned out to be a fully restored five thousand square foot mansion just two blocks from a private beach. Three stories tall, surrounded by palms on all sides, with a courtyard pool separating the main house from the manager's cabana.

A short walk to a city park. And a few blocks from Duval and the activities there.

It was the perfect setting.

I Googled RV storage lots and found a place on nearby Stock Island that could fit us in. We could park our RVs there and use Norah's car to get around Key West.

I called her with the good news.

"Norah, I found a place. A villa in Key West. We can move in tomorrow. Five bedrooms, a pool, and a house manager to prepare our meals. You can bring Biscuit. Will that work?"

"Are you kidding! You found a place? In Key West? And we can move in tomorrow? How is that possible?"

"I called a good friend and she made it happen. You'll meet her after we move in. Can you be ready to go tomorrow?"

"Yeah, I'm more than ready. Can I call Maddie and let her know?"

"Sure. Call her. Tell her it's all set."

I told her about dropping our RVs at the storage lot in Stock Island. We agreed to meet there around one. Maddie would be riding along with Norah.

Everything was set.

I got to the storage lot early and paid in advance for both RVs.

Maddie and Norah arrived an hour later. We all hugged, piled into Buttercup, and with Biscuit and Bob, headed for the villa.

It was far more impressive than any of us expected. The house manager, a woman of about forty, greeted us at the door and gave us the grand tour.

She said we could have our pick of any of the bedrooms in the main house. All had private bathrooms and views of the pool.

Maddie and Norah chose bedrooms next to each other on the first floor. I took one on the second, giving the two women a bit more privacy. For the next thirty days, we indulged ourselves in all the pleasures that Key West could offer.

During that time, we learned that the two men who crashed the Ferrari into the ambulance had survived. They were telling the FBI everything they knew about the operation. They even provided detailed documents and names of everyone involved.

Using what they learned, the FBI, without Maddie, raided several locations and rounded up most of the ambulance crews and the people who worked them.

The Iraqi national who was the mastermind of the criminal enterprise, lawyered up and through his attorney, claimed his innocence. The presiding judge set his bail at five million dollars. It was quickly paid, and the Iraqi flew out of the country. Probably never to be seen in the US again.

Norah enjoyed being in Key West. So much so, that she looked for, and found a nursing assignment in the hospital there. Francis Ford, who had dropped by to meet her, helped her find an affordable place to stay on a permanent basis.

Maddie, aka FBI Special Agent O'Connor, decided she too liked the Key West vibe, and terminated her employment with the FBI.

She soon found a temporary job crewing on one of Key West's sunset cruises. It didn't pay much, but the tips were good, and she was free to live the life she always wanted.

Francis Ford offered her a job as head of security of her hotel holdings. Maddie thanked her, but declined, saying she needed time to figure things out. Francis understood and said the job would be open should Maddie ever want it.

Agent Harris, who was on the mend from his gunshot wound, came to Key West and spent a day seeing the sights with Norah. I never did find out if he was married or not.

Even though I enjoyed my time in the Villa, I ended my stay early. The rowdy tourist crowds packing the island on the weekends weren't my cup of tea. Too many drunks making fools of themselves.

I missed being on the road. So after three weeks in the villa, I said my goodbyes to Norah and Maddie. I got the RV out of storage and Bob and I headed out on our next adventure.

One last note. Most of the stolen cars in the warehouse were insured by the same company. They specialized in covering high-end and expensive collectibles. They had offered a reward for information leading to the return of many of the cars in the warehouse.

After they were recovered, the insurance company decided the reward would go to Norah since it was she who had tracked down the crew whose trail eventually led to the warehouse and the ultimate recovery of the cars.

I never did learn how much the reward was, but did learn Norah offered half of it to Maddie.

Author's Notes

I'm supposed to say the people, places, and events mentioned in this book are not real. So that's what I'm going to say.

But if you search Google, you might find a few similarities between some of the places and events mentioned in this book. I'm not saying the book is based on them, just that much of what I write about in the Mango Bob series is based on the people and places I encounter while on the road.

If you've ever traveled in a motorhome, you probably know how this works. You check into a park, meet people and see things you never expected to see. Very often, these things can change your perspective on life.

Anyway, if you liked this book, please post a positive review on Amazon. Good reviews helps book sales and keeps me writing new stories about the adventures of Mango Bob and Walker.

Should you visit Florida and see a big orange tabby sitting on the dash of an RV going down the road, wave.

It might be Mango Bob. He likes all the attention he can get.

As always, thanks for your support.

Bill Myers

The adventure continues . . .

Other books in the Mango Bob series include:

Mango Bob

Mango Lucky

Mango Bay

Mango Glades

Mango Key

Mango Blues

Mango Digger

Mango Crush

Mango Motel

Mango Star

Mango Road

Mango Gold

You can find photos, maps, and more from the Mango Bob adventures at http://www.mangobob.com

Stay in touch with Mango Bob and Walker on Facebook at: https://www.facebook.com/MangoBob-197177127009774/